DARK QUEEN RISING

PAUL DOHERTY

BLACKTHORN

First published in Great Britain, the USA and Canada in 2019
by Black Thorn, an imprint of Canongate Books Ltd,
14 High Street, Edinburgh EH1 1TE

Distributed in the USA by Publishers Group West and in Canada by
Publishers Group Canada

First published in 2018 by Severn House Publishers Ltd,
Eardley House, 4 Uxbridge Street, London W8 7SY

blackthornbooks.com

1

British Library Cataloguing in Publication Data
A catalogue record for this book is available from the British Library

ISBN 978 1 78689 489 2

Typeset by Palimpsest Book Production Ltd., Falkirk,
Stirlingshire, Scotland

Printed and bound in Great Britain by Clays Ltd, Elcograf S.p.A.

DARK QUEEN RISING

Paul Doherty has written over 100 books and was awarded the Herodotus Award, for lifelong achievement for excellence in the writing of historical mysteries by the Historical Mystery Appreciation Society. His books have been translated into more than twenty languages and include the historical mysteries of Brother Athelstan and Hugh Corbett.

paulcdoherty.com

'To my dear friend Eve Khan.
Many thanks for your help and support.'

HISTORICAL NOTE

By May 1471 that most ferocious struggle known as the Wars of the Roses was reaching a fresh, bloody climax. Edward of York and his two brothers, Richard of Gloucester and George of Clarence, were determined to shatter the power of Lancaster. Henry VI, the Lancastrian King, was their prisoner in the Tower and marked down for death. Edward then moved swiftly to annihilate the Lancastrian army at Barnet before turning west to search out and destroy Henry VI's Queen, Margaret of Anjou, their son, also called Edward, and their leading general, the Duke of Somerset. The year 1471 was one of Yorkist victories, yet it also gave birth to forces intent on the total destruction of the House of York. *Dark Queen Rising* chronicles the beginning of this. Of course this is a work of fiction, yet most of this dramatic story is firmly grounded on evidence, as the author's note at the end of the novel will attest.

House of York
Richard Duke of York and his wife Cecily, Duchess of York, 'the Rose of Raby'.
Parents of:
Edward (later King Edward IV),
George of Clarence,
Richard Duke of Gloucester (later King Richard III).

House of Lancaster
Henry VI,
Henry's wife Margaret of Anjou and their son Prince Edward.

House of Tudor
Edmund Tudor, first husband of Margaret Beaufort, Countess of Richmond, and half-brother to Henry VI of England. Edmund's father Owain had married Katherine of Valois, French princess and widow of King Henry V, father of Henry VI.
Jasper Tudor, Edmund's brother, kinsman to Henry Tudor (later Henry VII).

House of Margaret Beaufort
Margaret Countess of Richmond, married first to Edmund Tudor, then Sir Humphrey Stafford and finally Lord William Stanley.
Reginald Bray, Margaret's principal steward and controller of her household.
Christopher Urswicke, Margaret Beaufort's personal clerk and leading henchman.

PROLOGUE

'On the evening the Duke of Clarence, contrary to his honour and oath, departed secretly from the Earl of Warwick to King Edward his brother.'

Great Chronicle of London

'And so kingdoms fall, thrones tip and crowns topple,' Melchior, a Barnabite friar from a village outside Cologne, a Rhinelander, solemnly intoned. He stared across at his two companions who had gathered with him in this small writing chamber deep within the precincts of Tewkesbury Abbey.

'Indeed it is so,' one of his companions replied, 'and we, the Three Kings as they call us, have the true knowledge to make that happen.' He placed his hands on the book of hours. 'I would swear to such as I would on that held by our brothers at St Vedast.'

'We are nearly finished,' Balthasar, the third Barnabite declared. 'We shall soon return to our friends in London.'

'Hush.' Melchior, their leader, raised a hand. 'Do you not hear it?' The chamber fell silent. The Three Kings listened intently. The great Benedictine abbey did not echo with any sound: no bells tolling, booming their invitation to prayer; no melodious plain-chant drifting on the early morning breeze, no patter of sandalled feet; nothing but an ominous, oppressive silence. Balthasar went to speak but Melchior shook his head and lifted a finger.

'There,' he whispered, 'the clash of armies. It has begun!'

His two companions strained their hearing and nodded in agreement as the clamour from the nearby battlefield rolled through the abbey. The armies of York and Lancaster were at last locked in deadly combat along the water meadows of the Severn river.

'Edward of York,' Melchior declared, 'and his brothers have brought the Lancastrians to account. Queen Margaret of Anjou hoped to escape across the Severn into Wales, but that will not happen. Instead, she will face defeat. Her general Beaufort of Somerset and all his host will be scattered as was pharaoh's army; they will be swallowed up in disaster.'

'But our master surely will remain safe even if his House is the victor?'

'Do not worry,' Melchior replied, 'George of Clarence is the King's own brother, a man who will not put himself in harm's way even if this day is vital to him and his kin.'

'He will be pleased,' Balthasar, the youngest of the Three Kings, declared, 'the secrets we have gathered . . .' He paused. 'Is it not time we shared the fruits of our work with him?'

'True, he gave us the seed for the sowing,' Melchior replied. 'But we are the ones who planted and tended the growth of this rich, bountiful harvest: a veritable treasure chest of intrigue and scandal.'

'But we have not finished yet.'

'No, we are not. I have received messages from Brother Cuthbert at St Vedast. He has discovered a porter who served Duchess Cecily and heard her scream certain words. Cuthbert has invited him to St Vedast.' Melchior grinned to himself. 'He will be rewarded, once Cuthbert has taken a verbatim account of what Duchess Cecily shouted when she discovered that her royal son, Edward of York, had married the Woodville woman.'

'Oh, rich indeed,' Caspar the third Barnabite whispered. 'And what else? What more could be done?'

'News has arrived,' Melchior turned to face Caspar, 'that Richard Neville, Earl of Warwick, has been defeated and killed at Barnet. He may once have been York's great friend and champion but, as we know, because of his hatred for the Woodvilles, he withdrew his allegiance and entered Lancaster's camp. Anyway,' Melchior continued, 'our King-maker has paid the price for such a choice and been despatched to his eternal reward. More importantly, Warwick left no male heir, only two daughters: Isobel, married to our Lord George of Clarence; the other, her sister Anne, will, in my view, be the object of affection for our master's younger brother, Richard of Gloucester. He will be in the thick of the fight today and, if he survives, if Gloucester is victorious, I am sure he will approach his brother the King and demand the hand of Anne Neville in marriage, along with half of her father's estates which are the richest in the kingdom.'

'But surely our master will oppose that?' Balthasar demanded.

'Of course.' Melchior sighed. 'And so my Lord of Clarence has asked us to provide a solution without,' he sighed again, 'without causing the death of that young lady.'

'What happens,' Caspar asked, 'if York loses the fight today? What then?'

'Oh, safe enough for us.' Melchior rubbed his hands. 'If Warwick deserted York, so did Clarence. He betrayed his brothers for a while and sheltered deep in the Lancastrian camp, and we went with him, we had to! Now,' Melchior pulled a face, 'if York loses, if my Lord of Clarence is killed, if Clarence survives and is taken prisoner, will not be the important issue. We have certain knowledge! We possess information, valuable information, precious little nuggets of scandal hidden away in a manner known only to ourselves. If Margaret of Anjou and Somerset carry the day, they will need us, and so we will still profit in so many, many ways.' He paused, listening to the growing clamour of steel against steel rolling across the abbey grounds. 'In the meantime,' Melchior murmured, 'we must act as if York will sweep the day. Remember, our master has asked us to keep another matter in mind as well as under close watch.'

'The little Beaufort bitch?' Caspar retorted.

'The same,' Melchior agreed. 'Margaret Beaufort, Countess of Richmond, late widow of Lord Edmund Tudor, mother of now possibly the sole Lancastrian claimant, Henry Tudor. If the stories are correct, the Beaufort bitch is to become a widow again: her husband Sir Humphrey Stafford is apparently not long for this vale of tears. Now the Beaufort woman also shelters here in this abbey with her leading henchmen, her steward Reginald Bray and her clerk, Christopher Urswicke. I understand she was visiting kinsmen in Wales before being caught up in this clash of armies.'

'Why doesn't my Lord of Clarence deal with her?'

'Oh, he will in time,' Melchior declared, 'and when he can!

Remember the Beaufort woman is protected by her husband Sir Humphrey Stafford, who has at his disposal all the support of his powerful kinsman the Duke of Buckingham. My master has not forgotten that. However, the woman is being closely watched. Indeed, my Lord of Clarence and his henchman Mauclerc claim to have a spy deep in the bitch's household. So,' he rose to his feet, 'let us see what is happening. The good brothers here chatter like birds on a branch: they'll have news from the battlefield as well as information about the Beaufort Bitch whom we may have to deal with.'

'And in London?' Balthasar demanded. 'Brother Cuthbert has orders on how to deal with the porter he has questioned.'

'Oh, do not worry. Cuthbert knows exactly what to do.'

Brother Cuthbert, a purported Barnabite friar, stood staring through the narrow window in the small chancery chamber on the second storey of the priest's house: this crumbling mansion adjoined the ancient, almost derelict church of St Vedast on Moorfields, that great wasteland beyond London's northern wall. The Barnabite peered through the narrow lancet, the dark was beginning to grey. He had done his duty, now it was time to bring matters to an end. Brother Cuthbert turned and walked back to Raoul Bisset, a former porter in the household of Duchess Cecily of York. The friar smiled and lightly touched the dagger hidden beneath his robe. He studied the porter carefully. Cuthbert was now satisfied that this small, greasy tub of an old man was no spy or threat; Bisset was simply desperate for money and ready to sell the priceless morsel of information he had treasured for many a year.

'So,' Cuthbert forced a smile, 'what you have told me,' the Barnabite gestured at the transcript on the table before him, 'is the truth. Duchess Cecily definitely said that?'

'Oh yes, Brother.' Bisset licked his lips and stared longingly at the wine tray on the chest in the far corner. Brother Cuthbert walked across, filled a pewter goblet, brought it back and watched as Bisset greedily drank.

'You were saying?' Cuthbert demanded.

'Brother,' Bisset licked his lips, 'the duchess had a fiery temper and a tongue which cut like a razor. She and her husband Richard of York were forever quarrelling and her tantrums only worsened with age. After her husband was killed at Wakefield fight, Duchess Cecily would lash out with both tongue and cane. The only person who could placate her was her favourite, her eldest, Edward who is now King. The duchess dreamed that her darling son would marry the princess of some great foreign house, be it France, Castile or some other kingdom. She boasted as much and would constantly lecture him and others on the need for such a marriage. Duchess Cecily detested the Woodvilles. She hated them with a passion beyond measure and would not allow them into her presence—'

'And this remark,' Brother Cuthbert interrupted, 'you were there?'

'Yes, yes, I stood outside her chamber. I was bringing up a parcel and I noticed the door was slightly open. The duchess, who was sheltering at Windsor, had just received a messenger who had been dismissed to the buttery.'

'The duchess was alone?'

'Oh no, no, no, her chamber priest was present. Well, that poor man has long since died. He fell down some steps. Anyway,' Bisset tapped the transcript before him, 'this is what I heard. Now, Brother, I was promised a reward. Good silver, freshly minted coins?'

'This chamber priest, was he hearing her confession?'

'He may have been,' again Bisset tapped the transcript, 'but this is what I heard. Now, Brother, my reward?'

'Yes, yes, of course, but it is not here. You see St Vedast,' Cuthbert waved a hand, 'is a derelict church, once the heart of a small village until the Great Plague wiped the hamlet from the face of the earth.'

'Yes, yes, we had the same outside Framlingham in Norfolk.' Bisset fell silent as the smile faded from Brother Cuthbert's face. 'I am sorry,' Bisset stammered, 'you were saying?'

'Moorfields is now the haunt of outlaws, wolfsheads and other malefactors, Master Bisset, so we hide our coin deep in the cemetery. Anyway come, come, I will take you to your reward.' He made to turn away but then came back and watched as Bisset struggled to his feet.

'What is it, Brother?'

'When you worked in the duchess's household, were you ever visited by Bishop Stillington of Bath and Wells? Did you ever hear his name being mentioned by the duchess or by any of the great ones who visited her?'

'Never.'

'And does the name Eleanor Butler mean anything to you? After all, you were a porter, you brought people and goods into the households and dwelling places where the duchess resided?'

'Brother, the name means nothing to me, nothing at all.'

'Are you sure?'

'Of course,' Bisset gabbled on, 'as in any great household, rumour and gossip were common enough. Stories about the duchess and her husband.'

'But you witnessed nothing first hand?' Cuthbert pointed back at the table. 'Only what you have just told me?'

'Brother, that's the truth, but now I am hungry and I would like to go. You promised me shelter and food as well as those coins.'

'Of course.'

Brother Cuthbert led Bisset out of the chamber, down the rickety stairs, along a passageway which swept past the small refectory and out into God's Acre; a gloomy graveyard which looked even more sombre with the river mist swirling in. Cuthbert walked briskly, gesturing at Bisset to hurry as he listened to the old porter's gasps and groans. They made their way along the pebble-strewn path which wound around the ancient headstones and decaying funeral crosses of that sombre house of the dead. They passed through a clump of yew trees and onto a stretch of wasteland, a tangle of weeds, briars and sturdy bushes. Brother Cuthbert stopped and bowed at two of his colleagues who stood resting on spades over a freshly dug grave. Cuthbert walked back to the porter, who stood sweaty and gasping, staring around.

'What is this?' Bisset exclaimed. 'Why have you brought me here? You don't keep coin . . .'

'Here's payment, my friend.' Cuthbert stepped closer and thrust his dagger deep into Bisset's belly, twisting the knife so the blade turned up, rupturing the flesh. Cuthbert dug and dug again as he watched Bisset gag on his own blood and the life light fade in the porter's eyes. The Barnabite withdrew his dagger and watched the dying man topple to the ground. Once Bisset lay silent, eyes staring, mouth gaping, the Barnabite turned to his two companions who had stood silently watching the killing.

'He has his reward,' Cuthbert snapped. 'Now bury him with the rest.'

PART ONE

'When both armies were too exhausted and thirsty to march any further, they joined battle near Tewkesbury.'

Crowland Chronicle

'Bless me, Father, for I have truly sinned. It is a month, yes, it was on the second Sunday of Lent that I was last shriven of my sins.'

Margaret of Beaufort, Countess of Richmond, widow of Edmund Tudor, mother of Henry, their only son, and now wife to a very frail Henry Stafford, paused in her prayers. Margaret crossed herself and desperately tried to recall her examination of conscience. She had sat in the lady chapel judging herself, weaning out her faults, but now she could not recall them.

'My Lady?' Brother Ambrose, priest-monk of the Benedictine community of Tewkesbury Abbey, was now quite alarmed. He moved the shriving veil which hung between the mercy pew where he sat and the prie-dieu against which the young countess leaned. Ambrose scrutinised Margaret's thoughtful face. She was not beautiful or even pretty, but she had a look of considerable charm; her complexion was pale and clear, her eyes grey as a morning mist beneath dark, arched brows. She was full lipped and generous mouthed; other monks judged her to be solemn, even severe. Brother Ambrose, however, could detect good humour, even merriment beneath that studious face, ever ready to smile even as the world turned against her. Ambrose realised that was now happening as Fortune's fickle wheel was about to be given another cruel spin.

'My Lady,' he whispered, 'I shall pray for you.'

The countess abruptly rose. She clutched a pair of doeskin gloves and used these to smooth down her fur-trimmed red dress. She touched her dark-auburn hair, as if to make sure it was almost hidden by the exquisitely bejewelled and embroidered headdress.

'My Lady?' Brother Ambrose rose but then fell silent as Lady Margaret raised a hand.

'Can you hear it,' she whispered, 'the noise of battle?'

'My Lord Edward of York and his brothers, Richard of Gloucester and George of Clarence are moving swiftly,' Brother Ambrose replied. 'Abbot John receives a constant flow of intelligence from the battlefield. York intends to put Queen Margaret of Anjou, the Angevin she-wolf and her son Edward to the sword. My Lady, our prayers are with you. I understand that your kinsman, Edmund Beaufort, Duke of Somerset, also intends to end all troubles and bring this war, short and cruel, to an end.'

Lady Margaret, however, was no longer listening, but moved to the window of the guesthouse chapel deep in the enclosure of Tewkesbury Abbey. Margaret pulled back the shutters; she turned slightly. 'What date is it?' she murmured.

'Saturday the fourth of May. The feast of St Pelagia and Florian . . .'

'. . . The year of our Lord 1471.' Margaret finished the sentence. 'Truly a day of destruction,' she added.

The countess broke off as a chapel door was flung open. Reginald Bray, accompanied by Margaret's chancery clerk, Christopher Urswicke, hurried into the small chapel. They paused just within the doorway and Margaret heard the distant but chilling sound of mortal combat; the vengeful, vicious crash and clash of steel. Sharp bursts of cannon echoed above the murmur of men roaring their hate and screaming their pain on this hot, early summer's day around the village and abbey of Tewkesbury.

'What is it?' Brother Ambrose demanded.

'Madam,' Urswicke ignored the Benedictine, 'madam, you must come now. We have news from the field. Somerset has broken. He and his army are in full flight.'

Margaret swallowed hard, the pain at what she'd just heard, despite her own secret dreams and ambitions, was a blow to both body and soul.

'How can that be?' she demanded.

'Urswicke is correct,' Bray declared, his harsh voice rasping and loud. 'Madam, do not busy yourself in prayer, but come.'

'To do what?' Ambrose protested.

'What can be done?' Margaret glanced to all three men. 'What can be done when worlds collapse and chaos sweeps in?'

'Come, madam.' Urswicke grabbed his mistress's hand: he nodded at Ambrose and hurried the countess out of the guest-house chapel. They hastened along paved alleyways where stone-faced saints and angels peered down at them from corners and enclaves. On the tops of pillars, the gargoyles, with their monkey-faces and snarling mouths, seemed to mock Margaret's mood. She decided not to look but kept her gaze down on the ground as they swept around the small cloisters. Here the air was sweet and heavy with the constant tang of incense and the flow of fragrant smells from the abbey kitchens. The day was drawing on and the abbey bells would soon toll, summoning the brothers to break their hunger before returning to the church for another hour of prayer. The battle raging in the fields around the great abbey was certainly making itself felt. Black-garbed monks, hoods pulled close, hurried backwards and forwards, caught up in a panic-growing fear. Margaret glimpsed Abbot John Strensham, deep in conversation with other senior monks in the small rose garden which stretched in front of the chapterhouse.

'Ignore them,' Urswicke whispered. 'Mistress, ignore them! Play the part! Play it now, for the game is about to change if York carries the day.'

Margaret stopped. She squeezed Urswicke's arms and stared into his face. He always reminded her of a choirboy, an impression heightened by his soft, precise speech. Urswicke was smooth-shaven with pale, almost ivory, feminine skin, light-blue eyes as innocent as any child's, merry-mouthed with a mop of dark-brown hair which he apparently never combed. 'A simple-faced clerk' was how someone had described Christopher Urswicke, son of Thomas Urswicke, Recorder of London. Margaret smiled faintly as she held Urswicke's innocent gaze. She looked at him from head to toe. He dressed like a clerk garbed in a dark-brown gown over a jerkin and loose-fitting hose, yet beneath the gown were dagger and sword, and the boots on his feet were spurred as if he was ready to ride at a moment's notice.

'My Lady?'

'I must remember,' she replied. 'There is more to a book than its cover, and that certainly applies to you, Master Christopher. But come . . .'

All three hastened down the cloistered walk and out into the warm sunshine. They approached the abbey church and entered through a postern gate, climbing the rough-hewn steps leading up into the great tower. Bray was insistent that they reach the top to see precisely what was happening. The steward's sallow, close face, pointed nose, thin-lipped mouth and square chin were laced with a fine, sweaty sheen. Hot and exasperated, Bray plucked at his chancery robe, running a finger around the neckline of his cambric linen shirt to clear the sweat coursing down his neck. Margaret noticed the cut marks on Bray's cheeks, a sure sign of her steward's agitation when Bray had shaved that morning. Margaret paused on the first stairwell.

'The page boy, Lambert, who brought messages from kinsman Tudor,' she whispered, 'how goes he in all of this?'

'Safely ensconced with the grooms in the abbey stables. Ignore him,' Bray hissed, 'and everyone else will. Start fussing and the world will fuss with you. Isn't that right, Christopher?'

Urswicke just pulled a face. Reginald Bray, chief receiver and principal steward in the countess's household, was regarded as most skilled in his trade, but his dark humour and blunt speech were equally well known. They continued to climb, becoming more aware of the strong breezes piercing the lancet windows. The horrid din of battle was also becoming more pressing. Lady Margaret, still praying quietly that her own boy would stay safe, listened to the gasping breath of her two companions, aware of the sweat now soaking her own clothes. She tried to distract herself by glancing at the bosses carved in the different stairwells and turnings. Most of these were heavy-winged angels, each carrying a musical instrument, be it the bagpipes, flute or trumpet.

'We need the protection of St Michael and all his heavenly cohort,' Urswicke exclaimed, following her gaze.

'I am sorry,' Lady Margaret paused, resting one hand on his shoulder. Bray stood just behind her ready to help. 'You are limping, Christopher?'

Urswicke turned and grinned. 'My ankle is slightly twisted but I am sure you have other concerns. Madam, we live in hurling times. Kingdoms are now lost and won in a day.'

They continued on till they reached the top of the tower, pushing back the heavy trapdoor, helping each other through the hatchway to stand on the gravel-strewn top. They crossed this and leaned against the moss-encrusted crenellations. All three stared out over the murderous mayhem spreading out across the abbey's great water meadow, fed by the twisting Severn glinting sharply in the early afternoon sun. The Lancastrian battle phalanx had buckled and broken; already both foot and mounted were streaming away in retreat, pursued by the fast-moving, vengeful Yorkists in full battle array. Even from where she stood, Margaret could glimpse the Beaufort standards and pennants quartered with the royal arms of both England and France. Other standards were also visible: those of Beaufort's allies such as the Courtenays of Devon and the De Veres of Oxford. The Lancastrian banner bearers, standards held high, were desperately trying to make a stand to mount a defence. The Yorkists, however, were pressing hard, breaking the Lancastrians up, filleting their battle formation like a butcher would a slab of meat. The bitter sound of the bloody conflict now carried stronger: shrill cries and screams, bellowed curses, shouts of defiance and the heart-stopping groans and moans of the wounded and dying. Margaret also glimpsed the streaming banners of Edward of York as well as those of his two brothers, Gloucester and Clarence, a host of Yorkist insignia, be they The Sunne in Splendour, the Bear of Warwick or the Boar of Gloucester. These billowed around the royal banner, which rippled in a gorgeous sea of colour: blue, scarlet and gold. The Yorkists had unfurled the sacred standard of England, usually kept behind the high altar of Westminster Abbey. Edward of York was using this to emphasise his right to the Crown, as well as his solemn assurance that he would show no mercy or pardon to the enemy fleeing before him. The course of the battle was becoming more distinct as the Lancastrians retreated even more swiftly and the Yorkists followed, spreading out to curve inwards so as to complete their encirclement.

The fresh, green grass of the great meadow was now decorated with the colours of the fallen; their tabards, pennants, shields, banners and standards. Columns of smoke smudged the horizon as other Yorkists broke off from the pursuit to pillage and burn the Lancastrian camp. Margaret shaded her eyes and prayed for her kinsman, Beaufort. Early that day Margaret had learnt how the Lancastrians had camped the previous evening at Guphill Farm, in a stretch of the twisting Gloucester countryside known as the Vineyards. The Yorkists were now pillaging this and Margaret wondered what had happened to the Angevin queen and her son. The roar of voices, men screaming their pain or laughing in their victory, made her close her eyes and whisper a further prayer. Beside her, Urswicke was threading his ave beads whilst Bray quietly cursed. A blood-chilling roar forced Margaret to open her eyes and stare down. The Lancastrian line had buckled and snapped completely. Any resistance had collapsed. Men were now retreating across the great meadow and the thick press of the Yorkist banner bearers were surging forward.

'They are fleeing,' Urswicke exclaimed. 'My Lady, your kinsmen are desperate to seek sanctuary here. Come, they will soon be below us.'

Margaret followed her two henchmen down from the top of the tower. She tried to curb the sheer terror welling within her. They reached the shadows of the northern transept. Lancastrian knights and footmen were already thronging through the main entrance, desperate to shelter in the abbey's cool darkness. Monks came hurrying along the nave, hands fluttering in agitation at the first sharp echoes of weaponry just outside the main door. The Yorkists had dismounted, fully intending to continue the slaughter even in these sacred precincts. Urswicke, quick-thinking and eager to escape what could be a bloody massacre, pushed Margaret towards a doorway, beckoning at Bray to follow them through into a musty, cobwebbed chamber, with steep steps leading up to a small choir loft. Urswicke turned the key in the lock and placed the bar in its slats before leading the countess and Bray up the narrow, spiral staircase. The choir loft was small and cramped, angled into the wall so the singers and trumpeters could clearly see what was happening just within the main doorway below, as well as the porch beyond: here processions would assemble before sweeping up the long, cavernous nave towards the majestically carved rood screen which shielded the sanctuary and choir beyond. No such procession would assemble now. Margaret stared pitifully down at the frightened, blood-streaked men surging through the main door, desperate to escape their furious pursuers who now edged in, shields locked, swords flickering out like the poisonous tongues of a host of vipers.

The fighting below grew more intense. Margaret glimpsed her kinsman Edmund Beaufort, helmet cast aside, as he backed further up the nave, his gloriously embroidered tabard with its glowing colours drenched in blood. On either side of the duke, his remaining household knights were desperate to mount a defence, but they broke up as the Yorkists pursued them further down the nave, hacking and hewing so blood swirled along the ancient paving stones. The struggle often became solitary, individual Lancastrians being surrounded by Yorkist knights. No mercy was shown. Margaret watched as one of Beaufort's banner knights fell to his knees in abject surrender. His tormentors simply tore his armour and weapons from him, pushed down his head and severed it with one clean blow. The Yorkists laughed as the head bounced across the paving stones, whilst the still upright torso spouted blood like a fountain before toppling over. The nave was no longer a Benedictine house of prayer, more like a butcher's yard in the Shambles.

Men shrieked in their death agonies under a hail of cutting blows from mace, sword and axe. The Lancastrians tried to hide in the chantry chapels along each transept, but the trellised screens of such small shrines proved to be no protection. Nor were the tombs of the former lords of Tewkesbury such as the Despensers and the Fitzalans. Margaret, standing in the corner of the choir loft, gripped the balustrade in sweaty fear as more and more vengeful Yorkists poured through the main entrance, as well as through the Devil and Corpse doors along the transepts either side. Abruptly trumpets shrieked, their noise braying along the nave.

'The King, the King!' a harsh voice bellowed.

Margaret peered down, twisting to see the three men who now strode into the church, all armoured and visored for battle. They stood like spectres from a nightmare; each of them had removed their war helmets, thrusting these into the hands of one of the squires milling about them. The central figure, his blond hair shimmering in the sunlight, lancing through the great windows of the nave, turned slightly. Margaret narrowed her eyes as she

recognised the smooth, tawny features of Edward of York, Edward
the King, the great killer of Margaret's kinsmen, the Beauforts.
Beside Edward stood his two brothers: on his left George of
Clarence, thinner than his brother, his wine-fat face laced with
sweat. On the King's left, the small, wiry, sharp-featured youngest
brother, Richard of Gloucester, his long, reddish hair framing an
unusually pallid face. All three princes were armed with sword
and dagger. Edward raised both hands in a sign of victory before
lowering them, pointing both sword and dagger down the nave.

'Kill them all!' Clarence bellowed. 'Show no quarter, give no
mercy!'

A scream answered his words as a Yorkist squire, holding a
dagger to his prisoner's throat, now drove it in. More shouts of
despair and cries of triumph broke the stillness, followed by a
clatter of weapons. This abruptly ceased as the abbey bells began
to toll, crashing out their peals as a deep-throated chanting rose
from the sanctuary. The heavy curtain across the rood-screen
entrance was abruptly pulled back. A hand bell rang as a line
of monks, cowls pulled close, left the sanctuary and processed
into the nave. A cross bearer and two acolytes together with three
thurifers preceded Abbot John Strensham who, garbed in all his
pontificals, walked slowly down the church. He had removed the
golden pyx from its silver sanctuary chain and now held this up
in both hands.

'Behold the Lamb of God,' he intoned in a hollow-sounding
voice. 'Behold the Lamb of God who takes away the sins of the
world.' He walked on, holding the pyx high as he gazed directly
at the King. 'I hold here,' he declared, 'the body and blood of
the Risen Christ. I hold it here in this terrible place which is
supposed to be the House of God and the Gate of Heaven. Yet
you, your Grace, have turned our abbey into a butcher's yard.
Look around you, do not pollute these sacred precincts. Desist!
The killing must end.'

Margaret could only agree as she murmured a prayer in repar-
ation at the abomination which now stretched along that
shadow-filled nave: wounded, tired men, broken in body and
shattered in soul, clinging to the pillars and trellised screens of
the different chantry chapels. Some of the wounded, terrified at the
prospect of immediate slaughter, crawled across the blood-drenched

floor in a vain attempt to hide amongst the long line of black-garbed Benedictines.

'Look,' Urswicke hissed, Margaret did so. George of Clarence was now walking forward, pointing his glistening, blood-wetted sword at the abbot.

'Be careful,' Strensham warned. 'These are sacred precincts, God's own sanctuary.'

'Tewkesbury,' Clarence bellowed back, 'does not possess such a right. It cannot grant sanctuary. The men who shelter here are traitors taken in arms against their rightful King, who has unfurled his sacred banner and proclaimed his peace. They have insulted that. They are blasphemous liars.' Clarence edged forward. 'These miscreants have sworn, on other occasions, to be loyal and true to my brother the King. They are oath-breakers as well as traitors and so deserving of death.'

'They are also,' Richard of Gloucester stepped forward to join his brother, 'murderers. They have the blood of our House and kin on their hands, including the unlawful slaying of our beloved father and brother after Wakefield fight.'

'Deliver them!' Clarence shouted, shaking his sword. Abbot Strensham walked as close as he could to the pointed blade.

'George, Richard,' Edward the King dramatically re-sheathed his weapons, 'our quarrel is with traitors, not Abbot Strensham and his Benedictines,' a note of humour entered the King's voice, 'and certainly not with Holy Mother Church. These malefactors, double-dyed in treason and treachery, men twice as fit for Hell as any sinner, have sought sanctuary here. Let them have it.'

The King stepped forward, one hand raised. 'Abbot Strensham, you have the word of your King.' Edward turned away and, escorted by his brothers who also re-sheathed their weapons, left the abbey church. The Yorkist knights streamed after them. Abbot Strensham gave a deep sigh, raised a hand, snapping his fingers. Two monks hurried forward to close the heavy, double portals, turning the key in its lock and bringing down the great bar whilst others of the brothers did the same at both the Devil's porch and Corpse door.

'Are you ready?' Urswicke bent down and stared at his pallid-faced mistress, mouth all puckered, her tired eyes watchful and wary. 'Abbot Strensham has arranged for you, and you only, to slip through the rood screen into the nave.' He gestured at Bray. 'Reginald and I will accompany you into the sacristy but no further. Mistress,' he added, 'be careful. You know you have to be. A person claiming sanctuary cannot, according to canon law, receive any visitors who might bring weapons, purveyance or comfort, be it physical or spiritual, to a sanctuary seeker. So be vigilant and remember the risks both you and the abbot are taking, not to mention your kin.'

'Yes, yes.' Margaret sighed. She got to her feet, took a deep breath, pulled up the hood of her gown and, with Urswicke leading the way, they left the guesthouse. Urswicke paused whilst Bray locked the doors behind them; they then continued along stone-paved passageways where harsh-faced angels, sullen saints and smirking gargoyles peered down at them from the shadows. An eerie silence had crept through the abbey, as if it was part of the thick river mist now seeping in from the Severn. All sound was dulled, the echoing song of plain-chant, the ringing of bells, the slap of sandalled feet on stone and the cries and shouts of the lay brothers working in the vast abbey kitchen and buttery. All this seemed to have been cloaked by an ominous silence. Occasionally black-garbed figures, robes flapping, would flit across their path. Now and again Margaret glimpsed peaked, white faces of monks peering out at them from some window or embrasure.

Edward of York's men were also there but Abbot Strensham had issued his own orders. The sacristan of the abbey did not fire the sconce torches, light the powerful lanternhorns or lower the Catherine wheels, their rims crammed with candles. This lack of light proved to be a real obstacle to York's soldiers, who did not know the abbey with its twisting runnels, narrow winding paths, different gardens, herb plots and flower beds. They had to thread themselves through a veritable maze of stone where it was so easy to lose their way. Urswicke, however, faced no such difficulty as he followed the precise directions provided by Abbot Strensham.

At last they reached the small door to the minor sacristy of the great abbey church. Urswicke knocked and Abbot Strensham himself ushered them in. He had a hurried, whispered conversation

with Urswicke and Bray ordering them to stay then, taking
Margaret by the hand, he led her out of the sacristy. They crossed
the darkened sanctuary, through the rood screen, down steep steps
into the nave and across to the chantry chapel of St Faith. Margaret
felt she was walking through the halls and chambers of the
underworld, where ghosts gathered and pitiful moans and groans
mingled with the whispering of desperate men. The light was
very poor and this only deepened the illusion that all of this
misery was part of some blood-chilling nightmare. At the entrance
to the chantry chapel Margaret paused and stared at the dark
shapes huddled along the nave.

'We do what we can for them,' the abbot murmured, 'but they
are all doomed men. Edward of York is intent on their deaths.
Both I and Somerset know that.'

The inside of the chantry chapel was opulently furnished with
blue-dyed turkey rugs. The polished woodwork of both the screen
and the chapel furniture gleamed in the light of the six-branched
altar candelabra. Edmund Beaufort, Duke of Somerset, the leader
of the Lancastrian host, sat slumped in the celebrant's chair, feet
resting on a stool. On the floor around him lay his battle harness,
his weapons stacked in the far corner. Margaret, aware of Abbot
Strensham leaving and the door closing behind him, walked softly
around and stared into the face of a great lord whom she knew
faced certain death. At first Somerset did not even acknowledge
her but sat cradling his head in one hand, the other tugging at
the sweat-soaked tufts of his blond hair which fell down to his
shoulders.

'My Lord,' she whispered, 'my Lord I am here. Margaret
Beaufort, daughter of the first Duke of Somerset.'

'Margaret, Margaret, Margaret.' Somerset's hand fell away.
He straightened up, removed his feet and pointed to the stool. He
then abruptly leaned forward. He grasped her hands, drew her
close and kissed her softly on each cheek before gesturing at
the stool. 'Margaret, my little Margaret.' He sat back in the chair.
'How long has it been?'

'Four years.' She smiled through the dark. 'Four years almost
to the day. You remember, the May Day celebrations?'

'Yes, yes.' Somerset gestured at his stained but still glorious
tabard lying on the floor beside him. '*Sic transit gloria mundi,*'

he murmured, 'thus passes the glory of the world, Margaret. My brother John was killed in today's battle, Courtenay of Devon likewise. God knows where the rest are or what the future holds for them! And as for you, the last of our line.' Somerset joined his hands in prayer. 'Little Margaret, since I heard of you visiting me, I have been reflecting. I shall give you a homily, a sermon on the times. Much of it you will already know but some of it points to the future. So Margaret, let me begin my sad story of kings. Remember the verse that all the waters of the sea cannot wash away the balm and chrism of coronation? A king is sacred! Henry VI, son of Henry V and Catherine of Valois, is God's vice-regent here in this kingdom. True,' Somerset wiped his sweaty, bewhiskered face, 'our enemies claim that Henry sits closer to the angels than any of us; that he is not of this world yet he is still our King. We Beauforts descend from John of Gaunt, son of Edward III and his mistress Katherine Swynford; we also have a claim to the throne. We are legitimate and have been declared such by both King and Parliament, yet we support the Crown. Henry VI, holy but witless, married Margaret of Anjou, the so-called Angevin she-wolf. She produced an heir, Prince Edward.' Somerset shook his head. 'A most unlikeable young man. Another killer! God knows what will happen now to Henry or his son because the House of York, also descended from Edward III, believe they have a claim to the throne, one superior to anyone else's. Richard of York was killed at Wakefield but his three remaining sons Edward, Richard and George have continued the struggle and so we are here. We have been brought to this pass. The Beauforts and the House of Lancaster are truly finished. Margaret of Anjou and her son will be captured and slain. Many of those who supported them, men such as Richard Neville, Earl of Warwick – the so-called King-maker – was killed at Barnet along with many of our comrades.' He paused and peered at Margaret. 'You will need protection. You are a Beaufort, Margaret. Your husband is Sir Humphrey Stafford?'

'Fought for York to protect us all,' Margaret replied. 'He too was at Barnet, and grievously wounded! I cannot say if he will survive. Thankfully his kinsmen the Staffords of Buckingham are well protected by Edward of York and sit high on his council.'

'And if Sir Humphrey dies, Margaret, as I too am going to die very soon. Oh yes.' Somerset held a hand up. 'I am reconciled with that. Edward and his brothers want to destroy Lancaster root and branch. You Margaret,' again he touched the back of her hand, 'you are the last sprig of our tree, or at least your son is, Edmund Tudor's golden boy. Where is he?'

'Safe.'

'Where?'

Margaret just stared back.

'Yes, yes,' Somerset whispered, 'it's best not to say . . . But to return to you. If Stafford dies, will you take a third husband?'

'God will decide.'

'Yes, *Deus vult*,' Somerset replied. 'Listen Margaret, your father, my kinsman, the first Duke of Somerset, died out of sheer despair. Some even claim that he took his own life.'

'Some are liars. Why do you mention that?'

'I just wonder if we Beauforts are cursed, whether we are doomed to fail. This morning I thought we would carry the day. I really,' he paused to control the stutter which marred his speech, a legacy, or so they said, of a powerful blow to the head during a tournament at Windsor, 'I truly thought victory was within our grasp. I plotted to clear the field and destroy York.' He clenched his fist. Margaret watched and recalled how Somerset was a man of bounding ambition and fiery temper: she secretly wondered if such faults played their part in his defeat and that of Lancaster along the meadows outside.

'Pity poor Warwick killed at Barnet. Pity your brother-in-law Jasper Tudor did not reach us in time. Pity that we were unable to ford the Severn.' Margaret flinched at the self-pity which curled through Somerset's voice. 'Pity us all Margaret.' Somerset, eyes closed, rocked backwards and forwards. A loud scream echoed down the nave and Somerset broke from his reverie. 'Be on your guard against Clarence.' He hissed. 'Clarence is a killer to the very marrow, a Judas soul bound up like Lucifer with his own ambition. He intends to kill you, murder your son and anyone else of Lancastrian blood. He will do all this and then, like the rabid wolf he is, turn once again on his own kith and kin. He will prowl both court and kingdom. Murder, treachery and ravenous ambition will trail his every footstep: these hounds of

Hell will be famished, hungry for the taste of blood and for Clarence's self-preferment . . .'

Christopher Urswicke gently removed Mauclerc's hand and pushed it away.

'What is the matter, Christopher? Are you not interested in the male as you are in the female? Do you not prefer the company of men to that of women or are you . . .?'

'Hush now.' Urswicke leaned over and pressed a finger against Mauclerc's lips. 'Remember why you are here,' Urswicke hissed to this most sinister henchman of George Duke of Clarence.

'Yes, here we are.' Mauclerc's voice was mocking. He fell silent as Urswicke drew his dagger: the blade gleamed in the light of the lanternhorn set on the garden table deep in a rose-fringed arbour overlooking the kitchen garden of Tewkesbury Abbey. Urswicke placed the dagger on the table before he twirled it; the blade spun, glittering and pointed. 'Do you threaten me Urswicke?'

Mauclerc leaned closer, the lantern light casting shifting shadows. Urswicke watched intently. Mauclerc was a dagger man and Urswicke wondered if others lurked in the darkness behind. He held Mauclerc's gaze, studying him carefully. Clarence's henchman had a wolfish face with those narrow, slightly pointed eyes, the hollow cheeks, squat nose, and a mouth which seemed unable to close fully around the jutting teeth. A man who wore a perpetual sneer, as if he had judged the world and found it wanting to himself. Mauclerc scratched his black, glistening shaven pate, then abruptly snatched at the dagger, but Urswicke was swifter. He grasped the knife, twisting it in his hand so it pointed directly at Mauclerc's face. Clarence's henchman smiled thinly.

'I've heard of that Urswicke.' He murmured. 'Fast you are, swift as a pouncing cat. A born street fighter, despite your delicate frame.'

'Or because of it? So Master Mauclerc, put both hands where I can see them and do not think of even touching either the dagger in your belt or the Italian stiletto in the top of your boot. Nor must you whistle or, indeed, make any sound to draw in your escort which must not be far from here. Good? Do you understand?' Urswicke didn't even bother to wait for an answer.

He re-sheathed his blade and leaned against the table. 'So we are,' he began, 'at the witching hour on this balmy May evening in Tewkesbury Abbey. A short distance away the corpses of the Lancastrians are being stripped and collected like faggots of wood for the fire. Here in this abbey, the remaining surviving Lancastrian leaders lie bloody and besmirched: their only defence is Holy Mother Church in the person of Abbot John Strensham—'

'They'll die,' Mauclerc interrupted. 'They will all die. Clarence my master is insistent on that.'

'Even though, for a while, he turned coat and fought for Lancaster, changing back to his royal brother when Warwick and Somerset seemed weaker?'

'My master,' Mauclerc retorted, 'had no quarrel with his brothers but only with the Woodvilles. The King's marriage to Elizabeth of that name offended many of the lords. The Woodvilles are grasping, a family greedy for power, deeply ambitious without the talent to match . . .'

'Like so many of our noble lords.'

Mauclerc drew his breath sharply. 'You insult my master?'

'No Master Mauclerc, I tell the truth, but enough of this fencing, this sham swordplay.'

'You talk of my master betraying his own brother,' Mauclerc jabbed a finger at Urswicke, 'yet you are here to act the traitor to your own mistress, Margaret Beaufort.'

'My loyalty is to the King,' Christopher insisted. 'My own father is Recorder of London, an important judge and the most fervent supporter of Edward of York.'

'Though your relationship with your father is hardly cordial?'

'We have our differences.'

'You mean he has his women who, I understand, drove your mother to an early grave . . .' Mauclerc paused as Urswicke's fingers fell to brush the hilt of his dagger.

'My father is my father,' Urswicke murmured. 'I am who I am, a clerk, a lawyer well versed in politics who now accepts his hour has come. The House of Lancaster, the fortunes of the Beauforts are finished, shattered and pushed into the dark.'

'We were not talking about them but your mother?'

'Leave that, Master Mauclerc. Let us concentrate on what's going to happen.'

'Oh, that's easy enough. The King, not to mention Gloucester and Clarence, are determined to pull Lancaster up by its rotten roots and consign that stricken tree to the fires of history.'

'And my mistress, the countess?'

'You mean your former mistress?'

'True.' Urswicke half smiled. 'But her fate?'

'She is married to a Stafford who, like many of his tribe, fought for our King, in particular at Barnet. Consequently she is safe providing she behaves herself. Her son is another matter. You see, once all this is over, the English court will divide. There will be the King, his wife Elizabeth Woodville and her brood. Close to them Richard of Gloucester and George of Clarence. Then there are the Yorkist warlords, men such as William Hastings, Stanley, Buckingham and the others and, of course, Holy Mother Church. We now deal with the Lancastrians. There is Henry VI, that holy fool who lies locked up in the Tower. He can stay there, he will never come out.' Urswicke tried not to flinch at the venom in Mauclerc's voice. 'Yes, yes Christopher, Henry VI will not be making any more royal progresses through the kingdom. He can stay imprisoned, pattering his prayers and preparing for his own funeral. We, however, are going to hunt for his Queen, Margaret of Anjou, and the bastard Edward, her son. We want to capture them. In the meantime, those who have taken sanctuary here must die and my master intends to kill any other remaining Lancastrian with even the weakest claim to the throne.' Mauclerc pushed his face closer. 'And that includes your mistress's son, Henry Tudor, the offspring of her former husband Edmund who was, as you know, half-brother to that holy fool Henry. What we now want to know are the whereabouts of your mistress's son?'

'In a while,' Urswicke replied. 'We must not travel that road so swiftly. We must proceed at a canter, not at a gallop.'

'Time is passing, Urswicke. You must make choices. As I have said, Somerset and the others are for the slaughter. You want protection from my master and you shall have it, but it comes with a price . . .'

'It always does.'

'Or it can be interpreted as a token of good faith by yourself.'

'I offer you three such tokens.'

'And what are these?'

'The whereabouts of Margaret of Anjou and her son.'

Mauclerc's surprise was palpable. He half rose, gasping for breath. 'Nonsense.' He breathed. 'How can you?' Mauclerc sat down. 'Why should she . . .?'

'Margaret and her son are desperate to cross the Severn and seek the protection of my mistress's brother-in-law, Jasper Tudor, who hides behind the vast fastness of Pembroke Castle where, by the way, her own son also shelters. So,' Urswicke waved a hand, 'you have two tokens, take them or leave them.'

Mauclerc stretched out a hand, Urswicke clasped this. Mauclerc squeezed, let go and got to his feet. 'Hold.' Urswicke peered up through the dark as he gestured with his head towards the abbey. 'The Lancastrian defeat, so swift, so crushing. What happened? And I might be able to give you another token.'

'Edward of York,' Mauclerc paused as if gathering his thoughts, 'Edward of York,' he replied, 'came on fast, passing through Southwick, aiming like an arrow for this abbey. Margaret of Anjou and her army were desperate to cross the Severn but they failed. She and Somerset had no choice but to advance to meet us. The Lancastrians divided their host into three battle groups. Prince Edward and Lord Wenlock held the centre. Somerset their right, Courtenay of Devon their left flank. They advanced swiftly through the Vineyards and reached the south of the abbey.'

'And King Edward's army?'

'Also divided into three phalanxes. King Edward held the centre, Gloucester the left, Lord Hastings the right. What the enemy didn't know was that King Edward had hidden a host of two hundred mounted spearmen on a wooded hill a little to the south of Gloucester's phalanx.'

'We heard the sound of cannon fire?'

'Yes. King Edward brought up his artillery and archers to deliver a shower of missiles on Somerset's battle line: this proved to be a sharp and deadly hail. Somerset was left with no choice but to attack, and became embroiled with Gloucester and the King's phalanxes. The Yorkists held the attack until the spearmen King Edward had hidden on that wooded hill charged out to smash into Somerset's line, forcing it back. The Yorkists then began to roll the Lancastrian line up as you would a piece of piping . . .'

'But the Lancastrian centre, surely . . .?'

'Ah.' Mauclerc tapped the side of his nose; he paused as an owl hooted hauntingly through the dark.'

'Three times!' Urswicke exclaimed.

'Three times what?'

'If an owl hoots three times through the dark, it's a prophecy for those who hear it. If there are two people in the same place, one of them will die and the other will be the cause of it. Do you believe that, Mauclerc?'

'Aye, as I believe harridans fly through the air and the Hounds of Hell prowl this abbey. I don't believe in such babble talk.'

'The battle?' Urswicke asked, quickly trying to conceal his own unease.

'Ah,' Mauclerc laughed abruptly, 'the Lancastrian centre should have come to Somerset's aid but Lord Wenlock froze, God knows why?'

'I do,' Urswicke replied. 'And here's your third token. I met Wenlock secretly on his march to the Severn. I pretended to be sending messages to the Duke of Somerset from his kinswoman, my mistress. Anyway, Wenlock who, as you know, once fought for the House of York, was open to suggestion. After all, King Edward had once appointed him to be captain of the English fortress at Calais. My couriers delivered messages informing Wenlock that if the battle went against Lancaster and he survived, my mistress would intercede for Lord John Wenlock and so would her husband, Sir Humphrey Stafford.'

'So that explains it,' Mauclerc interrupted. 'Wenlock didn't freeze, he just didn't commit his forces to confront the Yorkists who inflicted great damage along the Lancastrian battle line. Courtenay of Devon was killed in the bloody hand-to-hand fighting, as was Beaufort's brother John. Somerset was furious. He left the battle and galloped up to Wenlock to remonstrate. Wenlock argued back, so Somerset, and he has a fiery temper, smashed Wenlock's head with his battle-axe.'

'God and all his angels,' Urswicke breathed.

'The Lancastrians witnessed this savage clash: their leaders were killing each other whilst the rest were being cut down as you would lop branches in an orchard. The Lancastrians broke. They fled towards Abbot's Mill, one of the Severn tributaries, but this was swollen due to recent rains. Many were drowned, the others tried to flee across the sunken water meadow only to be cut down. A day of great slaughter. Parts of the meadow were knee-deep in gore; there was enough spilt blood to float a boat. Edward's victory was complete, a sign of God's pleasure for the House of York. Now we must go.' Mauclerc beckoned. 'Our masters await.'

Urswicke picked up his cloak lying over the table and followed Clarence's henchman out of the arbour and across the kitchen garden. He made Mauclerc, who carried the lanternhorn, walk ahead of him. Urswicke watched the moving circle of light as they made their way under the looming mass of Tewkesbury Abbey. Night had fallen but the abbey didn't sleep. Knots of well-armed household knights, sporting the blue and yellow of York as well as the personal coat of arms of the three royal brothers, guarded all entrances to and from the abbey.

Urswicke and Mauclerc eventually left the precincts by a postern gate. They hurried down a narrow trackway into Tewkesbury village, its usual silence and tranquillity broken by the mass of soldiers camped out in the streets which led into the market square, dominated by a soaring stone cross. Edward and his brothers had taken over a merchant's house overlooking the market area, a majestic three-storey mansion built out of honey-coloured Cotswold stone; both its door and windows were flung open in a blaze of candlelight. The royal brothers were gathered in the long, wood-panelled dining hall. They lounged at the top of the common table, Edward the King slouched on a throne-like chair, his brothers either side of him. Further down, clerks of the royal chancery copied and sealed letters, proclamations and inden-tures. The hall was perfumed with the sweet smell of scented candles and the rich odour of melting wax. Around the room stood York's leading henchmen. Urswicke recognised Lovel, Catesby, Ratcliffe and others of Gloucester's household, as well as those of the King, such as William Hastings who played such a prominent role in the Yorkist's victory. The royal standards and other banners filled one corner of the hall. Strewn on the floor beside them were those of the defeated Lancastrians, besmirched with urine, faeces and other dirt. Urswicke glimpsed the Lilies and Portcullis of Beaufort and hurriedly glanced away. Mauclerc told him to stay before handing the lantern to a retainer and hurrying up to kneel between the King and Clarence, with Gloucester leaning over to listen to what Mauclerc whispered as he pointed back towards Urswicke. The King raised a hand, snapping his fingers, gesturing at Urswicke to approach. Mauclerc brought a stool, placing it where he had knelt. Urswicke went to bend the knee.

'No need,' Edward barked. 'Not now. Time is passing.' The King's light-blue eyes creased into a smile. 'I know you, Christopher, or rather your family. Your father's loyalty provides great comfort to me and mine. Now.' Edward raised himself out of his chair, 'Hastings!' he shouted. 'Clear this room. You sirs,' Edward bellowed at the clerks further down the table, 'gather your manuscripts, get out and do so quickly.' Edward rose and clapped his hands, the hall swiftly emptied. Urswicke glanced at the royal brothers. All three had stripped themselves of their mail and armour and now wore puffed, sleeveless jerkins, displaying the blue and yellow of York, over stained cambric shirts. The royal brothers were still blood-streaked and, as they moved on their chairs, the spurs on their boots jingled like fairy bells. They had taken off their broad, studded warbelts and hung these over the back of the chairs. Waiting for the hall to be fully cleared, Urswicke studied all three brothers closely. Edward the King, he concluded, certainly deserved the title as the handsomest man in the kingdom. Despite the exertions of the day, Edward still looked serene and composed, his beautiful face seemed slightly burnished as if with gold dust: Edward's nose was thin and aquiline, his lips full and merry, his blond hair closely cropped and sheened with sweat whilst the light-blue eyes were bright with mischief and merriment. The King had retaken his seat and now sat, mouth slightly open, staring down the hall, a heavy-lidded look as he watched Hastings usher a bevy of young damsels out of a window seat towards the door. Clarence looked almost identical to his elder brother, though sharp observation would soon notice the reddish, vein-streaked drinker's face, the mouth slightly slobbery, lips twisted into a perpetual pout. Clarence, Urswicke concluded, believed the world owed him much and still had to pay. Richard of Gloucester was remarkably different from both his elder brothers. He had long, reddish hair which framed a pale, severe face with watchful eyes and tight-lipped mouth. Rather small in height, Richard sat slightly twisted as he favoured a birth injury to his back. He kept drumming his fingers on the table while staring around the hall, as if he suspected enemies still lurked nearby. A man of nervous energy, Richard of Gloucester was totally devoted to his eldest brother, as well as to the memory of their beloved father, slain at Wakefield. Over the last few months Richard had emerged as a fierce warrior skilled in battle and totally ruthless in the pursuit and destruction of the enemies of his House. Richard turned and caught Urswicke staring at him. He winked and Gloucester's severe face creased into a genuine smile which completely transformed him.

'Christopher Urswicke.' Gloucester leaned across, hand extended for the clerk to clasp. He did so, moving to the side as Edward sat back in his own chair to allow Christopher to respond. Abruptly Urswicke felt his shoulder tightly gripped. He turned. Clarence pushed his face close, lips glistening with red wine, which drenched his breath as well as the front of his doublet. 'And how's your mistress little Meg? We will deal with her and her by-blow, the imp Henry Tudor. She cannot hide behind the Staffords of Buckingham forever. We will . . .'

'George.' Edward leaned over and gently prised Clarence's hand away. 'First,' the King beamed at Urswicke, 'we must deal with troubles of the day. Yes?'

Urswicke nodded his agreement. Deep in his heart, however, he would certainly remember what the King had just said. 'First we must deal . . .' He glanced quickly at Clarence. Then what, he wondered . . .?

'I have thrown the dice in my last game of hazard.' Somerset took his hands away from his face and stared up at the cross above the chantry chapel altar. He had described the battle outside, freely confessing how he had committed one mistake after another, explaining in detail his execution of Wenlock. 'Our only hope,' he murmured, 'is that the Angevin crosses the Severn, to be welcomed and protected by Jasper Tudor. If not . . .' His voice trailed off. 'If not,' he repeated, 'you Margaret and your boy are the last remaining hope of Lancaster. Now listen.' Somerset stared around the chantry chapel. 'You know, Margaret, that George of Clarence, like Neville of Warwick, clashed bitterly with the Woodvilles. Both nobles were furious at Edward's secret marriage to Elizabeth Woodville, an insult which has rankled deeply. Warwick and Clarence left the Yorkist camp in open rebellion. However, the Queen Mother, Cecily, the Rose of Raby, successfully persuaded George and Edward to be reconciled.' He paused at the cries of some wounded man further down the nave, a shriek of agony at the pain as well as the despair which now darkened the souls of all those facing imminent death. 'Soon,' he whispered, 'we will be past all sorrow.'

Margaret, despite her revulsion at Beaufort's arrogance, which had brought him and thousands of those who trusted him to this sorry pitch, leaned over and stroked Somerset's blood-streaked wrist. He grasped her hand and gently squeezed her fingers.

'Anyway,' he released his grip, 'you know the rest. Warwick and Anjou invaded, only to be brutally defeated. Clarence, as usual, survived. As I warned you, be most wary of that most sinister prince of blood. When Clarence was with us, I heard strange rumours, stories and whispers. Some of these concerned you and yours . . .'

'In what way?'

'Apparently Clarence boasted how he has a spy deep in your household: I suspect this is most probable because Clarence is committed to the total destruction of the Beauforts and all whom we hold dear. However, Clarence nurses a diabolic pride, a real hubris which could bring him down. Such a weakness would give you the power to meddle in his affairs. Trust me, Margaret. I confess I have been guilty of following my own pride, of not listening to more subtle counselling. However, here on my death watch, let me assure you: Edward of York's greatest weakness is his own family, his queen and the Woodvilles, a pack truly hated, cursed and reviled. Clarence will not change his nature. He is as committed to their destruction as he is to yours. The Woodvilles will supply all the necessities for the coming conflagration.'

'And Gloucester?'

'Loyal to his brother: "loyalty is mine" is Richard's motto.

He will stand by Edward for as long as Edward lives. What might happen if Edward died?' Somerset pulled a face. 'To return to my argument, Clarence is the real weakness in the Yorkist defences, his soul burns with ambition. He sees himself as the rightful Lord of England. When he was allied to Warwick and the House of Lancaster, he actually proclaimed himself King. He will now return to such idle boasting like a whore to her trade.' Somerset wiped the sweat from his face. 'And so we come to the Secret Chancery. Clarence's cabal of clerks, three in number, Rhinelanders in origin, former friars. Clarence depends on these for providing grist for his mischief.'

'Which is?'

'We do not know, except the clerks are called "the Three Kings", after their city of origin, Cologne where, according to tradition, the Three Kings mentioned in the Gospel lie buried. They also take the saints' names: Caspar, Melchior and Balthasar. You may well ask, Margaret, why should I, a duke, a prominent leader of the Lancastrian cause, be interested in Clarence's Three Kings . . .?' Beaufort rose and crossed to the wall recess where the cruets were placed during Mass. Beaufort picked up an earthenware jug and drank greedily before offering it to Margaret who shook her head. 'A gift from the abbot,' Beaufort whispered, coming back to his chair. He sat down cradling the jug. 'From the little we have learnt,' he continued, 'The Three Kings have drawn up a book, a manuscript, a secret document called "Titulus Regius".'

'The Title of the King,' Margaret murmured.

Beaufort stared at his young kinswoman, the last true surviving Beaufort. He wondered if she would be safe, surrounded as she was by the different wolf packs which prowled the Yorkist court. Despite the poor light, Beaufort glimpsed a shift in Margaret's clever eyes as she stared back. A knowing look, as if Margaret Beaufort had studied the Duke of Somerset and knew his true worth. A small nun-like woman, Beaufort reflected, and again he wondered how she would cope with the victorious, vicious Clarence, who would watch her and her household with his spies and paid assassins.

'The "Titulus Regius".' Margaret demanded: 'What is it?' She paused as a door was flung open further down the nave. Margaret sprang to her feet and hurried out of the chantry chapel. She feared armed Yorkists might have broken in but it was only Abbot Strensham. Apparently one of the wounded Lancastrians, realising he was in danger of death, had pleaded with one of his companions who, in turn, had begged a sympathetic Yorkist guard to fetch a priest so the dying man could be shriven. Margaret watched the shifting shapes of Abbot Strensham and his prior, who followed the lead of the bobbing light from the sacristan's lantern-horn down the nave. She froze at another fierce cry which was answered by raucous singing from the Yorkist soldiers outside. Margaret returned to the chantry chapel where Somerset was drinking from the wine jug.

'Remember this,' he continued as Margaret sat down, 'our three Yorkist warlords have a strange family history, or so rumour has it: their mother, Cecily Neville, daughter of the Earl of Westmoreland, was apparently an outstanding beauty, so much so she was called the Rose of Raby. She also has a hideous temper. Rumour has it that Clarence, using the Three Kings as searchers and scribes, is investigating his own family hunting for this and that.'

'Why?'

'God knows, but Clarence is continuing such searches. I am not too sure what he wants to prove but, to get his own way, Clarence would go down to Hell and challenge the Lord Satan. Believe me, kinswoman,' Somerset pulled his chair closer, 'if you can, strike back, meddle in his affairs. Clarence is undoubtedly doing the same to you and yours but he's even a greater threat to the House of York. Ah well,' Somerset gestured with his head, 'Abbot Strensham is still tending to that poor comrade. He might as well shrive me for by this time tomorrow; I will be brought to judgement before God's tribunal . . .'

Margaret rose, she kissed her kinsman and crept out of the chantry, silent as a shadow back up the sanctuary steps and into the sacristy where Bray was waiting. He explained how the abbot, prior and sacristan were still in the church so he would escort her back to the guesthouse. They left the abbey precincts and made their way along paved passageways, tunnels of stone lit by the occasional lantern. They crossed the cobbled courtyard stretching in front of the guesthouse, clearly lit by sconce torches fixed to the walls. Margaret heard a sound from the sloping, tiled roof of their lodgings. She glanced up and stared in amazement at the blaze of fire which came hurtling through the darkness towards her. She pushed Bray to the left even as she darted the other way. The flaming bag of oil crashed onto the cobbles, followed by another and then a third; all three bursting into spouts of flame and fiery oil. Bray raised the alarm screaming, 'Harrow! Harrow!' The door to the guesthouse was flung open and Owain Mortimer, principal squire to the Countess Margaret, darted out, followed by his twin sister Oswina. Margaret, gasping for breath, pointed up at the sloping roof. Once her trembling had subsided, she beckoned at her companions to follow her down the narrow gulley which ran along the side of the guesthouse. They turned into the backyard, a place where the refuse was piled; a stinking, slimy midden heap, home for a horde of rats which squealed and scurried away at their approach. Margaret and Bray stopped by the narrow siege ladder leaning against the back wall of the two-storey guesthouse. Bray immediately climbed this to examine the broad ledge against which the rest of the roof rested. He glanced swiftly around and clambered down.

'So easy,' he gestured at the roof, 'especially for a trained assassin. He took those satchels of oil, each primed with a slow-burning fuse. He then crouched on the ledge before climbing up the tiles. Easy enough; he could rest against them and wait. He knew we would have to return here. He hears our approach, sees us clear in the light of our sconce torches. He takes his tinder, the first is lit and . . .'

'The back of this guesthouse is blind.' Owain Mortimer pointed up the wall. 'All the chambers are to the front. No one inside would even hear or see anything amiss. No one,' he repeated wearily in his sing-song voice, 'no one at all.'

'We were abed,' his twin declared, 'though we were not sleeping, I was worried about you mistress.'

Margaret held up a hand as she stared at the ladder. 'Let us go inside,' she declared. 'It's best to be there.'

They returned to the stark parlour close to the guesthouse entrance. Oswina busied herself lighting candles whilst Owain poured a jug of breakfast ale into four stoups on a wooden tray.

'Is Christopher back, has he returned?' Margaret asked, sipping her drink.

'No he's not here,' Owain replied, 'and nor should we, so close to your enemy; the rest of the household agree, they have gone to their chambers and locked themselves in. God knows mistress, what will happen on the morrow. The Yorkists will drink deeply tonight. They will all be in a bloodlust and looking for vengeance. Have you decided, Mistress – what we should do next?'

'Not yet,' Bray retorted.

'Then when?' Oswina replied.

Margaret, still holding the tankard, sat back in her chair. 'The assassin,' she spoke, her voice sounding harsher than she had intended, 'the evil soul who tried to burn me alive, who could it be? Why now? Why now? Though I suspect,' she put down the tankard, 'that those fiery missiles were the work of York, Clarence in particular.'

'They wish to root out the Beaufort tree.' Bray lapsed into his usual homily, a whispered tirade against the House of York. Margaret sat back in the cushioned chair and let her mind drift. She had to curb the fear curdling within her. She closed her eyes and prayed for her husband Humphrey Stafford, now lying grievously wounded after Barnet. The news she had received from her manor at Woking was most disturbing. Humphrey, never the strongest of men, suffered from a life-long skin corruption, St Anthony's fire, which some leeches likened to leprosy, so much so that four years ago, she and Humphrey had joined the confraternity of Burton Lazars. Margaret had bought statues, triptychs and other paintings celebrating St Anthony's life to decorate the solar of her manor house, praying constantly beneath them, yet these supplications had not worked any miracle. Now the household leeches reported how the contagion had been grievously affected by the wounds Sir Humphrey had received: a knife cut to the thigh and a sword blow which had glanced off his shoulder. Margaret murmured another prayer and opened her eyes. She really should return to Woking but not until the present business, vital to her, was completed in London.

Margaret half listened to Bray and Mortimer's heated whispering and her mind went back to her manor house, wondering what was happening there. She loved her Woking estates; she had inherited them as part of a legacy from her grandmother, the

redoubtable Lady Holland, along with a rich collection of manuscripts and delicately inscribed psalters and other devotional
literature. Margaret tried to recall the manor in an attempt to
soothe her humours: how her residence was screened by copses
of ancient oak, beech and copper set in lush, fertile parkland.
The house itself was twice-moated; the outer one contained the
poultry runs, livestock sheds, warren, granges and a small deer
park. The inner moat, crossed by a drawbridge leading through
a fortified gateway, contained the manor itself, with its great hall,
large pantry and spacious buttery. Then there was a chapel,
chancery office and, above all, a range of private chambers overlooking the herb and flower gardens, a well-stocked stew pond
and lush orchards.

Margaret felt her eyes grow heavy and she sank into a half-
waking sleep; as she did so, the different visions which always
swept in, returned clear and precise. Margaret felt as if she was
staring at a finely etched painting or the brilliant illumination
in some psalter. She sat and watched herself struggling through
snow which had drifted heavily. There were trees, bushes and
rocky outcrops, and she was sure that she was in Pembrokeshire.
She was hastening towards a great iron wall which soared up
into the wine-coloured sky. The wall was at least sixty yards
high, entered through a fortified gateway guarded by snarling,
black-haired war dogs. Margaret was not frightened of these; she
was more anxious about what was waiting for her beyond the
wall. She turned and glanced piteously at the corpses which
sprawled against the hard-packed snow. She recognised that of
her father, stretched out as they had found him in his chancery
chamber; the goblet of wine he'd been drinking had rolled close
to her dead father's head, turning his blond hair blood-red, as if
he had been struck a grievous blow. She also recognised the other
corpses, her first true husband, the beloved Edmund Tudor. He
was lying all crouched as he had on his deathbed, consumed by
a raging fever. Other corpses littered the snow, men and women
of her family and household. She wanted to go back to them but
the snow dragged at her, its whiteness hurting her eyes. She was
sure she could hear her son crying from behind the soaring iron
wall whilst the harrowing baying of wolves somewhere around
her seemed to be drawing closer . . .

'Mistress, mistress?' Margaret opened her eyes. Bray was staring beseechingly down at her. 'Mistress, you were chattering. Father Prior is here. He is very concerned.' Margaret blinked, rubbed her face and sat up in the high-backed chair and smiled at Prior Anselm, who took the stool placed in front of her, his bony, angular face wreathed in concern.

'My Lady,' he began, 'the good brothers have had their horarium severely disturbed; the abbey is full of armed men, more blood stains our flagstones than dust. Violence stalks the cloisters, our choir stalls, even the great sanctuary itself. Now we hear reports of fiery missiles being thrown down into the courtyard outside – that's true, isn't it? I have inspected the cobbles; they reek of burning oil whilst scraps of scorched leather scatter like leaves. One of our brothers glimpsed this as he hurried to fill waterskins from the well. What is this, why now?' The prior joined his hands in prayer. 'God knows what further mischief will raise its sinister head like some deadly vicious serpent – because that is what Satan is, he and his many legions.'

'Father Prior?' Margaret grasped the old monk's right hand, raised it to her lips and kissed his thick, copper ring of office. The prior blushed.

'I am sorry,' he muttered. 'But the truth is we are all terrified. We are not men of war.'

Margaret, throwing a warning glance at Bray, Owain and Oswina, quickly described what had happened, offering the conclusion that the assailant was probably some drunkard eager to do hurt to a Beaufort or a Lancastrian fugitive furious that a Beaufort should be sheltering amongst Yorkist warlords.

'You see, Father Prior,' Margaret gently touched the back of his hand, 'I am living proof that you cannot serve two masters.'

The prior laughed and clambered to his feet. He walked to the door then paused and glanced at Margaret's three companions. 'I recognise you, Master Bray, as the Lady Margaret's steward, but these young persons? They look alike. They must be brother and sister?' The prior cocked his head sideways like some curious sparrow. 'Yes, night-black hair, smooth, sallow faces, large eyes and full-lipped mouths. You must be Welsh, yes? We have some of those from the southern tribes here in the abbey.'

'Owain and Oswina Mortimer,' Margaret replied, gesturing

at the twins to grasp the prior's proffered hand. They did so hurriedly, then stepped back as if shy at the attention now being shown them. 'They are kinsmen of the noble Mortimer family, orphans raised by my brother-in-law, Lord Jasper Tudor.'

'Ah,' the prior sighed, 'a man the Yorkists would love to seize. And he is where?'

'Pembroke Castle,' Margaret retorted, 'where he will stay until he can take ship to France.' Margaret shrugged. 'Jasper entrusted Owain and Oswina to me. They, along with Reginald Bray and Christopher Urswicke, are my privileged chamber people.'

'Urswicke, ah yes. We have heard about him. A brother saw him leave for the town where more excitement is brewing. The King has taken over Merchant Stratford's house. A party of horsemen have been despatched on urgent royal business. I understand Urswicke was one of them. Now my Lady, take care. I understand my Lord of Clarence has insisted that he visits you to present his compliments.' The prior sketched a blessing in the air and then left.

Margaret would have loved to retire. She felt sweat soaked, heavy limbed, her mind fraught with anxiety which gnawed at her peace of mind, the prospect of meeting Clarence only sharpening this. She tried to compose herself, putting on a brave face while she and her chamber people hastily prepared the parlour. Clarence arrived and Margaret wondered at the sound of heavy cartwheels across the cobbles, the clatter of sharpened hooves and the deep neigh of dray horses. Owain volunteered to go and see. Margaret shook her head saying that he should stay at table and eat the light repast the refectorian had left in the small adjoining buttery.

Clarence arrived, he almost kicked the door open, mincing in like some court lady. He'd wrapped a bottle-green cloak around him which caught on the jingling spurs of his war boots. Clarence, grasping a wine goblet in one hand, simply tore the cloak free. He snapped his fingers and pointed at a stool. One of the three shadowy figures who accompanied him hastily brought this across. Clarence sat down with a heavy sigh, his sweaty face creased into a false smile, lips glistening with wine, eyes bright with malice. He stroked his finely clipped moustache and beard, dragging at the bits of dry wine caught there.

'My Lord,' Margaret turned in her chair to face him squarely.

'My Lady.' Clarence bowed mockingly, raised his goblet in toast and drank deeply. 'Oh, by the way,' he pointed at the shadowy figures behind him, 'these are my chancery clerks who manage my Secret Seal.'

Margaret glanced up at them and tried to hide her fear at the three sinister figures garbed in hoods and blue-black robes. She recognised the colour and cut as belonging to some minor order of friars but she could not recall their name. These three were certainly not men of prayer. They stood, menacingly silent, hands up the voluminous sleeves of their robes which, Margaret suspected, concealed a dagger, stiletto, or some other such weapon. One of these leaned down to whisper in Clarence's ear and, as he did so, Margaret, with her keen sense of smell, caught the odour of oil and smoke and she wondered if one – or all – of these macabre figures had been responsible for the recent attack on her. Margaret shifted her gaze from Clarence and stared hard at his sinister companions, refusing to be cowed or frightened by them. She found it difficult to distinguish individual features but she was aware of heavy-lidded eyes and noses as sharp as quill pens. All three were thin-lipped which, with their bulging foreheads and tight-lipped grimace, gave them an odd fish-like appearance. Wolfsheads, Margaret concluded: whatever their garb or whatever Clarence said about their status, these were predators ready to strike.

'Three brothers,' Clarence whispered, as if revelling in their company. 'Excellent clerks!'

'I have heard of them.' Bray spoke up. 'Former friars, the Three Kings from Cologne.'

'Others call them that.' Clarence lifted his goblet. 'To me they are just the most faithful of retainers who accompany me here, there and everywhere. They do my bidding like the loyal lurchers they are. Now,' Clarence smacked his lips, 'I have brought you something, little Meg.'

'That is not my name. I am, sir, the Lady Margaret Beaufort, Countess of Richmond.'

'Which makes you a kinswoman to the Beaufort traitor and other vile miscreants lurking in the abbey church.' Clarence, face seething with hate, jabbed a finger. 'Where is your brother-in-law, the traitor Jasper Tudor and your dearly beloved son Henry? Little Henry?' Clarence's voice became a squeal of mockery. Bray's hands went beneath the table, close to the long, stabbing dagger in his belt. Margaret glanced up. One of the Three Kings had brought his hand from the sleeve of his gown. Margaret glimpsed the glitter of the long, thin blade.

'My brother-in-law,' Margaret retorted quickly, 'resides in Pembroke. So does my beloved son.'

'Do they now?' Clarence taunted.

'My Lord.' Margaret fought to curb the almost overwhelming desire to claw at Clarence's false, fat, glistening face. 'My Lord,' she repeated, 'I am tired and I need to retire.' She made to move. 'I should do so now.'

'Oh no, no, no.' Clarence fluttered his fingers in her face. 'I must show you something before you sleep. You must say goodbye before they leave.'

'Who?'

'Come, come! You must see this.' Clarence rose to his feet and swept out of the guesthouse, Margaret felt that she had no choice but to follow. She stopped however, just before the threshold, and stared at the great war cart which stood in the centre of the small bailey. On each corner of the cart a cresset torch flared against the cold night breeze, the flames illuminating the horror displayed there. The sides of the cart were nothing more than sharp poles lashed together. Their sharp, spear-like tips provided gaps for archers inside to loose, whilst the poles would serve as a sturdy defence. Now these sharpened posts had been used to display, on all three sides of the cart, a row of severed heads thrust on the tips like so many ripe apples. The breeze shifted, rippling the hair of the decapitated heads, and Margaret caught the salty tang of dried human blood.

She walked slowly forward, fascinated by the abomination. She recognised some of the dirty, gore-stained faces, their hair pulled back and tied in a topknot so each face could be clearly seen. Margaret immediately glimpsed the once handsome face of John Beaufort, Edmund's younger brother, now contorted by a savage, bloody death. Clarence grasped Margaret by the elbow, a tight clasp as he moved her around the cart so she could clearly see the severed heads of Lancastrians killed in battle, their corpses decapitated in preparation for being tarred and poled above the gateways of different cities. As she passed the tail of the cart, she glimpsed the blood-drenched sacks of severed limbs, which would also be displayed and proclaimed to the sound of horn, trumpet and bagpipe. Margaret could take no more. She turned, gagged and retched, going down on her knees. Clarence crouched beside her. Bray protested and tried to come between them. Clarence drew his dagger.

'Enough George, enough!' Clarence clambered to his feet as Richard of Gloucester strolled out of the darkness. 'George, the King needs you. My Lady?' Gloucester pointed to Margaret resting on Bray's arm. 'I bid you goodnight and good rest.' He came closer, in the juddering light. Gloucester's harsh face seemed softer and Margaret glimpsed genuine pity in those ever-shifting eyes. 'George,' Richard lifted a gauntleted hand, holding Margaret's gaze as he spoke to his brother, 'You have no further business with this lady, the hour draws on. Judgement awaits, come.'

Clarence backed away from Margaret, fluttering his fingers in mock farewell before spinning on his heel and following his brother into the darkness, his three sinister guards close behind. Margaret watched them go as she tightly gripped Bray's arm.

'Master Reginald,' she hissed, 'I swear by the light I will kill that demon incarnate and all his ilk. How dare he threaten my beloved son?' She turned and Bray, who knew his mistress's secret soul, was frightened by the look of intense fury which had transformed her usually placid face.

'Master Bray,' she whispered hoarsely, 'this is truly *à l'Outrance, usque ad mortem* – to the death, whatever form that death takes.'

PART TWO

'Queen Margaret was taken and securely held.'
Crowland Chronicle

Urswicke reined in with the rest of the Yorkist war band before the gate of Little Malvern Priory. He stared around at his companions. In the main they were Clarence's henchmen, professional killers; a few royal knight bannerets had also joined the cohort led by Sir Richard Crofts, a local magnate who knew the twisting, sunken lanes, narrow trackways and coffin paths of Gloucester as he did the veins on the back of his hands. For a while the cohort just sat, horses snorting, shaking the sweat out after such a vigorous ride, sharpened hooves scraping the ground.

'They must know we are here,' Mauclerc called out over his shoulder. He dismounted, drew his sword and pounded on the gate. '*Les Roiaux!*' he shouted, 'we are King's men, open in his name. Open, I say, or we'll force the gate.'

Lights appeared on the crenellated wall above them, moving circles of dancing torchlight. One of Mauclerc's riders primed his crossbow and loosed a bolt. Others did the same to the scrape of swords leaving their scabbards. The crossbow bolts were aimed at the pools of light which swiftly disappeared. Urswicke heard a horn bray followed by the rattle of chains and the scraping of bolts. The great gate was thrown open and Urswicke joined the charge into the entrance bailey which stretched up to the main priory buildings. Mauclerc had despatched members of his war band to search the priory's two postern gates: these must have met some resistance as the clatter and clash of arms echoed from the other side of the priory. They all dismounted. A monk carrying a cross in one hand and a lantern in the other hurried through the darkness and sank to his knees. Mauclerc and Crofts showed him no mercy. Clarence's henchmen seized the monk's head between gauntleted hands and squeezed hard, shouting questions at him. The monk, gasping with pain, dropped the lantern and pointed back to a two-storey, grey-ragstone building with lights glimmering between the shutters. Again Mauclerc shouted questions then pushed the monk away. The man stumbled to his feet and pointed at the shutters of what Urswicke believed was the guesthouse; these were flung open followed immediately by the sharp whirr of crossbow bolts cutting the air. Most of these fell short but the monk seemed almost to stumble onto one, taking the barb deep in his chest.

Mauclerc's party, weapons drawn, charged towards the building, racing across the cobbles so as to distract the aim of the bowmen sheltering in the guesthouse. More bolts whistled sharply, most missed their target. Urswicke, panting and gasping, felt one whip past his face. At last they reached the door and the bowmen above found it difficult to loose, let alone find a target. A bench was found and used as a battering ram to smash the ancient door off its leather hinges, then they were inside. Men-at-arms wearing the blue and white livery of Lancaster confronted them, thronging in the hallway, along the gallery, as well as on the stairs leading up to the solar. A savage hand-to-hand struggle ensued, sword grinding bone, dagger piercing flesh, mallet, war axe and morning star crushing heads and faces. Flesh was ripped. Blood gushed to the devilish cacophony of shouts, screams and heart-rending yells. No quarter was asked. No mercy shown, until the remaining defenders threw down their weapons and fell to their knees, hands raised in surrender. Mauclerc and Croft screamed at their own men to respect this. Urswicke, who had managed to avoid any real danger by keeping to the rear of the press, watched the surviving Lancastrians being disarmed and pushed out into the darkness. Mauclerc ordered most of his cohort to stay whilst he, Urswicke and a select few climbed the stairs to the solar. Mauclerc kicked open the door and went inside. He stood, sword drawn, staring at the group huddled before the hearth.

Urswicke immediately recognised Queen Margaret of Anjou, the Angevin, resplendent in blue and gold, surrounded by her principal ladies whom Urswicke knew by sight: Anne Neville, the Countess of Devon, Katherine Vaux, and other leading lights of the Angevin's court. Urswicke felt a pang of pity as he wondered if all these ladies knew they were now widows, their husbands being cut down at Tewkesbury. Beside the Queen stood her son Prince Edward, resplendent in silver Milanese armour, his ornate plumed helmet on the floor beside him, his warbelt lying across his mother's lap. He walked towards Mauclerc with all the arrogance of a peacock, his mouth twisted in contemptuous anger.

'What business!' He paused before Mauclerc. 'Sir, what business have you here?'

Mauclerc lurched forward and struck the prince full in the face. He then hit him again and again, ignoring the screams and cries of the Queen. The prince tried to resist but the knights who had accompanied Mauclerc seized the young man and also pummelled him with blows and kicks.

'Strip him!' Mauclerc yelled. 'Take his foolish finery as plunder.'

The knights did so, tearing off the prince's breastplate, greaves and the chainmail jerkin beneath, until the prince was reduced to standing in his linen shirt and leggings. A pathetic young man, now aware that he truly was in the hands of his enemies. Queen Margaret rose and hurried towards her son, hands out, pleading and begging. Mauclerc struck her repeatedly in the face, pushing her back, shouting at his men to strip her to her shift. He then ordered his retainers to bind the hands of both mother and son. The royal couple were hustled like Newgate felons out of the solar, down the stairs and out into the yard where a cart was waiting. Both royal prisoners were pushed into this; an archer lashed their hands and feet to the slats.

Mauclerc went back into the priory to inform the fallen Queen's ladies that they must fend for themselves, whilst their men-at-arms who survived the furious mêlée were to be stripped of all their weapons and possessions then be released. Nor did the monks escape unscathed. Mauclerc yelled how they had sheltered sworn traitors so they should look after the wounded and bury the dead. Urswicke used the confusion, the to-ing and fro-ing, to climb into the cart to sit beside Prince Edward who slouched, eyes half closed, mouth dribbling. The young prince was deep in shock like his mother. Urswicke stared piteously at them. Once these were the Golden Ones, the Mighty of the Land: they had wielded great power with legions at their beck and call. Now it was all finished. The old King Henry VI, Margaret's saintly husband, was locked in the Tower. The Yorkist warlords had put him on a sorry-looking nag and paraded him through London, showing the people that he may be holy but he was no warrior king. Henry's armies were shattered: his captains of war either killed or soon to be. The few who had escaped, such as De Vere of Oxford, were to be put to the horn and exiled for life.

The fallen Queen was muttering to herself. Now and again she would sit up, stretch across and try to stroke her son's head. Again she seemed unaware of what was really happening. For a while she sat, eyes blinking, lips moving soundlessly. She scratched her face, clawing back her greying-gold hair and peered at Urswicke.

'I know you, sir.' The Angevin's voice was surprisingly harsh. 'You're clerk to Lady Margaret Beaufort.' She laughed so abruptly behind her raised bound hand, Urswicke wondered if her wits were wandering. 'You are,' she continued, 'aren't you, little Margaret's clerk? Her son Henry is the last of us. Oh, they will hunt him down, they will pursue him like dogs would a deer through wood and thicket till they capture and kill him as they have my beloved . . .'

Prince Edward lifted his head and turned to Urswicke. 'What do you advise, sir? What do you say that I do?'

Urswicke hid his surprise at being asked about what he intended to offer. 'Defiance,' Urswicke retorted. 'Defiance! You came back to this kingdom to claim what was yours by birthright and lawful descent. You are the King's heir and they are traitors, as was their father Duke Richard, executed after Wakefield fight. So play the man,' Urswicke urged in a whisper. 'Do not ask for mercy for, I assure you, none will be shown.'

'I am a French princess,' Margaret slurred. She now sat crookedly, sifting her hair through her fingers. 'I will demand to be treated as such.' She straightened up abruptly, hands on her lap, adopting a regal pose, as if she was attending a crown-wearing ceremony at Westminster. She turned and, eyes full of hate, glared at Urswicke. 'And who are you, varlet?' She mocked. 'You are Urswicke? Your father is a Recorder of London, a fervent adherent of Edward of York. What are you doing here?' She moved her tied hands, stretching her wrists as if to snap the rough twine binding them.

'You'd best leave,' the prince whispered hoarsely. 'My mother must be left alone. Soon she will begin her rants and there will be little reasoning with her or peace for ourselves.' He half smiled at Urswicke, his handsome face now bruised and tearstained, his light-blue eyes full of fear. 'This will end in blood,' he whispered, 'certainly for me. You'd best leave.'

They reached Tewkesbury just as the greyness began to fade and the sky was scarred by fiery streaks. War had engulfed that small market town, and all the demons which trailed in its wake were making their presence felt. Huge yawning burial pits were being hurriedly dug outside the town. The dead, their dirty ghost-like flesh displaying all the gruesome wounds of battle, were piled on the ground like slabs of pork on a flesher's stall. Some of the womenfolk of the slaughtered men desperately searched amongst the fallen for the corpse of a beloved, their grief and mourning made all the more bitter by the raucous abuse and lewd invitations from the Yorkist men-at-arms preparing the pits. Many of the Lancastrian camp followers had already been seized and ravished. As Urswicke rode by an alleyway he glimpsed one woman on her knees before a group of soldiers, their hose all unlaced and pulled down around their ankles. Plunder was rife and the royal marshals were eager to retrieve all the precious objects seized from the Lancastrian camp. The air was thick with smoke from the many campfires and the makeshift pyres where the corpses of the horses killed in the battle had been doused in cheap oil and placed on stacks of wood. These had been fired, the flames shooting up before the foulsome, black smoke billowed in filthy clouds, spreading a horrid stench across the town.

Couriers and messengers galloped along the narrow streets, bringing news of what was happening both north of the Trent and, more importantly, London. From there the news was grim. The capital was now being threatened by a fresh Lancastrian army and a flotilla of war cogs under Thomas Neville, the Bastard of Fauconberg. Urswicke overheard all of this when a chamberlain of the royal household joined their cavalcade. He also insisted that the two royal prisoners wear thick cloaks and cowls pulled over their heads so they would not be recognised. Once they reached the royal quarters, the mansion house of Merchant Stratford, the prisoners were dragged from the cart and pushed down the cellar steps to be imprisoned in a store chamber. The doors to the great hall were closed and guarded by a host of royal knights, one of whom informed Urswicke that the King, together with his brothers, Lord Hastings, Norfolk and other Yorkist leaders, were deep in discussion.

Urswicke tried to excuse himself, pleading that he should return to the abbey, but Mauclerc, jubilant at what he described as 'the best night's work ever', insisted on Urswicke accompanying him back out into the streets and across the square to The Golden Lion, a spacious, black-and-white timber tavern. The market had now been cleared of its stalls and a soaring execution platform was being constructed. The royal carpenters were feverishly working to put the finishing touches to this macabre scaffold. The rage of York was apparent. Even though this execution ground was not fully completed, it had already been used to carry out summary punishment. Lancastrian captains had been hustled up and killed just before dawn, their blood-drenched cadavers quartered, salted and tarred before being tossed into large vats beside the scaffold, their heads thrust into barrels to be pickled. Other prisoners had been hanged on the railing around the gibbet: nooses put around their necks before they were summarily pushed over to jerk and dance until they hung, swaying slightly in the breeze, wafting a host of disgusting smells around the market place. Urswicke felt as if he was in a nightmare. Hideous death pressed all around him, yet some of the carpenters were whistling and singing as they went about their business, totally oblivious to their gruesome surroundings. Tewkesbury was now possessed by the full terror of war which assailed, sight, sound and smell. Urswicke abruptly felt nervous, a spasm of fear which made him wonder if the path he was following was the correct one, a twisting, tortuous, snake-like trackway. Would this, he wondered, end in disaster, or the realisation of his mistress's dream?

'We are here!'

Urswicke broke free from his reverie. They had entered the sweet-smelling taproom, a spacious chamber; fresh green summer rushes strewn with herbs covered the floor, these exuded a spring-like fragrance to mingle with the delicious tang from the hams hanging in white nets from the rafters. The meat and other foods would dangle there until they were cured by the smoke and steam billowing out of the great kitchen, as well as the constant fragrances from the huge spit being slowly turned in the majestic hearth.

Mauclerc had a word with minehost who whispered back and pointed across to the stairs. Mauclerc and Urswicke went up these into a well-furnished chamber where three individuals were waiting. Urswicke suspected these were the Three Kings, the clerks of Clarence's Secret Chancery. They lounged in chairs or on the broad settle which served as a window seat. They rose as Mauclerc and Urswicke entered. One of them, Melchior as he introduced himself, hurriedly swept documents and manuscripts from the chamber's writing table, pushing these into a chancery coffer reinforced with steel bands and protected by three locks. The other two pulled back their hoods. One of them gestured at a stool close to the table before offering Urswicke some wine and cheese from the food platter on a side dresser. Urswicke asked for a little wine and a piece of cheese wrapped in a linen cloth. These were handed over as introductions were made. Once these were finished, Mauclerc talked to the Three Kings in what Urswicke suspected was German, a spate of harsh, guttural words. All Three Kings listened carefully, nodding and saying *'Ja! Ja!'* in agreement. Occasionally they would glance at Urswicke and smile thinly. He acknowledged their greeting but pretended to be more interested in his food and drink than anything else. Urswicke felt he had the measure of Mauclerc, a mailed clerk, a man of war, a ruthless henchman. The Three Kings, however, despite their pale, sharp, bony faces, seemed pleasant enough. They were apparently skilled in tongues by their own admission, whilst their ink-stained fingers and the spots of wax on their robes showed they were chancery men. Once Mauclerc had finished talking in German, all four gathered at the table.

'You must be curious?' Melchior demanded.

'Of course,' Urswicke ruefully admitted. 'You have a reputation. A good one,' he added hastily. 'Skilled scriveners, shrewd clerks, loyal henchmen. You are not from this kingdom, so how did you enter my Lord Clarence's service? Three brothers, yes? Friars?'

'Former friars,' Melchior retorted. 'Members of a community, the Barnabites, who had a small house outside Cologne. A lovely, peaceful place until we heard our mother had been arrested and burnt as a witch in Karlstadt, our home town, a true place of dark suspicion. Apparently she had been taken up to be interrogated, tortured, tried and executed. We received the news too late but we journeyed back to Karlstadt.' He paused, smiling slightly at Mauclerc and his two brothers.

'And?'

'As I said Meister Urswicke, we were too late. Our mother had been tried and convicted. Nobody spoke in her defence. She had been burnt alive in a market square. They didn't even give her the comfort of a swift garrotte by the executioner. Nor were pouches of gunpowder tied around her neck to hasten her end. The woman who bore us, our mother, was reduced to ashes which were then strewn on a dung heap. Nobody would talk to us. You would think we were lepers rather than friars. So what could we do? We were regarded as learned men, very skilled in tongues, proficient in the chancery, but our mother they treated as you would a piece of filth, something to be burnt, totally destroyed. So what could we do?'

'And what did you do?'

Melchior smiled a wolfish grin, his white teeth strong and pointed. 'Oh Meister Urswicke, we exacted punishment. We killed the *Ritter*, how would you say it? The lord of the town? We cut his throat in the dead of night along with those of his wife and children. We did the same to all who had sat in judgement on our mother; be they judges, jury or prosecutor. Finally we seized the executioner, a stupid burly butcher whom we drowned in his own cesspit. We then set fire to the church and city hall and fled as fast as we could to the sanctuary church of Dordrecht in Hainault. You must know it, Meister Urswicke, a busy port where, by chance, my Lord Clarence was resting during one of his many . . .'

'One of his many journeys abroad.' Mauclerc took up the story. 'My master became deeply intrigued by the story of these three brothers, warrior clerks, very skilled with the pen and the knife. He visited them in sanctuary and they talked. Indeed, my Lord spent a great deal of time in that church. A true friendship was formed, a bond made; unswerving loyalty promised. My Lord Clarence managed to settle matters. My comrades here would leave sanctuary and enter his household. They would take oaths of fealty, to serve their master body and soul, day and night, as long as they lived.'

Urswicke nodded and sipped from his goblet.

'You are shocked by what we did?' Melchior demanded.

'Oh no! Your mother was innocent?'

'Certainly not,' Melchior replied. 'She was as guilty as we are. Our mother was a self-proclaimed witch who raised three warlocks. We entered the Roman Church to gain advancement, acquire knowledge, learning, and so secure preferment. Our mother and our good selves are certainly not innocent of anything.' Urswicke nodded as Mauclerc and the others laughed, softly clapping their hands in appreciation at what had been said.

'Beyond the Rhine,' Balthasar, the youngest of the Three Kings spoke up, 'the old religion still holds as fast as the oaks of the ancient Teuterborger forest; its roots go very deep. Much more profound than the influence of fat priests, noddle-pates and peasants who certainly don't practice what they preach.'

'Enough!' Mauclerc clapped his hands. 'Comrades, you now know the excellent service Master Urswicke performed on our behalf. The Anjou wolf and her whelp have been seized and they are for the dark. Master Christopher Urswicke is now one of us, a trusted henchman of my Lord Clarence, even though he will continue to dance attendance on the Beaufort brat. So . . .' Mauclerc rose, crossed to the door, opened it and bellowed for a servant. A short while later, minehost brought up platters of food; vegetables fried in duck fat, strips of pork covered in mustard, morsels of venison garnished with herbs and salmon from the Severn ponds. The jug of wine proved to be the best from Bordeaux. Urswicke joined his new comrades as they ate and drank until their hearts' content whilst outside echoed the ominous beat of both mallet and hammer as the execution platform was finished. Urswicke realised the meal was being used in order that he could be observed, questioned and judged, so he adopted the guise of a father confessor, listening carefully and nodding wisely.

The conversation flowed around what was to happen next and Urswicke learned more about the violent disturbances which had broken out in Kent. How some of the rebels were common robbers who, according to Balthasar, wished to dip their filthy hands into rich men's coffers. Other rebels were farmers who had donned their wives' smocks and wore cheesecloths on their heads to demonstrate their resentment at the low prices Londoners were paying for their dairy products. More ominous, however, were the intrigues of the nobles and gentry of the surrounding shires: these had raised the black banners of anarchy and the blood-red standards of revolt. The rebel lords were now preparing to aid and assist Thomas Neville, the Bastard of Fauconberg, as he prepared to bring his fleet armed with cannon and culverin up the Thames. Fauconberg was an ardent Lancastrian: Urswicke listened carefully and wondered how he and his mistress could exploit this growing chaos.

'The King has undoubtedly heard all about this,' Mauclerc observed. 'He will be ruthless. He will crush all opposition . . .'

Urswicke drained his goblet and declared he was tired; he added that he would rest for a while, accepting Mauclerc's offer of using the settle as a bed. He swiftly fell asleep and was later roughly woken by Mauclerc shaking his shoulder.

'You slept like a babe at the breast,' Mauclerc hissed, 'but our master has summoned us, he wants us with him.'

Urswicke rose and left the chamber for the garderobe. He then returned to splash cold water over his face and hands at the wooden lavarium. The hour candle on its spigot in the corner showed it to be five hours after midday. Urswicke dried himself, making sure he was presentable. He could tell by the hurried preparations of the Three Kings that they too had been sleeping off the heavy effects of food and wine. They all left the tavern. The market square had fallen strangely silent, like a mausoleum reeking of dead things and pregnant with fresh horrors brewing. The scaffold was draped in black and purple cloths, the entire square being ringed by royal archers and men-at-arms.

Merchant Stratford's mansion was similarly guarded. Inside, the great hall had been changed, its furniture swept aside. A gleaming Arras tapestry displaying all the insignia of York and the royal household covered the wall opposite the door; this served as a dramatic backdrop for the canopied throne placed on a makeshift dais. Edward now sat on this, flanked by his brothers together with their leading henchmen, the Woodvilles, Hastings, and others of their ilk. Banners and standards displaying the Boar of Gloucester, the Bull of Clarence, the Bear of Warwick and the White Lion of Norfolk clustered close to the throne.

Edward sat in half-armour, his face cleanly shaven, his trimmed hair oiled, his tawny skin gleaming with perfumed nard. He wore his crown with a drawn sword across his lap, symbols that the King was prepared to deliver judgement. Urswicke joined the rest of the henchmen gathering to the left of the throne. He sensed that some bloody masque was about to unfold. A trumpet blared and the hall fell silent. A servant hurriedly placed a stool before the throne. A side door opened and Queen Margaret of Anjou and her son, still garbed in dirty, dishevelled linen shifts, were pushed into the chamber. The former Queen was ordered to sit on a stool whilst Edward beckoned the young prince forward.

'Why?' Richard of Gloucester rose to his feet. 'Why did you invade our realm and cause great hurt to the King's peace?'

'To assert my claim and that of my saintly father,' the prince retorted, stepping forward as if he wanted to shake off all traces of captivity. 'My father,' the prince yelled, following Urswicke's whispered advice, 'is the true King of England. Your father was a usurper, a mere baron of York, a rebel, justly executed after the battle of Wakefield, him and his whelp Edmund—'

He got no further. Edward the King sprang from his throne and struck the prince full on the mouth with a savage blow from his gauntleted hand. The prince staggered back, blood pouring from his split lips and bruised mouth. Margaret of Anjou struggled to her feet but the Yorkist lords closed in, knocking her half-conscious to the floor. Daggers were drawn. The prince, realising the peril he was now in, screamed at Clarence for mercy, but that lord struck with his dagger time and again at the prince's exposed chest and neck. Others, including Gloucester, joined in the blood-splattering hail of knife thrusts and dagger blows. The long blades rose and fell, glittering in the light. The prince, dying from a host of wounds, collapsed to the floor, his blood sparkling around him. Even then the Yorkist lords, led by Clarence, continued to stab, kick and punch until the King's trumpeters brayed for stillness and the heralds shouted for peace. The blood-drenched lords, chests heaving, mouths gasping for air, stepped back. The victim was no longer a man, just a sodding heap of gore; his mother, soaked in her son's blood, tried to crawl towards

him, moaning piteously, her hand going out to caress her dead
boy's face. Edward the King shouted something, waving his hand
as if he wanted to be free of the gruesome mess on the floor
before him.

'Clear the hall.' Howard of Norfolk, Earl Marshal of England,
stood on the edge of the dais, hands raised. 'Clear the hall,' he
repeated. 'His Grace wishes to be alone.'

Once outside the mansion, Urswicke leaned against the wall,
drawing deep breaths as he swiftly crossed himself.

'You are well?'

'I am well.' Urswicke patted Mauclerc's gloved hand resting
on his arm. 'I am well but I need to rest . . .' And, not waiting
for a response, Urswicke, his flushed face all sweat-soaked,
walked across the square, averting his eyes from the cadavers,
the corpses of those hanged earlier in the day, dangling on ropes
like flitches of ham in a butcher's shed.

Urswicke forced himself to think on other matters, to recall
sweet memories, to clear his mind and calm his heart. He drifted
back in time to his beloved studies in the halls of Oxford; evening
walks through the Christchurch meadows and, above all, sitting
with his mother in their high-walled garden of his father's mansion
just off Cheapside in the heart of the city. Urswicke's mother
called this 'her paradise, her garden of Eden'. It certainly was.
Urswicke's father, if he did anything well, furnished his wife and
son with the finer things of life. The garden was a true pleasance,
well stocked in length and breadth, like the great meadow of the
abbey. A sea of greenery, flowers and herbs pleased the eye and
turned the air constantly sweet. A most delightful place to wander
with its small fruit orchards, flower beds, herb plots, rose-
garlanded arbours, comfortable turf seats, stew ponds and carp
tanks with small fountains carved elegantly out of stone.

The garden was a retreat where he could escape the sly
lechery of his father and the constant pain such flirtation caused
Christopher's mother. When the weather was fine they would
go out and she would make Christopher sit and read to her. She
had a special love for the tales of Arthur and the verses of
Petrarch, which had reached England and were being avidly
translated and transcribed, along with Boccaccio's *Decameron*
and the 'Devotia Moderna' – a radical new approach to religion

coming out to the Low Countries in a number of thought-provoking treatises.

Once he had left Oxford, Urswicke had hurried home, hiring himself out as a clerk to different households. He had been greatly helped by the Countess Margaret, who was a firm, hand-fast friend to his mother. Margaret often visited the Urswickes, sometimes in the company of his mother's brother Andrew Knyvett, who served as physician to the countess's household. More often than not, Margaret's visits were by herself and, when Christopher's mother fell ill of some evil humour of the womb, the visits became more frequent. The countess even held his mother as she died quietly and peacefully in her chamber. Shortly afterwards, the countess asked to see Christopher by himself. She informed him that his mother, just before she died, had begged her to take Christopher into her household. Urswicke would never forget that meeting, standing at the foot of the four-poster bed, its curtains pulled back, the casement window thrown open to help his dead mother's soul on her journey into the light. Countess Margaret had grasped his hands and drew him close.

'Christopher,' she declared – her eyes had that fierce stare which always appeared over something deeply passionate to her – 'I loved your mother dearly and I love you as much. You are now flesh of my flesh, the very marrow of my bone and part of my heart's blood. From now on I will be your countess but I shall also be your mother, your sister, your comrade. I will stand next to you in the great shield wall of life, shoulder to shoulder, ready to confront the monsters who crawl out of the darkness and, believe me, they will . . .'

'Master Urswicke?'

He stopped, startled out of his reverie, and realised he'd entered the abbey precincts which lay silent all around him: no patter of sandalled feet, no bells or chanting, not even the usual noises from the kitchen, buttery or bakery. Nothing but an ominous, watching stillness. Abbot Strensham, fearful about what might happen, must have ordered his brothers to stay in their cells. Again Urswicke heard his name called and turned as the countess's squire Owain stepped out of the shadows.

'What is it?' Urswicke hurried towards him. 'The countess . . .?'

'She is well.' Owain drew closer, his long, dark face wreathed in concern. 'Our mistress has secretly left. She does not think it is safe here. She is journeying as swiftly as she can to London where she hopes to lodge at her husband's riverside mansion . . .'

'Yes, yes,' Urswicke snapped, 'I know where that is.'

'She also mentioned that she might visit a secret place. What is that, Master Urswicke? My mistress was insistent that you be given this message.'

'Nothing, nothing,' the clerk murmured, glancing around. 'Nothing to concern you. And what else?'

'The rest of the household are following behind. The countess, together with Master Bray and two outriders, left hurriedly. Before she departed, she asked if you would stay until the business here is completed and then join her.'

'Yes, yes I will.' Urswicke stared at the Welshman's close face, even as he prayed that the countess would exercise great caution as she entered the city. Owain pulled the gauntlets from beneath his warbelt; he put these on and stretched out a hand.

'Master Urswicke, I was instructed to wait for you. Make sure you receive the message and that you are well. I have done that. Now I must leave and join the rest before nightfall.'

Owain withdrew his hand, raised it in farewell and hurried back into the shadows along the cloister path. Urswicke made his way over to the guesthouse, now strangely quiet. The countess's retinue, together with other guests, had fled in full expectation that the bloody affray at Tewkesbury was certainly not finished. Urswicke went up into the different chambers to find them swept clean. He peered through a lancet window.

'The day is drawing on,' he whispered to himself, 'and I should be gone from here!'

He returned to his own closet chamber with its paltry sticks of furniture and narrow bed. He sat on the edge of this, lost deep in thought. He felt himself grow sleepy and shook himself awake. He glimpsed the half-full goblet of wine and drained it to the dregs before taking off his cloak; he wrapped this around him and stretched out on the bed. Darkness had fallen when he was awoken by a persistent rapping on his door. He drew his dagger and, slightly stiff, edged towards it.

'Who is it?' he called.

'Brother Norbert, remember me, sir?' the voice whined through the door. 'I am here with Brother Simeon, remember? You despatched us as messengers to Lord Wenlock whose crushed head is now poled in the market place.'

Urswicke felt a chill of apprehension. He opened the door and the two cowled figures slipped into the room. He indicated that they should sit on the edge of the cotbed whilst he drew up a stool close to them. Urswicke half suspected that these two worthies, whom he had used to convey messages, in particular to Lord Wenlock, were intent on mischief.

'You wish to speak?' Urswicke spread his hands. 'The hour is late and tomorrow beckons.'

'And it will bring more blood,' Norbert intoned lugubriously. 'Rumour has it that King Edward is determined on settling scores with all those who took sanctuary in our abbey.'

'And why should that concern me?'

'No, what should concern you, Master Urswicke, is that you are a Judas man who seemingly betrays both houses. You sent us with messages to Lord Wenlock. We now know what he did and how he died. Moreover, this abbey is clothed in darkness but we know its maze-like paths and we can thread the labyrinth. You would not even know we were there. We have watched you scurry here and scurry there. You meet the likes of Mauclerc. Even we know who he is, a man hot for devil's work. So who do you really serve, York or Lancaster?'

'I have done invaluable work for our Lord King.'

'Oh yes,' Norbert simpered, 'I was hiding in the garden when you and Mauclerc were whispering your treachery. Did you have a hand in the capture of the young prince? How will the House of Lancaster view that? Not to mention your meddling with Wenlock. And why is your mistress scurrying off so swiftly to London? What is she hiding?'

Urswicke stared hard at these two lay brothers. Abbot Strensham had chosen them because both had served as royal messengers before being granted a pension and a corrody in this abbey. Urswicke ruefully admitted he had underestimated this precious pair: they had served as royal couriers, a breed of officials with a reputation for prying and eavesdropping, ever ready to collect juicy morsels of valuable information. Both of these villains apparently hunted together and he wondered if they had used the same guile on the abbot and the other brothers.

'And so what?' Urswicke asked.

'You pay us in good pound sterling and,' Norbert rubbed his hands together, 'our little secret becomes a case of eye has not seen, nor has ear heard, nor will it enter into anyone's heart what mischief you have truly perpetrated.'

Urswicke nodded, taking a deep breath as he considered the possibilities. He did not flinch at the blackmail against himself. What worried him was any threat to his mistress. King Edward suspected her, whilst Clarence was her sworn enemy ready to believe any allegation levelled against a Beaufort. More chillingly, these two malefactors had stumbled upon the countess's great secret. She was, at this moment in time, harbouring something precious, and the lay brothers had referred to that. He did not want Mauclerc leading a swift-riding comitatus to pursue the countess and her household and thoroughly question them. Urswicke stared down at the floor and tried to recall what he knew about the abbey and its buildings. He thought hard and made a decision.

'Very well.' Urswicke pointed to the hour candle in its horned shell. 'When the flame marks the midnight hour, I will meet you out near the piggery.'

'Why there?'

'Because that's where I hid my money belt. Guesthouses lie open. Thievery is commonplace even,' he added sarcastically, 'in a house of prayer. A hundred pounds sterling, no more, for that's all I have. Take it,' he shrugged, 'or do your worst.'

Norbert glanced at Simeon who nodded his approval.

'In an hour then.' Urswicke rose, opened the door, and his visitors shuffled out into the night. Once he was sure they were gone, Urswicke hurriedly made his own preparations to leave. He packed his saddlebags with what he needed and went down to the abbey stables, where a sleepy-eyed groom promised to prepare his horse for a journey to London.

Urswicke returned to his chamber and plotted what he should do. He knew where the piggery was. Urswicke always carefully walked any place he lodged in, as a constable would his castle, looking for those places to hide, points of strength or possible weaknesses. Tewkesbury Abbey was no different. He checked the hour candle and, at the appointed time, slipped out of the guesthouse and made his way across the abbey grounds. He tried not to meet the gaze of the stone-carved gargoyles, *babewyns*, saints and angels, who glared down at him in mournful expectation, almost as if they knew what he plotted. Urswicke, however, felt composed. He had not created this situation, yet for his mistress's sake he had to resolve the challenge which confronted him.

He reached a wooden fence, climbed it, and crossed the abbey meadow, passing the cattle byres which reeked to heaven and eventually reached the hog pens where a large herd of pigs massed together, snuffling and grunting as they snouted the filthy ground. Urswicke, ignoring the stench, took up the position by the gate and waited. He half listened to the pigs, feral creatures always hungry and ever vigilant for food. The hogs sensed him, and every so often would crash against the poled fence or the iron-plated gate, stirring up the mud to thicken the cloud of filthy smells. At last Urswicke glimpsed the light of a lanternhorn bobbing through the darkness. The monks approached, almost swaggering, eager for their prize. Urswicke lifted the heavy, leather saddlebag and put his hand inside to grasp the small arbalest already primed. He moved his hand and felt the leather strap of a second crossbow.

'Well Urswicke, you have summoned us here . . .?'

The monk stopped as Urswicke abruptly brought out the crossbow and, stepping closer, released the catch so the barb sped to smash Norbert's face to a bloody, bony mess. The lay brother, still holding the lantern, crumpled to the ground. Urswicke stepped around him, dropping the first arbalest as he grasped the second. Simeon just froze, shocked to a stony stillness as Urswicke swept towards him and, with the crossbow within inches from his opponent's face, released the barbed quarrel, taking Simeon in the forehead, smashing his skull and piercing his brain. Urswicke watched his enemy slump to the ground. Certain that both men were dead, he put the arbalests back in their leather sack. He then took each of the blood-soaked corpses, dragged them to the fence and tossed them over. The second cadaver had hardly sunk into the thick, oozing mud of the piggery when the hogs, who had already smelt blood, surged in a frenzied attack to rip and tear at this unexpected, gore-smeared banquet: their squealing and grunting rose like some unholy hymn. Urswicke grasped the saddlebag and hurried into the night.

'You were correct,' he whispered over his shoulder, 'eye will not see, nor will ear hear, nor will it enter the heart of anyone about what I truly did.'

Urswicke eventually reached the stables and, as he approached the stall where his horse stood ready and waiting, a shadow slipped into the pool of light thrown by a lanternhorn on its hook close to the stable door.

'Master Urswicke,' Mauclerc stepped closer, 'I have been searching for you. You are leaving?'

'Urgent business in London.'

'Oh yes, the Lady Margaret has already left; she did so without royal permission.'

'Did she need it?'

'No but, as a courtesy, she really should have approached the royal chancery, but never mind. Everything is in a state of flux. We have received intelligence from London that the unrest there is much more serious than we first believed. We trust only a few men of power in the capital. One of them is your father. He and his comrades will have to stand like a door of steel against the rebels surging through Kent.'

For the first time in many a year, Urswicke thanked God for his father, yet he held himself tense. 'So what now?' he demanded.

'Matters move swiftly to judgement,' Mauclerc retorted. 'The King intends to force the issue here at the abbey early tomorrow. Our master also has need of you, not only here but in London as well. So, for the moment, you must stay, Master Urswicke, and see whatever the new day brings.'

Urswicke discovered that the day brought bloodshed: swift, cruel and terrible. Along with other Yorkist henchmen, he was roused roughly just before dawn, the abbey bells already tolling their dire warning, a loud protest against the King's intended actions. Edward, however, had his way. The abbey doors were forced. Yorkist soldiers flooded into the nave, searching out and seizing their enemy who sheltered in the chantry chapels, even behind the high altar. A few resisted, fighting back, but at last all the prisoners were chained and led like common felons out of the church. Abbot Strensham tried to protest but Clarence, surrounded by knights of the royal household, their swords drawn, rejected the abbot's protests. Clarence loudly declared that Tewkesbury Abbey did not enjoy the right of sanctuary. Moreover, the captured men were no ordinary felons but dyed-in-the-wool traitors who had been taken in arms against their rightful King. They were guilty of heinous treason and should answer for it.

Urswicke mingled with others of Clarence's coven and joined them as they escorted the prisoners out of the abbey precincts and down to the market place. Here the execution platform had been fully prepared. The common hangman, face all masked, stood by the execution block with a huge wicker basket beside it. A glowing brazier fanned by the morning breeze flared and smoked, the flames leaping up in bright tongues of fire. Some townspeople had also gathered to watch. A few of these, prompted by Clarence's henchmen, hurled curses and whatever refuse was at hand. In the main, however, the crowd just watched the pitiful masque unfold.

A line of broken, wounded men being herded into the square towards a great log table set up in front of Merchant Stratford's mansion. The table, now a court bench, was covered in a dark-green baize cloth. The symbols of royal justice, the royal sword and mace, rested there, along with a black, stark crucifix and a book of the Gospels. Urswicke glimpsed Edward the King standing at an upstairs window of the mansion. The King was peering down at this summary court of 'Oyer et Terminer', hastily assembled to dispense swift retribution. Behind the table sat the judges, Richard of Gloucester, who was also High Constable of England, on his left the Duke of Norfolk, the King's own marshal, and on Richard's right, Lord William Hastings, the Crown's special commissioner to the West Country and along the Welsh March. Clerks and scriveners sat ready to record a faithful account, parchment unrolled, quill pens at the ready. Gorgeously garbed heralds unfurled the royal standard as well as the banners and pennants of the three judges. These were placed behind Gloucester and his colleagues in specially prepared sockets on the three, throne-like chairs. Other heralds dragged the standards of the accused and placed these across the mud-strewn cobbles, creating a macabre carpet stretching from the table to the steps of the execution platform. A trumpeter blew a shrill blast, then, in a loud voice, proclaimed how the King's justices of Oyer et Terminer were ready for judgement.

The ceremonies and protocols eventually ended and the process began; it brooked no opposition and provided little hope for the accused. Each of the prisoners was dragged in front of the table to hear the charges read out by a clerk in a bell-like voice; every indictment was one of high treason and so worthy of death. Somerset was the first to hear this, and when asked for a reply he simply spat at his judges and cursed them now and for eternity.

'It will not be long,' he shouted, 'before you Yorkist vipers follow your father into the dark . . .'

Richard of Gloucester would have sprung to his feet but Norfolk, a cynical smile on his face, just grasped the young prince by his arm, whispering into his ear. Richard nodded as if in agreement and glanced over his shoulder up at the window where his brother the King was watching. Urswicke glimpsed Edward raise his hand. Richard turned back.

'You,' he pointed at Somerset, 'are attainted and so are worthy of death.' Gloucester then banged the table with his left hand as his right gestured at the guards to take Somerset away. The Lancastrian leader was seized and pushed up the steps onto the execution platform where he was forced to kneel before the block. Somerset's jerkin and shirt were roughly ripped and pulled down so his neck and head were fully exposed. The duke's hands were tied behind his back, even as the executioner's assistants forced Somerset to turn his head before thrusting it down onto the block. The axe man lifted his two-bladed weapon, brought it back in one glittering flash of sunlight then down, cutting the neck so sharply, Somerset's head bounced away as his torso jerked and spurted an arc of blood which drenched the entire platform. Somerset's head was then lifted, the executioner grasping it by the hair as he held it high, walking to the edge of the platform so that the judges could clearly view the half-closed eyes still blinking, the lips slightly twitching. The executioner then turned to the left and right so all could see, as a herald proclaimed, 'The fate of all such traitors.'

Urswicke was standing just behind Clarence and watched the Yorkist lord clap and jump, as if this was all some childish game put on for his pleasure and entertainment. Other prisoners, such as the Courtenays of Devon and the prior of the Hospitallers, were also tried and condemned. They too were hustled up the steps, forced to kneel, and then the great, gleaming execution axe whirled, followed by a sickening thud as it severed bone, muscle and flesh. The head would roll away before being displayed and placed in the waiting basket. The execution platform swirled in blood which seeped over the edge, into the gaps, to snake amongst the cobbles, drenching the Lancastrian banners left strewn there. After each execution, Clarence would clap his hands and chortle with glee as he performed another jig. Once the executions were over, however, Clarence became self-important, snapping his fingers for Mauclerc, the Three Kings and Urswicke to follow him across the slippery cobbles, back into The Golden Lion and up to the chamber they'd used before. Servants brought bowls of hot potage, chunks of meat and croutons in a highly spiced sauce, along with freshly baked manchet loaves and a jug of the tavern's finest Bordeaux. Clarence insisted on serving this himself, praising its richness and repeating how fitting that such blood-red wine should be drunk on the same day as the enemies of his House went under the axe.

'But now for fresh fields.' Clarence sucked on his fingers and pointed at Urswicke. 'My brother and I want you in London,' he leaned across the table, 'to keep the sharpest eye on that little bitch Meg of Richmond. You must also deliver a message to your redoubtable father, the Recorder.' Clarence shook his head. 'Thomas Neville, the Bastard of Fauconberg, intends to seize the city. You, your father and other loyal souls must prevent him. If London falls, our cause is seriously injured . . .'

Margaret Beaufort, Countess of Richmond, had left Tewkesbury on Sunday morning, reaching London late the following Tuesday to find that the news of the Yorkist victory at Tewkesbury and the summary execution of her kinsmen and others had swiftly preceded her. Margaret paused to rest and think in an ancient church just inside Aldgate. At first she busied herself lighting tapers before a statue of the Virgin, as well as paying a chantry

priest to sing three requiem masses for all those slain at
Tewkesbury. Afterwards she sat in the shadows, watching the
shifting light as the candle-flame before the different shrines and
statues flickered vigorously before guttering out. Margaret strove
to compose herself as she stared at a fresco on the pillars: this
depicted the Wheel of Fortune, how it would raise prince, priest
and prelate only to cast them down again. Margaret did not want
to be part of that wheel. Indeed her struggle was more dangerous.
The mighty Beauforts had, apart from herself, been annihilated
and wiped off the face of God's earth. She had to survive if
only for her son. If she went down, he would certainly follow.
And who would do this? The Yorkist warlords, Clarence in
particular, were her mortal enemies. In the first instance, she
would have to confront Clarence and destroy him, both root and
branch. Yet how?

A plan was forming, like a snake uncoiling, though slowly.
She had to remain cunning, prudent and patient. If she struck,
when she struck, she must not make a mistake. She heard a voice
raised further down the church and recalled the herald standing
on a cart just inside Aldgate. This city official proclaimed the
news from Tewkesbury as well as the more dangerous reports:
that the Bastard of Fauconberg's war cogs were sailing up the
Thames, whilst the men of Kent were gathering to storm through
Southwark and seize the southern gate of London Bridge. Of
course such proclamations caused deep unrest, yet Margaret was
relieved. All this upset might distract the Yorkist lords and their
ilk in the city. Margaret was determined to ensure that her beloved
son remained safe, as well as plot for the future. She wondered
about the 'Titulus Regius'. Margaret suspected that this document,
from the little that Somerset had told her, was highly injurious
to the House of York. She determined to seize such a manuscript
and use it to sow discord. Somerset was correct; Clarence may
be her avowed enemy, but he was also, albeit secretly, the implac-
able enemy of his own House and family.

Margaret threaded her ave beads through her fingers. Now and
again she would lapse into prayer as she wondered about whom
she could truly rely on and trust? Thanks to her marriage to Sir
Humphrey, she had the full protection of the Stafford family and
their leader the Duke of Buckingham. However, Sir Humphrey

was a truly sick man, made weaker by the hideous injuries sustained at Barnet. So how long would he live? Whom else could she trust? Was Somerset correct? Was there a spy deep in her household?

The countess knew she had two shield comrades, especially Christopher Urswicke. She crossed herself and prayed that her clerk would remain safe in that wolf's lair at Tewkesbury. The other stalwart was Reginald Bray, the steward and controller of her household. She glanced over her shoulder. Bray was sitting on a wall bench, legs apart, head down deep in thought. Margaret smiled to herself. Urswicke was astute but still young. He had complete loyalty for her, born out of his deep love for his mother as well as a burning resentment against his father and the heartbreak he had caused. Margaret also knew that Christopher was deeply grateful for what she had done to ease Urswicke's mother during the last painful months of her life.

Bray was different, a man who lived deep in the shadows. Ostensibly Reginald was her steward, a man with ink-stained fingers, well versed in matters of the chancery and the Exchequer. To all appearances, a faithful retainer, skilled in administration. Margaret, however, knew the full truth. There was a gap in Bray's service as a clerk when he, by his own confession to her, had fought in the King's array across the Narrow Seas as well as along the Scottish March. He was a veteran soldier and had risen to be one of the 'Secreti, the Secret Men' who went before the King's army to discover intelligence, spy on the enemy and, if they could, inflict damage on enemy leaders, be it through some ambush or secret attack at the dead of night. Bray was a master bowman and just as proficient in the use of the dagger and the garrotte. In truth, Bray was an assassin, a man who could become a shadow, to flit fiercely and silently where other men feared even to tread.

Margaret shifted in her seat, eyes on the dancing candle-flame even as a stratagem, subtle and complex, began to emerge in her teeming brain. She was determined to play the little maid, the court lady but, in truth, she would carry the war into the enemy's camp. She recalled her study of the classics and the writings about the Roman senate; how they would vow to wage war by land and sea, by fire and sword: that is what she would do! At times, if she could, she would cause public unrest but, in the main, her war would be secret yet just as devastating. She desperately wanted to visit her secret place, The Wyvern's Lair, but that would have to wait. At the moment the situation was too dangerous. Margaret knew she was under surveillance. As they had passed through Aldgate earlier that afternoon, Bray, sharp of mind and keen of wit, had whispered how he had glimpsed the scrutineers, informers paid by the city council, to observe and report on who entered and left the city. They must have noticed her and sent information by the street swallows, urchins who could be hired and taught to learn some message by rote. The Lords of the Soil at the Guildhall must already know that Margaret Beaufort Countess of Richmond had entered the city and would act accordingly. She crossed herself for a final time.

'Reginald,' she murmured, beckoning her steward forward. He crouched down beside her and she smoothed his cheek. 'Tell the rest of my household, now they have joined us, to go direct to Sir Humphrey's house in Queenhithe. The steward there is waiting and I am sure chambers will be ready. Tell Oswina and Owain to ensure everything is settled.'

'And you, Mistress?'

'You and I Reginald, are off to that grim house of war.'

'My Lady?'

'The Tower!'

A short while later they left St Katherine's. Dusk was falling as they made their way down Mark Lane to Thames Street. Margaret kept herself cloaked and cowled whilst Bray, sword drawn, strode beside her. The lanes and streets were narrow, a maze of arrow-thin alleyways where the upper storeys of the houses on either side leaned forward to block out both light and air. Shop signs creaked and swung precariously just above their heads, and they had to guard against the constant rain of slops from the upper windows. The stench of the refuse rotting in the lay stalls as well as the crammed open sewers running down the centre of the street was so offensive Bray had to buy pomanders from a chapman. Margaret held one of these over her nose and mouth, trying not to glance at the bloody battles being waged in and around the steaming midden heaps by cat, rat and dog. A pig which had attacked a child had been caught, tried, its throat cut, and had been hung from a three-branched gallows, the other two nooses being occupied by the corpses of housebreakers; apparently these had been caught red-handed by the bailiffs who had stripped them, placed a rope around their necks before kicking away the barrels the two wolfsheads had been forced to stand on.

Such sickening sights were common. London life in all its rawness bustled on; traders, tinkers and shop-men touted raucously for business. Hot-pot girls, sent out by the nearby taverns and cook-shops, tried to entice passers-by with what was on offer: minced chicken in pastry, beef brisket, honey-coated pork along with little beakers of ale, cider and wine. Beggars whined, clacking their dishes. Whores pouted and simpered in doorways where they stood in their garish, striped gowns and fiery-red wigs. Margaret grew accustomed to such sights and sounds, closing her ears to the raucous din, be it the wail of bagpipes, the screams of children and the constant strident cat-calling by those who thronged the streets. The countess, however, sensed something else: a palpable tension, as if the city knew that it was about to be drawn into the bloody conflict which had raged at Barnet and Tewkesbury.

Men-at-arms, hobelars and archers thronged about, all garbed in the royal livery or the blue and yellow of York. Carts crammed with weaponry were being pulled down to the different gates of the city, and Margaret even glimpsed culverins and cannon being dragged on sledges to the principal quaysides along the Thames such as Queenhithe and Dowgate. Knights in half-armour grouped at the different crossroads, where city men-at-arms were fastening chains to be dragged across the mouth of the main streets as a defence against enemy horsemen. News from Tewkesbury was being proclaimed time and again by professional chanteurs, who stood on barrels or casks to regale the passing crowd, embellishing their tale with bloodthirsty stories from that fierce battle.

They left the city, moving into Portsoken, a desolate area between the Abbey of the Minoresses and the Church of St Mary Grace's. Here the unlicensed troubadours, minstrels and actors could perform free without being troubled by city bailiffs. A travelling troupe had set up a stage and mummers, their faces hidden by hideous masks, were busy playing out the execution of the Lancastrian lords in Tewkesbury market place. They used figures fashioned out of straw, buckets of pig's blood and baskets of offal to make their account more gruesome. Margaret swiftly averted her eyes and murmured a requiem. Bray now held her arm in this squalid place of fleshers' yards and tanning sheds, which flooded the area with filth and attracted savage dogs, a real threat to the weak or unwary.

Margaret heaved a sigh of relief when they reached the great postern gate to the rear of the Tower. This was now protected and barricaded with war carts, palisades and sharpened stakes driven into the ground. Banners and pennants floated in the breeze, their gorgeous insignia besmirched by the smoke billowing from fiery braziers. Men-at-arms and mounted archers patrolled the entrance under the command of knight bannerets, and all who approached were challenged. Margaret, resting on Bray's arm, walked carefully towards the table which spanned the narrow gap between the two sides of the barricade. A royal clerk, dressed in the livery of the King's household, looked Margaret and Bray up and down from head to toe before imperiously lifting his hand, snapping his fingers at them to approach. One of the knights behind the clerk recognised Margaret as she pulled back the hood of her cloak and, leaning over, whispered heatedly into the clerk's ear. The man changed in an instant, he rose, smiling from ear to ear, beckoning her closer and tactfully refusing the warrants and licences Bray produced from his wallet.

'My Lady,' he bowed, 'you are most welcome.' He turned and spoke to one of the soldiers behind him. The man hurried off and the clerk waved Margaret and Bray through the barrier into a small enclosure. Margaret raised a hand in thanks to the young knight who had recognised her, then followed the clerk into a sparsely furnished pavilion pitched before the Tower gate.

'My Lady,' the clerk grated, 'I have sent for the constable. Lord Dudley will be here shortly.'

Margaret made herself comfortable, Bray standing behind her. She listened keenly to the conversation amongst the officers who stood close by talking about the looming threat. How the Bastard of Fauconberg intended to sweep the men of Kent into London, recalling the turbulent days of Wat Tyler and Jack Cade, when the city suffered all the horrors of attack, sack and rapine. Nevertheless, despite the impending menace, Margaret truly believed that the civil war was finished. Edward of York, that golden-haired English Alexander, would tip the scales and carry out the total destruction of his opponents. He had fought them for years: his recent victories had annihilated most of his enemies, and those who had survived would be marked down for death. Despite the sinister Clarence, she quietly prayed that the Yorkist King did not consider her to be one of these. The pavilion emptied. Bray, who stood close to the entrance, walked across and leaned over.

'Mistress,' he whispered, 'Christopher Urswicke, should he not be here?'

'He tends to urgent business in Tewkesbury,' she replied.

'His business or ours?'

'You don't trust him, Reginald?'

'My Lady I do but, if I discover that I am wrong, I shall kill him.'

'And Urswicke has said the same about you.' She grinned impishly up at him. 'Trust is trust, Reginald. You stand by it or you fall. Believe me, you and Christopher are my shield companions. If I go down, so do you. If you fall, you could very well drag me with you . . .' She broke off as Lord Dudley, Constable of the Tower, a tall, balding man with a thick bushy moustache drooping at the corners of his mouth, entered the pavilion. Margaret made to rise.

'My Lady.' Dudley raised a hand. 'Please, it's an honour to see you.'

Margaret allowed the constable to kiss the tips of her fingers; she then introduced Bray. Once the pleasantries and introductions were finished, Dudley, dressed in chain mail and half-armour, took a stool and sat down. He rested his elbows on his knees, hands joined as if in prayer. He scratched his forehead then stared long and hard at Margaret, a fierce look but Margaret held his gaze. She had met Dudley before at some court celebration and knew him to be a good soldier of some integrity. She noticed the fresh scars to his face and moved to look at those on the side of his neck. Dudley grinned in a display of broken yellow teeth. He gently tapped his bloodied skin.

'River pirates,' he declared, 'as they once were. All gone now: their souls despatched to judgement, their corpses impaled on a row of sandbanks along the Thames.' He grinned wolfishly. 'Yes, I fought with John Tiptoft, Earl of Worcester, or so he was, until he supported the wrong side. He was caught and executed. Worcester fought in Wallachia around the city of Tirgoviste, in the service of the Lord Count Drakulya. A fearsome warlord, my Lady, who took no prisoners. Tiptoft learnt about impalement and how effective it is. More striking than a corpse dangling from the end of a rope or,' he shrugged, 'heads being severed in Tewkesbury market place. Yes, we have heard the news. King Edward is preparing to leave for London and he is issuing proclamations by the day which are posted at the Conduit in Cheapside and the Great Cross in St Paul's graveyard.' He took a deep breath. 'For what it's worth, my Lady,' he crossed himself, 'the list of dead is also being posted, and again, for what it's worth, I am truly sorry for your loss. The Beaufort family,' he sighed, 'have suffered grievously.' He fell silent, tapped his boots on the ground and glanced up. 'Margaret of Richmond, I know why you are here.'

'I wish to see the old King.'

'Many, including myself, do not see him, speak to him, or even allow ourselves to be seen consulting with him.'

'I want to.' Margaret steeled herself. 'And I need to see him soon. Edward of York and his brothers march on London. Henry is a problem Edward must address. I suspect he will, sooner rather than later. Consequently, sir, I wish to have words with a dying man. You cannot refuse me that. I must add that he is a kinsman of mine. I beg you sir, I need to have words with him.'

Dudley bowed his head; when he glanced up his cheeks were tear-soaked. 'I know,' he murmured, 'but I am concerned.'

'His Grace the King, and he was crowned that,' Margaret asserted herself, 'is half-brother to my late husband Lord Tudor. You know what is going to happen. I need to speak to the old King before the clouds gather and this fortress of yours becomes shrouded in mystery, if not murder. I am no threat to you, Edward of York or any of his ilk. I am here out of sheer compassion.'

Dudley nodded and rose, barking orders at his henchmen who had gathered close by. Margaret and Bray, surrounded by men-at-arms, were led out of the pavilion and through the sombre, cavernous postern gate into the Tower. Night was falling, but that grim fortress was frenetically busy. Men-at-arms milled around. Catapults, mangonels and trebuchets and all the other hideous engines of war were being prepared. The air was riven by the screech of cordage, the clatter of armour and the cries of officers. These all mingled with strident squealing from the hog pens, where the pigs were being slaughtered, their guttered carcasses being prepared, smoked and cured in preparation for a siege. The women of the garrison were busy around the wells filling water pots. The Tower was preparing for war and the imminent attack by the Bastard of Fauconberg's forces, be it across London Bridge or from the river.

Margaret's escort marched swiftly and they were soon in the great cobbled bailey where the formidable White Tower soared up above them, stark against the early summer sky. Margaret expected to be taken there. Instead, they were led across the execution yard, past the Church St Peter Ad Vincula and into the Wakefield Tower. Here the escort left them. Lord Dudley seized a ring of keys, led them up some steps, unlocked a door and waved them into a grim, grey circular stone chamber with a small enclave which served as an oratory. A murky place, the only light being provided by lancet windows and a few tallow candles fixed on spigots. The cowled prisoner sitting at the chancery table, strewn with manuscripts and books, sighed noisily and rose to greet them. A tall, angular figure garbed in dark clothes and shabby slippers. He shuffled forward. Margaret was immediately struck by how surprisingly young he looked; a pleasing countenance with a broad forehead, well-spaced eyes and rather pallid skin which seemed to emphasise his very pointed chin and protuberant lower lip.

'Your Grace.'

Margaret and Bray sank to their knees. Henry VI, King of England, God's anointed, hastened towards them.

'Not now, not now.' He half stuttered. 'Who are you? Emissaries from my wife?'

'Your Grace, this is Margaret Beaufort, Countess of Richmond, and I am her steward Reginald Bray. We have come to pay our respects.'

'Of course, of course.' Henry gestured at Dudley to prepare the chamber, a chair for himself and stools for his visitors. At last all was ready. Margaret glanced pleadingly over her shoulder at Dudley; the constable bowed, snapped his fingers at his escort and left the chamber, closing the door behind him. Margaret sipped at the cup of posset she had been served. Bray stood close to her, fingers resting on the hilt of his dagger. 'Come, cousin.' Henry stretched forward, hands extended. 'You are so kind. You have come to visit your poor kinsman.' He smacked his brow with the heel of his hand. 'So many Beauforts, good, generous people,' he lifted his head, tears brimming in his eyes, 'all gone into the dark. Oh, the years pass and I have seen them go.'

'Your Grace,' Margaret replied, pulling her stool closer, 'time is short. You have heard the news fresh out of Tewkesbury?'

'I have.' Henry sat all slack, mouth half open, eyes fearful. Margaret stared pitifully at this poor excuse of a king. She recalled what one of her kinsmen had said, 'Poor stock breeds poor stock.' Henry's paternal grandfather had been a leper: his French grandfather had suffered fits of madness believing he was a glass vase which could crack at any time. Henry had now reigned for fifty years, a period of decline and decay. As King he had been reviled, seized, mocked and humiliated the length and breadth of his kingdom as he passed from the hands of one violent warlord to another. He certainly wasn't born to be a king, more of a monk than monarch. A saintly man who loved his book of hours, psalter and ave beads, murmuring his prayers or, if he was lucid enough, poring over ancient manuscripts.

'I have heard the news,' Henry repeated, fingers going to his lips. 'I fear for my son and beloved wife.' His hand fell away. 'You know what they say? That the prince is not truly mine but the by-blow of one of my wife's lovers?'

'It's a lie, your Grace.'

Henry peered closer at Margaret. 'Yes, yes you would say that, wouldn't you? And how is your boy, the offspring of my darling half-brother Edmund?' Margaret just stared back. Henry abruptly turned sideways, peering at her out of the corner of his eye. 'I know, I know,' he whispered, 'this is the killing time. The wheel is being turned once more.'

'Your Grace,' Margaret gestured at the chancery desk, 'you

have parchment, wax, ink, pen and signatory ring. I need a writ under your seal that it pleases you to allow the bearer of such a warrant to do as he or, in this case she . . . well, whatever I want. I need to thread my way across this city and, more importantly, find a path through the murderous maze of court politics. Your Grace, my pardon, my apologies but, as you say, the killing time is here.'

Henry sucked on his lips and nodded. 'Yes, yes, it so pleases me,' he murmured. He rose, crossed to the table, beckoning at Bray to join him. The writ was scrawled and sealed with the King's signet ring. Henry then sat down, rubbing his lips with bony fingers.

'So, sweetest cousin, what do you want?'

'The Titulus Regius?' Margaret retorted. 'The Title of the King?'

'Ah yes.' Henry smiled. 'Searchers have been busy looking for that, industrious in discovering information. Somebody told me that.' He paused. 'Everybody searches for secrets. They look for lies, sometimes the truth, which they can use against their enemies. Now.' He became all brisk. 'The Titulus Regius is the creation of George of Clarence and, if the truth be known or, so my wife hinted, it is an attack on the Yorkist claim to the Crown of England.' He licked his lips. 'It's either that or a document which shows that George of Clarence should be King of England.' Henry seemed to find that amusing and he began to laugh softly.

'How do you know that?'

Again Henry's fingertips brushed his lips and his eyes lost that knowing look; his expression grew more vacant, vacuous and slack.

'Your Grace?'

'Oh yes, oh yes.' Henry breathed out noisily, staring over his shoulder at the chancery desk. 'When my wits returned and my beloved wife held the reins of power, I learnt a great deal about George of Clarence. You see Clarence changed sides, didn't he? Flitting like a shadow, or slinking like a rat, between his own kin and the House of Lancaster. A man who blows hot and cold. He can be your firm friend on Monday and your deadly enemy on Tuesday. Anyway, during the time Clarence was in the Lancastrian camp, he insinuated that he knew great secrets. How he himself should be King. Wasn't a proclamation issued declaring that? Anyway, anyway,' Henry fluttered his fingers, 'according to my wife, Clarence later hired three clerks skilled in collecting chatter and gossip. They were making careful note of all this in a secret chronicle. I believe others helped them but I forget the details.' Henry took ave beads out of his belt pouch and began to thread them through his fingers. 'God save us, God save us. Clarence even gathered scandal about his own parents, but I forget the details. My wife could tell you more if she dare.' He glanced fearfully at Margaret. 'I shouldn't even be discussing this. If the Yorkist lords discovered . . .'

Margaret nodded understandingly; she knew all about the old King's shifting moods. How he could lapse into sudden silence, totally withdrawn from the world, or indulge in hysterical fits bordering on a frenzy. Once Henry began to change, there was little sense to be had out of him. Margaret suspected that was about to happen. She glanced at Bray, who quietly nodded, as if he'd read her thoughts and agreed with her. It was time to leave. Margaret rose and made her farewells but Henry now seemed unaware of anything and, bowing his head, he intoned the opening verse of Vespers.

'Oh Lord come to my aid. Oh Lord make haste to help me . . .'

Margaret glanced pityingly down at this broken King who'd been deprived of his crown, his kingdom, his wife, his heir, his liberty and, undoubtedly once the Yorkist lords swept into London, his very life. She left Henry to his prayers.

Dudley was waiting in the stairwell and escorted her back down through the postern gate. Margaret and Bray hastened through the bustling crowd towards the Tower quayside. They walked carefully to avoid the carts and sumpter ponies being led up to the fortress with food and munitions for the garrison. Bray wanted to hire a barge but the crowd thronging around the quayside steps meant that they would have a long wait. Moreover, Margaret's mood changed. She believed, and Bray agreed with her whispered warning, that she had a deepening conviction of being quietly followed, watched and scrutinised. She tried to stifle the fear which coursed through her. The hunters were out, she was sure of that, but even worse, why were the dogs so close? Did they know something about what she intended? Of course she had been seen entering London through Aldgate, her presence would be noted, but this was different. She truly felt she was being closely scrutinised, her every step noted. Margaret prided herself on how her days at court had sharpened her ability to sense danger, threats as well as the means to avoid them. Of course that had been at court where she could count on powerful protection, but the power of the Beauforts had been shattered. So what did the hunters search for? Did they suspect what was hidden away in her most secret plans? Once again she recalled Somerset's warning in the chantry chapel at Tewkesbury. Did she really nurse a Judas close to her breast? Did this traitor, whoever he was, work for someone else? That must be Clarence and his coven. Was that why the King's brother hinted and baited her about her precious son?

'Mistress?'

Margaret stared fiercely at Bray who stepped back in alarm.

'Mistress,' he repeated, 'I did not mean to startle you.'

'We are being watched, Reginald, so let us play them at their own game. We must go.'

She turned, going back up Tower Street which led them into East-cheap, the great fish market around Billingsgate. The place stank of the fish, salt and offal strewn across the cobbles where cat and dog fought with the hordes of tattered beggars over the different scraps. The pillories and stocks set up in this foulsome place were being well used, especially for fishmongers who had tried to sell stale produce and were now being forced to stand, head and hands clasped, with the rotting carcasses of fish slapped across their faces. Margaret pretended to turn to look at these and slipped as if she had lost her footing. She used this to stare around, as did Bray who hastened to help her. Nevertheless, they could detect nothing amiss until they entered a narrow lane leading down to Candlewick. Bray stopped to turn back to give a beggar boy a coin when he glimpsed a sudden darting movement along the roof of a house further down the street. A small furtive shape skilfully treading the sloping, tiled roof. Bray smiled to himself and walked back to join his mistress.

'Sparrowhawks.' He murmured. 'Little street urchins who can scramble across the roofs better than any rat, cat or squirrel. They have us under watch so . . .'

He pulled Margaret into the dirty, dingy taproom of a tavern, a low-beamed room smelling of ale and fried food. Bray summoned the landlord, offered him a coin and quickly explained what he wanted. The man nodded and led both Margaret and Bray across to a door with eyelets high in the wood.

'Stay there.' The landlord tapped his barrel-like belly. 'Stay there,' he repeated, 'peer out. Let us see who comes.'

He opened the door; the small chamber was no better than a musty, cobwebbed cupboard, though it had a seat built into the wall. Margaret sat whilst Bray peered through the slats and waited. He was about to turn away when he quietly cursed, beckoning at Margaret to join him. She did so, peering through the eyelets. The noise of the taproom had stilled. No one moved but froze, staring at the men-at-arms garbed in city livery who'd slipped into the alehouse. Margaret reckoned there must be at least a dozen and she certainly recognised their leader Roger Urswicke, Recorder of London and the estranged father of her clerk Christopher. The landlord acted his part, running up to greet the visitors, fingers fluttering, face beseeching, eyes eager to help. Yes, he assured the Recorder, a man and woman had just entered his tavern but they had slipped across the kitchen garden and out through the wicket gate which fronted the alleyway beyond. Urswicke nodded, snapping his fingers at the men-at-arms to follow. Once they'd gone, the landlord busied himself around the taproom until one of the slatterns hurried in and whispered, pointing in the direction of the garden. Minehost rubbed his hands in glee and hurried across to open the door, gesturing at Bray and Margaret to come out.

'Gone.' He breathed. 'They have all left. I hate the bloody Guildhall and its nosey judges, the arrogant aldermen and clever-tongued lawyers. I say that, sir,' he peered at Bray, 'yet I apologise if you are lawyer; you look like one.'

'I am, but not of that ilk,' Bray retorted. 'However . . .' He slipped the landlord another coin and led Margaret out into the alleyway.

Margaret could glimpse no movement along the rooftops or at the mouth of the narrow runnels. They moved on, eager to hide amongst the crowd surging up from Cheapside where the long range of stalls offered everything under the sun. Trading was vigorous, as if the merchants of the city could not care which warriors fought, who was victorious, who rose and who fell. Margaret had learned a very salutary lesson in her life, something she treasured close to her heart. How the patronage of the arts, the pursuit of knowledge – be it in the cathedral schools or the halls of Cambridge – were part of the very fabric of life which any worthy prince should foster. The hideous slaughter at Tewkesbury was a grievous sin which threatened that fabric and should be curtailed at all cost. She wanted her darling son to learn the lesson, that trade not war, learning not battles were the true business of a prince. Margaret broke from her reverie as a group of bailiffs shrieked at a cutpurse and plucked him out of the crowd. Every day men were taken up and arrested, Margaret reflected, determined that would not happen to her, young Henry or any of those close to her heart. She was determined to weave the web she wanted and the most important part of this was the removal of her son from any danger.

PART THREE

'King Henry was secretly assassinated in the Tower.'
Milanese State Papers

They reached the corner of St Andrew's Street. Across from this, a chanteur, his skin as dark as night, stood on a barrel, trying to entice passers-by to listen to his tale about the fate of the great city of Constantinople. How swarms of Turcopoles had filled its wells with corpses and soaked the streets of the great city in blood. Margaret swiftly scrutinised him but he seemed genuine enough, hardly a spy in the employ of the Guildhall or Clarence. Nevertheless, she still had that chilling feeling of being closely watched. Bray, however, who stood staring up and around, whispered the danger was past. They continued halfway down the street, stopping at The Wyvern's Nest, a nondescript alehouse. Bray led Margaret in as he bellowed for Hempen the landlord, a fat, bustling, grey-haired tub of a man with a cruel red scar around his throat.

'Are we safe?' Bray demanded.

'Yes! Come!' Hempen led them out of the porch and across the taproom. In the corner he lifted a trapdoor, which stretched down to murky cellars. Margaret followed the taverner, a man who had nearly died of hanging until her late husband Edmund Tudor had cut him down from the gallows. Hempen was a retainer whom Margaret trusted with her life: one of the few men who would do all he could to help her and her beloved son.

The taverner, muttering to himself, led his guests along the mildewed passageway, an ancient tunnel leading from The Wyvern's Nest, across the alleyway above, and into the cellars of the house directly opposite. Margaret and Bray squeezed themselves through the narrow gap which Hempen cleared by pulling away a stack of timbers. They entered the gloomy, wet-walled cellars, a place reeking of mould and damp, a deep-cold blackness broken only by the dancing light from the lantern Hempen carried. He led them up steep steps and pushed hard at the door concealed behind a heavy dust-strewn arras: this opened and Hempen waved them into a small, shabby solar, where two individuals were sharing a bench before a meagre fire in the mantled hearth. The man, dressed in travel-stained jerkin, hose and boots, rose and warmly embraced his sister-in-law.

'Jasper,' Margaret breathed, 'thank God you reached here safely and you, light of my life,' Margaret crouched to embrace Henry, a narrow-faced, pale-skinned boy with large, pleasing eyes, smooth cheeks and a dimpled chin. She lightly touched his black hair, now nothing more than stubble, his head had been so closely shaved. 'I hardly recognised you,' Margaret smiled, 'and yet,' she lapsed into Welsh, 'I know you to be the very beat of my heart and you shall always rest at the centre of my soul.' She grasped the fourteen-year-old's arms and rubbed her hands up and down. 'He is well?' Margaret glanced sharply at Tudor.

'I am well,' Henry declared before his uncle could reply, 'and Mother, I am so pleased to be with you. I had a sickness of the belly as we have travelled far and fast. But now I feel better. I am pleased to be off the roads.' His face became more serious. 'Uncle Jasper warned that we are in great danger.'

'Yes you are,' Margaret whispered and stood up. 'But we will keep you safe.' Margaret eased herself down onto the bench, Bray standing behind her. Jasper sat on her left, her son on the other side. Margaret peered out of the corner of her eyes at him. Henry looked a little pale and thin but he seemed healthy enough. She stretched out her hands to the fire as she repressed a shiver of fear. Hempen coughed, making to leave, but Margaret gestured at him to stay, politely refusing his offer of wine and food.

'Master Hempen,' she smiled at her son, 'was not of that name when he was held over the baptismal font in his parish church at Powys. He received his new name when he was caught up in the fierce clan wars which rage along the Welsh valleys. Hempen was taken prisoner and his opponents were actually hanging him from a branch when your father, my husband, like some knight from the tales of Arthur, galloped up and cut him down.' Margaret rocked herself gently, eyes half closed, 'but that was my Edmund, a true knight. Anyway, he took my good friend here into his service. Is that not true, Master Hempen?'

The landlord nodded, rubbing the great, red weal around his neck. 'The noose did this,' he declared, 'burning like a flame from Hell. I forsook my old name and assumed a new one, Hempen, as a constant reminder of my foes and a token of remembrance for my saviour. Oh yes.' The more the landlord spoke, the more sing-song his voice became, distinctly echoing the accent of a Welsh valley-dweller. 'Lord Edmund,' he continued, 'was insistent that I leave Wales with him. He supplied me with good coin and letters of introduction to the Vintner's Guild here in London.'

'My late husband encouraged Hempen to purchase The Wyvern's Nest, and he also bought this house which stands directly opposite. Edmund knew about the secret tunnel stretching between the two, a relict of smuggling days. People can enter the The Wyvern's Nest and promptly disappear if the tavern is raided and searched.' Margaret pointed to a bell under its coping, high in the corner of the solar wall, just above the door. 'Twine is fastened to that and snakes back to the tavern: if the taproom is raided, the cord is pulled and the bell will ring its warning.' She smiled thinly. 'Edmund always had to be wary when he visited London.' She shrugged elegantly. 'And so it is now. Nothing has changed. Amongst the powerful, the Beauforts and the Tudors are regarded with disdain. However, you are here. More importantly,' she patted her son on the shoulder, 'our enemies think both of you are locked up in the fastness of Pembroke Castle. Long may they continue to believe that. I am sure Edward of York, urged on by his two brothers, will despatch troops into Wales.'

'They'll still think we are there,' Jasper broke in. 'We slipped very quietly out of the fortress and we have created the pretence that we still shelter within.' He paused. 'I did muster troops, a host of Welsh horse and foot advanced as if they intended to cross the Severn and assist the Angevin.' He waved a hand. 'Smoke in the wind. Margaret of Anjou's cause was doomed. You received my cryptic message from Lambert the page boy, my courier?'

Margaret nodded.

Jasper spread his hand. 'However, I agree with you, sister, it is only a matter of time before Edward of York lays siege to Pembroke and his war cogs appear off the coast.'

'Would the Yorkists,' Bray demanded, 'really besiege by land and sea? Pembroke is a formidable fortress. It could take months if not years before it fell.'

'Oh the Yorkist lords know that,' Jasper half laughed, 'but they would only be too pleased to keep the fortress locked up so that no one can get in or get out. And now we will use that to our own advantage. Though,' Jasper rubbed his face, 'it's only a matter of time before some traitor sells the news that we have flown the cage.'

'And in your journey here, how did you travel?'

'Master Bray, you are looking at two pilgrims who suspect they may suffer some affliction of the belly, their humours severely disturbed. So, we intend to visit Becket's shrine at Canterbury and then move north to the Blessed Virgin's house at Walsingham. Of course now we are here, we intend to take a ship abroad. I understand that the Breton cog, *The Galicia*, is about to berth at Queenhithe, its master has agreed—'

'No, no, no,' Hempen intervened. 'It is not as simple as that. We must be prudent, careful. The watchers and the scrutineers, as thick as lice on a dog's fur, are out along the streets and quaysides. Searchers carry the city commission and have been appointed and despatched to watch out for any from the House of Lancaster trying to flee the realm.'

'Yes, yes, we have already encountered the same.' And Bray swiftly told them about the sparrowhawks and the appearance of no lesser person than the Recorder of London, Thomas Urswicke, eagerly searching for someone or something.

'And that could be young Henry,' Hempen retorted. 'We know a few of the searchers and sparrowhawks. There is a rumour that they are looking for someone important,' the landlord pointed at Henry, 'and I suspect that is you.'

'We should move,' Bray murmured.

'No, no,' Hempen retorted. 'As I have said, the ports, quaysides and river steps are plagued by spies. South of the river, the men of Kent are stirring. Fauconberg threatens the city. We must not move while such storms swirl. We could be caught up in them and trapped.'

'We must wait.' Margaret rose and beckoned her son into her close embrace and then kissed the bristles on his shorn head. 'God keep you.' She whispered urgently. '*Pax et bonum*, my son. You must prepare yourself for sudden flight. We need Urswicke here. I am certain he is on his way.'

'Mistress,' Bray cleared his throat, 'Mistress,' he repeated, 'Urswicke's father is leading the hunt for us. It is all too close for comfort. Mistress, I beg you . . .'

Margaret lifted a hand for silence even as she winked at her son. 'Christopher,' she replied, 'I trust him with my very life. We will wait. Urswicke will help us . . .'

Christopher Urswicke made himself comfortable on the chancery stool before his father's writing desk in a gloomy chamber on the second storey of the Guildhall, its windows overlooking the great market of Cheapside. Urswicke had arrived in London the previous day but kept himself discreetly away from either The Wyvern's Nest or Sir Humphrey's riverside mansion. The clerk knew he would see his mistress in good time but that had to wait. Other pressing business demanded his attention, not least the urgent messages he carried in his courier's pouch from Edward of York and his two brothers.

The noise and smells of Cheapside seeped through the window, the perfumed fragrances mingling with the fetid stench from the slaughter sheds. He rose, crossed and opened the small door window peering down at the crowd thronging about, a sea of constantly shifting colour and noise. Urswicke, on his walk to the Guildhall, had also caught the tension, a growing fear of the impending storm gathering to the south of the city. Rumours were flooding through London that the men of Kent were now in Southwark, whilst Fauconberg's war cogs, armed with culverin and cannon, would unleash a hail of fire against the north bank of the Thames. As if to express this growing tension and mounting hysteria, a travelling chanteur, perched on his box, bellowed a warning in a powerful, carrying voice.

'The waves of death will surge about us,
The torrents of destruction shall overwhelm us,
The snares of the grave shall entangle us,
The fear of death confront us.

'Citizens of London,' the chanteur continued, 'fire and brim-stone will rain down on this city. A sea of flame sweep through your dwellings. On your knees, and prepare yourself by prayer and fasting against the day of the great slaughter.' The chanteur immediately broke off as a group of city men-at-arms surged through the crowd to arrest him, but the chanteur picked up his box and ran, still shouting his chilling warnings.

'Dire indeed.' Urswicke spun around; his father had entered the chamber, closing the door quietly behind him. Thomas Urswicke, Recorder of London, pointed down to his soft, wool-edged buskins. 'I have always been silent, soft-footed.'

'A necessary talent,' Christopher replied, 'for when you slipped down the stairs to the servant maids' quarters.'

'Now, now.' Thomas Urswicke's smooth, jovial face creased into a knowing grin, his sharp green eyes bright with life, his mouth twisted into that merry smile which Christopher knew was a mask for a mind that teemed like a box of worms and a heart full of lechery and deceit. Thomas Urswicke scratched his thin-ning blond hair and adjusted his gold-threaded guild robe. He fingered the silver chain of office around his neck, the other hand thrust through the ornamented swordbelt with its costly copper stitching and embroidered dagger scabbard. Nervous gestures! Christopher idly wondered if his father had been tumbling some wench in one of the many deserted enclaves of the Guildhall.

'Well.' The Recorder tried to assert himself, stretching out a hand. Christopher ignored this; he undid his chancery satchel, took out the sealed documents and handed them over. His father, mood all changed, snatched these, muttering to himself as he kissed and broke the seals. He read quickly, lips mouthing the words: he glanced up, staring at Christopher as if seeing him for the first time.

'Good news out of Tewkesbury.' The Recorder straightened up and preened himself. 'His Grace the King and his beloved brothers put great trust in me: these messages hint that I may be dubbed a knight.'

'For what?'

'For holding this city against rebels and traitors. I am glad to see,' his father added archly, 'that you have come to your senses. You may pretend to work for the Beaufort bitch but my Lord of

Clarence says you did great work in capturing the Angevin she-wolf and her whelp.' The Recorder sat down in his chair. 'The messages talk of a desire to impose order, to bring the violence to an end.' He tapped the documents. 'According to these, the killings at Tewkesbury included other victims. Two lay brothers were found mauled and eaten by hogs. Abbot Strensham is furious. Do you know anything about such killings?'

'How could I? The armies of both York and Lancaster contain professional killers, men of blood; mercenaries who fear neither God nor man. Father, we live in a time of war! Murder, treason and betrayal prowl the roads of this kingdom like starving, rabid dogs.'

'Aye, and talking of prowling the roads, so do traitors. We have information that Lancastrian rebels may well slip in and out of the city to foreign parts. Some of this information hints that your mistress harbours outlaws, fleeing Lancastrians—'

'Such as?'

'We don't know. Just hints that her own son, together with her traitorous kinsman, Jasper Tudor, might be amongst those she actively harbours and protects.'

'Henry Tudor!' Urswicke exclaimed. 'Never! He and his uncle shelter behind the fastness of Pembroke. Who gives you such information?'

'Anonymously,' his father replied. 'In the entrance to the Guildhall you must have seen the two lions carved out of wood, heavy statues, their mouths open in a roar. Citizens, good honest citizens, are encouraged, indeed exhorted on their allegiance to the Crown, to give any information they learn about the whereabouts and doings of traitors, malefactors, outlaws, whatever their status or station. Of course most of the intelligence is given without seal or signature. This system is valuable, especially when allegations are laid against a Beaufort: that she shelters traitors, even if these be her own son and kinsman.'

The Recorder seized the blackjack of morning ale on the table before him and drank noisily before offering it across to his son. Christopher just shook his head as he tried to school his features and curb the agitation curdling in his stomach. 'And you believe all this?'

'Yes, Christopher, I do. The Beaufort bitch certainly acts

mysteriously. I myself have ordered her to be watched most carefully and, from personal observation, since her return to this city, she acts in a highly suspicious fashion. I went hunting for her but lost my quarry. Now you are back in the city, such a pursuit should be your prime duty.' The Recorder waved a hand. 'The Beauforts are spent. Nevertheless, my Lord of Clarence wants you and me to be in at the kill, the utter destruction of that damnable family. However,' the Recorder leaned across the table, eyes all excited, 'we must also prove our loyalty and deal with other problems which beset us. The Bastard of Fauconberg has landed in Kent and sweeps towards the city. He leads seasoned troops from the garrison at Calais, men harnessed for war, well furnished with horses, weaponry and cannon. Fauconberg styles himself "captain and leader and liege lord to King Henry's people in Kent". Accordingly, Fauconberg demands to be allowed safe passage through the city so he can seek out and destroy – and these are his own treasonable words – the usurper Edward of York and his ilk.'

'And the city's response?'

'Stockton our mayor and myself have rejected Fauconberg and all his works. We have informed him that the Lancastrian generals Warwick, and his brother the Marquess of Montague, were slain at Barnet; their corpses lie exposed in St Paul's. We have also sent Fauconberg a second letter proclaiming our King's great victory at Tewkesbury. And so, my son,' Christopher caught the sarcasm in his father's voice, 'we have tasks to complete.' He rose, came round the table, placing a hand on Christopher's shoulder, leaning down so close that Christopher could smell the ale on his father's breath. 'The hurling time is here, Christopher. Stay close to me and our family will rise like the evening star. Keep the Beaufort woman under close watch and, at the appropriate time, betray her. Lancaster is finished, yes?'

Christopher nodded and rose quickly to his feet so his father had to withdraw his hand. 'I swear,' Christopher held his father's gaze, 'that at the appropriate time, I shall betray the usurper.'

'Good, good. Now to these seditious commotions . . .'

For the next week, Urswicke busied himself around London, ostensibly at his father's behest, taking messages to Earl Rivers and other Yorkist commanders. Secretly, Urswicke kept a sharp eye on the quaysides and realised that for the moment it was nigh impossible for anyone to steal out of London.

Fauconberg eventually emerged but his first assault was paltry. One of his war cogs fired against an especially fortified gate at the Southwark end of London Bridge, whilst a barge, packed with his soldiers, set fire to some houses close by. Both attacks were easily beaten off. What secretly impressed Urswicke was the work of his father and other Yorkist leaders such as Lord Dudley, Earl Rivers and Mayor Stockton. They had prepared hastily yet greatly improved the city's defences. The gates at both ends of London Bridge had been strongly reinforced with bristling bulwarks. At the same time, the entire north bank of the Thames was being fortified from the Tower right up to Castle Baynard, with a barricade of wine pipes filled with sand and gravel, on which cannon, trebuchets and culverin were positioned so as to sweep the river approaches with a veritable firestorm.

Despite the emerging crisis, being busy on this or that task proved to be Urswicke's best defence and protection. He acted the bustling retainer though he realised he was being watched. In his journeys around the city he would stop to eat and drink in a variety of taverns or alehouses and concluded that he was being followed by different people at different times in various places. A swift glance around a taproom and he would search out an individual on his own, always busy on something; be it fixing a scabbard, cleaning a boot or sharpening a knife on a whetstone. Such people always made the same mistake. Urswicke would rise and cross to the counter or jake's room and the watcher would also make to move.

For the rest, Urswicke lodged at The Sunne in Splendour in Queenhithe ward with Mauclerc and the Three Kings. They had returned with him into the city, hiring chambers at this spacious, majestic tavern. Apparently its owner Minehost Tiptree was a former member of Clarence's household. The landlord intrigued Urswicke; a bland-faced, balding man, thin as a beanpole. He seemed gushing and welcoming, but Urswicke sensed the taverner's deep unease. On the one hand he was patronised by the most powerful lord in the kingdom, yet Urswicke would catch Tiptree staring at Mauclerc with a barely concealed disdain. Urswicke was also intrigued by what the Three Kings were actually doing, his curiosity sharpened even further by the secrecy surrounding their chancery chamber; this was always closely guarded by one of the Three Kings and Urswicke was rarely invited to enter. He also noticed how the tavern was visited by strangers dressed in the brown and blue garb of what Urswicke reckoned to be that of an obscure order of friars. These mysterious figures, hooded and masked, would usher the occasional visitor, similarly cloaked and cowled, into the tavern and up to the chancery chamber, where they might stay for hours, before being just as quietly taken away. Urswicke was tempted to eavesdrop or even send messages about it to the Countess Margaret: in the end he decided not to give Mauclerc any grounds for suspicion, as Christopher was certain that those who prowled behind him in the city were in the pay of Clarence's devious henchman. Mauclerc wanted to be certain of him so Urswicke decided he would wait for the countess to approach him.

On 14 May 1471, with fresh rumours sweeping the city, Urswicke decided that the countess must have moved to contact him. He gave his pursuers the slip and made his way down to St Peter's-at-the-Cross in Cheap, an ancient church, its lancet windows so narrow the nave was cloaked in perpetual darkness. Urswicke, silent as a ghost, crept up the transept to the statue of St Peter where he glimpsed the small scroll pushed into a wall niche directly behind the statue. He took this out, unrolled it and noticed the dates, 9th, 12th, 14th. Urswicke slipped the scrap of parchment into his belt wallet and strode out of the church. He walked swiftly, turning and twisting along the needle-thin alleyways like a hare in a cornfield. At last Urswicke reached the The Wyvern's Nest, where Hempen immediately took him down the cellar steps, along the tunnel into the house opposite. Countess Margaret, Bray, Jasper Tudor and the young Henry were breaking their fast in the solar. Urswicke was warmly greeted, hands clasped, and then Urswicke sat down, staring hard at Margaret's young son.

'I know what you're thinking,' Bray followed Urswicke's gaze, 'it's difficult, nigh impossible to get out of the city.' Bray stared challengingly at Urswicke whom he did not fully trust.

'It's made even more difficult,' Margaret declared, 'because you Christopher, myself and Reginald are followed, inspected and scrutinised. To be out on the streets is to be noticed. If we take young Henry into London, we would all be seized. Yet,' Margaret tried to keep her voice from turning tremulous, 'we cannot stay here. We may have a spy, a traitor in our own household who busily searches out our secrets.' Margaret let her worry hang like a noose in the air. Young Henry glanced nervously at his uncle, who grasped him by the shoulder and pressed reassuringly, whispering in Welsh. Urswicke studied Jasper Tudor, the Welsh lord's unshaven face and worn clothing. Tudor had disguised both himself and young Henry very cleverly and, as he stared at them, an idea took root, a subtle plot which Urswicke was sure he could bring to fruition.

'You are accepted by Mauclerc and his master the Earl of Clarence?' Margaret broke into his thoughts. 'He thinks you have done good work for the House of York?'

'Yes, I informed him about the agreement we tried to reach with Wenlock. I also gave Clarence precious information about the Angevin she-wolf and her son. The messages delivered to Wenlock were in a cipher: he replied in kind about the whereabouts of Margaret of Anjou.' Urswicke ignored Jasper Tudor's sharp intake of breath.

'Do not be shocked or surprised, kinsman,' Margaret retorted. 'We had to clear the field. The Angevin has had her day in the sun: her time and that of her arrogant, bloodthirsty son are over. Now,' Margaret spread her hands, 'this war has raged for over sixteen years not only in this kingdom but in France, the Low Countries and along the Narrow Seas.' She pushed back the platters on the table before her. 'Much of the same,' she continued, 'this war could have gone on for ever and ever Amen. Margaret of Anjou could have escaped from Tewkesbury and fled abroad with her son to continue this tedious, wearisome struggle. More invasions, armies marching, days of slaughter, of blood and mayhem: this will not happen now. The Sun of York is in its ascendency. However, one day young Henry here, and those who accept him, will emerge from the shadows. We must prepare for that. We must nurse and nurture our opposition.'

'And the old King?' Jasper Tudor abruptly paused as Margaret banged the table with the flat of her hand.

'God forgive me, God forgive us,' she retorted, 'but the old

King's day is also finished. Edward of York will soon be in London and any further threat to his rule will be ruthlessly destroyed. The old King will die of some sickness or a fall, or by a cause known only to God, but Henry will certainly die. We must make sure that his one and only legitimate heir,' she pointed at her son, 'escapes to plot his return to seize what is rightfully his.'

'And how do we do that?' Jasper paused at a clatter on the stairs outside and Hempen burst into the chamber.

'The searchers!' Margaret exclaimed, springing to her feet.

'No, it's Saveraux, master of the Breton cog *The Galicia*. He's in the tavern.'

'Bring him up,' Margaret ordered.

'Do you trust him?' Bray demanded.

'With my life,' Margaret snapped, then she smiled up at Bray. 'Reginald, we need to trust the few we really trust and we must act on that trust. Saveraux's sons and two brothers were hanged on Flamborough Head by Richard of York, Edward's father. They were executed on a special gallows which soared black against the sky. York falsely accused them of piracy. They were tried but given no opportunity to reply. Sentence was imposed and immediately carried out. Now Saveraux is a blessing, a Celt like you, Jasper: he has invoked the blood feud and taken the blood oath. He is the mortal enemy of Edward of York and all his kin. So yes, I trust him, Master Hempen, show him up.'

Saveraux was a balding, bulbous-eyed, burly mariner who stank of fish, tar and oil. He was garbed in dark-brown leather jacket and leggings with thick-soled, salt-encrusted sea boots. He swaggered into the room, thumbs thrust under his warbelt which sported a sword and two daggers. He bowed to Margaret, nodded at the rest and stood scratching his chin.

'Valuable information, my Lady, you may use it as you wish. But first let me tell you. I am moving *The Galicia* further down river, close to the approaches to the estuary.'

'Why?'

Saveraux grinned. 'Ah, that's my valuable information. Fauconberg and his allies are about to launch a surprise attack on the city. The assault will be two pronged. Fauconberg is to occupy St George's Fields, that great open space between

Lambeth and Southwark. He intends to range cannon and culverin along the riverbank opposite the city. He hopes to invade the city from the south whilst another host of rebels will force the northern defences to break through into Aldgate and Bishopsgate.'

'And your source for this?' Bray demanded.

'Wars come and go,' Saveraux retorted, 'but the sea remains. We mariners are a brotherhood with loyalties which have nothing to do with York, Lancaster or anybody else. To cut to the quick, one of Fauconberg's captains, a mercenary in charge of a war barge, came to warn me to move both my ship and my crew.'

'I believe you.' Margaret snapped her fingers at Urswicke. 'Christopher, swift as you can. Hasten to the Guildhall, tell your beloved father what you have learnt here. Do not betray your source but depict yourself, yet again, as a stalwart for the House of York.'

Urswicke did so. He reached the Guildhall safely where his father gave him a warm welcome. He listened carefully to Christopher's news and almost did a jig of joy. He summoned his clerks and, with Christopher lounging in a chair, despatched messages to Clarence and the other Yorkist commanders. Urswicke decided to stay with his father and learn as much as he could. He wondered about Saveraux's warning, yet the Breton captain was soon proved correct. Fauconberg's attack on the city was swift and savage. He secretly transported a force across the Thames to capture and hold both Aldgate and Bishopsgate so he and his henchmen could use these gateways to funnel more troops into the city. The attacks were led by two of Fauconberg's principal captains, Bardolph and Quintain.

Urswicke was despatched with messages to the Yorkist captain responsible for defending both of these city gates. The clerk, armed with sword and dagger, picked his way through the streets. As he approached the once-bustling towered gateways, Urswicke smelt the burning and glimpsed black columns of smoke streaming up against the clear summer sky. Many citizens had fled. The streets were deserted, though littered with the detritus of battle. Apparently the outworks of Aldgate had been forced, the fighting so savage and bitter, they'd been forced to drop the heavy portcullis on both defender and attacker. About six of the latter had been trapped inside the walls, caught and summarily executed, their headless cadavers impaled upside down on the approaches to the city gate.

The area around the defences was strewn with the dead. Corpses sprawled everywhere; faces and heads smashed, bellies ripped open, bones shattered, dreadful wounds caused by hand-guns and sharp arrow-storms delivered at close quarter. Smoke billowed to obscure the view so Urswicke simply followed the raucous din of battle. The fog of powder and fire parted and Urswicke glimpsed his father in sallet and mailed jerkin mounting a warhorse in preparation to lead a counter-attack. The destrier was caparisoned for battle, eager to charge, its sharp hooves impatiently scraping the cobbles. Around the Recorder milled men-at-arms and archers wearing the city livery. Urswicke glimpsed his son and pointed his sword at him, lifting the visor which protected his mouth.

'We will drive them back!' he roared. 'Christopher, go down to the bridge, see what is happening there. For the rest . . .'

Christopher's father lifted his sword and the soldiers around him shouted their approval. The entrance to Aldgate was cleared and the Recorder and his troops surged through. One of the men-at-arms, left behind because of wounds to his arms and face, informed Christopher that the rebels were in full retreat, falling back on St Botolph's Church. Urswicke thanked him, turned away, and hurried down towards the Tower, threading the streets where makeshift barricades, bulwarks and bastions had been hastily assembled. Stout cords and chains had been dragged across the streets and alleyways to impede the enemy. Urswicke was also warned to be wary of the caltrops strewn across the cobbles; sharp, cruel traps to bring down both man and beast.

Using the warrants his father and Mauclerc had provided, Urswicke safely negotiated his passage. He pushed his way through the press of city militia as well as the mob, a swarm of cutpurses and thieves who'd crawled out of their filthy dens to see what mischief could be had. As was usual during any unrest in the city, foreigners were singled out for punishment. Makeshift gallows set up at street corners were decorated with the dirt-strewn, twisting corpses of Flemish prostitutes seized from the nearby brothels; mouldy, mildewed mansions which had been sacked and put to the torch. More respectable foreigners had flooded into the churches to seek sanctuary or hidden in the houses of merchant friends along Cheapside.

Urswicke eventually reached the bridge where city troops massed under their captains, a moving horde of heavily armoured men, packing the approaches to the river. Engineers pushed their bombards, culverins and cannons down towards the Thames. Dirty-faced street urchins who served as powder monkeys for the engineers, scampered around the huge war carts. Stacks of corpses killed in the furious affray which had raged across the bridge ranged two yards high, though now it was all over. The rebels had seized the first gateway on the Southwark side and burned a number of houses. Urswicke, however, soon realised that Fauconberg's troops had been severely defeated, beaten back by the bridge defenders as well as city troops who had crossed the Thames by barge and were now threatening to encircle the rebels. The attack was over and Urswicke realised it was time to rejoin the countess . . .

By 18 May, the rebels had fled the city. Yorkist forces, together with the levies raised in the city, pursued the rebels deep into Essex and Kent. Urswicke decided to act. He begged Saveraux to bring *The Galicia* to Queenhithe, berth it there and act as normally as possible. Urswicke personally checked the Breton cog, a large, deep-bellied two-masted ship with a lofty stern and prow. Once he was sure *The Galicia* was safely berthed in Queenhithe, Urswicke asked the countess to hold an urgent meeting of her small council. They all gathered in the solar of the narrow house opposite The Wyvern's Nest. Night was falling, the only light being that from candles and flickering lanterns. Once assembled, Urswicke described his plan, adding that they had to act now. Saveraux and his ship were ready, whilst Edward of York and his entire host would soon be in the city. Once he arrived, an even closer guard and watch would be imposed over the quaysides, whilst the length and breadth of the river and all its ports would be ruled by martial law, and that included the likes of Saveraux, his ship as well as other foreign cogs.

The Breton loudly agreed with Urswicke, adding that he would have to flee before any attempt was made to detain him. Bray, ever cautious, argued heatedly for doing nothing, but Urswicke, his mind and wits sharp as a razor, countered that.

He argued that the difficulties raised were nothing compared to the real danger of following any other path. If Lord Jasper and young Henry fled back to Wales, Urswicke declared, there was a strong possibility of being captured and summarily dealt with. A savage, swift death was all they could expect in some desolate spinney or lonely wood. Even if they reached Pembroke safely, what then?

Urswicke described how Edward of York was already laying siege to the castle by land and sea. How could Lord Jasper and the prince enter the castle, and would they be really safe there? If they stayed in London, the net would tighten. Sooner or later they would make a mistake, the danger being all the sharper if there truly was a traitor in the countess's household. Nor must they forget the watchers in the street, the spies swarming everywhere, the sharp and observant street swallows and sparrowhawks. True, the city was a mass of winding, stinking alleyways, but what would happen if Edward of York imposed martial law, sealing off each ward and conducting a house-by-house search?

Urswicke argued long and persuasively. He could tell by her silence that the countess was listening most intently to his suggestion and eventually she agreed, adding that, if this stratagem went awry, they could always devise some other subtle way forward. They were committed. The countess, Lord Jasper Tudor and the now fearful Henry realised there was no better plan. The Yorkist bloodlust was up. Already rumours were seeping in that royal troops were pursuing the rebels into Essex and Kent, inflicting dire punishments on all those who'd taken up arms. Individuals such as Nicholas Faunte, the Mayor of Canterbury who had decided to support Fauconberg, suffered the full penalty for treason, being hanged, drawn and quartered in the market square of his own city. The tarred, torn remnants of his corpse, along with his head poled above the city gates. Urswicke urged Jasper and Henry to prepare themselves by the evening of the following day, adding that he would counsel and advise them on what they must do so as to be ready to depart on 20 May.

Early on the chosen day, Urswicke presented himself in his father's chamber at the Guildhall. The Recorder, still brimming with glee and good humour at what he described as 'the city's great victory against the rebels', didn't realise at first the full significance of what his son was telling him. He sat, mouth gaping, and then asked Christopher to repeat what he had said. Urswicke did. He explained how downstairs in the Guildhall parlour were a man and his son, wandering beggars, scavengers along Queenhithe who had glimpsed well-garbed strangers being brought secretly aboard a Breton cog, *The Galicia*. The Recorder stared down at the tabletop, rubbing his hands, then he lifted his head and smiled at Christopher.

'We will surely profit from this, my son.' And, springing to his feet, he called a servant and told Christopher to wait until his good friend, as he described Mauclerc, came striding into the chamber. Clarence's henchman swaggered in booted and cloaked, a broad warbelt strapped around his waist.

'Master Christopher,' he exclaimed, 'what is this, what is this?' Urswicke repeated his story and Mauclerc demanded that the beggars, both father and son, be brought up for questioning. Urswicke agreed; going down to the parlour he ushered up the two informants, shaven and shorn, garbed in filthy rags, their bare feet slapping the floor. Urswicke introduced Ragwort and Henbane, father and son, who'd assumed the names of herbs. The beggars spent their lives scavenging backwards and forwards across the quaysides of London, especially Queenhithe, begging for what could be had and desperate for any opportunity to earn a coin or a platter of food. Both Ragwort and Henbane, dancing from foot to foot, filthy faces set in a manic grin which showed yellow, blackening teeth, listened intently. They both nodded vigorously as Urswicke described how they earned a living and, like others of their brotherhood, were paid by him to report anything suspicious.

'And?'

Thomas Urswicke, summoning up all his authority as Recorder, strode round the table and advanced threateningly towards the two beggars, who fell to their knees, hands joined in supplication.

'And?' the Recorder repeated. 'What?' He crouched down before the beggars. 'What did you see?'

'We were collecting pieces of coal which a barge had brought up, Your Magnificence. It was after the present troubles.' Ragwort was almost gabbling as he placed a hand on his son's bony shoulder. 'Henbane here glimpsed it – sharp he is,' Ragwort continued in a sing-song voice, 'keen as a knife, even though his hearing and tongue are not what God wants them to be. Anyway,' Ragwort scratched his son's balding skull and gently pushed him away, 'sharp-eyed, he glimpsed two men, well garbed, faces and heads hidden. They were shepherding a youth whose hood fell back, tugged by the river breeze, before he pulled it up again. Perhaps a youth no older than Henbane himself, fourteen to fifteen summers. They pushed him swiftly up onto a Breton ship. We drew closer and watched. We learnt its captain was Saveraux and the cog is called *The Galicia*. We only saw them for a few heartbeats as they disappeared up the gangplank. We set up careful watch: those strangers, hooded, visored and in a hurry, never came off that ship. Nothing more than that.' Ragwort sniffed and wiped his nose on the back of a dirty hand. 'We heard about the proclamations,' Ragwort's whining voice stumbled over the words, 'we glimpsed the watchers, the spies,' the beggar licked his lips, 'we've also heard of the great reward . . .'

He paused as Thomas Urswicke drew his dagger and pressed the tip under Ragwort's chin. 'If you are lying,' he grated, 'you will suffer the consequences.'

'Let us find out.' Mauclerc strode swiftly to the door and shouted orders to his retainers thronging outside. He turned. 'Master Thomas, you are with us?'

'As always.'

The Recorder beckoned at Christopher and ordered two men-at-arms, standing guard just within the doorway, to take Ragwort and Henbane into custody. 'You,' the Recorder pointed at the two beggars, 'will come with us.'

Mauclerc came hurrying back. 'I have sent urgent messages,' he declared, 'to the royal cog of war, *The Morning Star*, moored in port, to sail down to Queenhithe. It is to keep *The Galicia* under strict scrutiny and, if necessary, make sure it does not slip its moorings. We also have men-at-arms and hobelars assembling. Come, Come.' Mauclerc snapped his fingers. 'We will seize and search the Breton ship.'

A short while later Mauclerc led the Urswickes, the two beggars and a phalanx of armed men, both retainers and city liveries, out of the Guildhall gates. They pushed their way through the morning crowd, the soldiers clearing the path in front of them with spears, halberds and drawn swords. The air was cool, a faint river mist still curled around the stalls being set up for a new day's trading. Chapel bells clanged their summons to morning mass. Trumpets, horns and bagpipes wailed as bailiffs led the captive roisterers, night-walkers and other violaters of the King's peace down to the stocks, thews and pillories. Every one scattered at their approach. The streets, alleys and runnels leading down to the river swiftly emptied as the dark-dwellers slunk back into their dens and mumpers' castles. A deathly stillness greeted Mauclerc's war band. The Yorkist victories, as well as the abrupt and humili-ating retreat of Fauconberg along with other rebels, had imposed a watchful peace over the city. The Guildhall had issued procla-mation after proclamation how any disturbance would be regarded as treason against both Crown and city.

They eventually reached Queenhithe; the quayside was awash with the guts and heads of fish netted earlier in the day. These turned the ground underfoot greasy and slippery, whilst the air reeked of fire, brine and other more fetid odours. A sharp breeze tugged at their cloaks. Mauclerc shouted and pointed to the great war cog, *The Morning Star*, making its way out to mid-river before it turned and drew closer to the quayside. *The Galicia* had already cleared its berth and was ready to sail when Mauclerc ordered one of his soldiers to blow three blasts on a powerful hunting horn. Saveraux, now aware of the armed cohort on the quayside, as well as *The Morning Star* bearing down fast, imme-diately hove to. Sails were quickly reefed and the Breton brought his cog back along the quayside. The royal warship followed, drawing so close that *The Galicia* could only leave with its permission. A great deal of shouting ensued. The Recorder lifted his warrants to display their seals whilst a herald shouted that Saveraux's ship could only sail with permission of both Crown and city.

At last the Breton cog was fully berthed. A section of side rails were moved and a gangplank lowered. Christopher Urswicke led the charge across this, the soldiers spilling out and, following Mauclerc's orders, immediately broke into the small captain's cabin beneath the stern whilst the Recorder demanded to see the cog's licences, warrants and manifests. Screaming and gesticu-lating how, despite the fact that he was in an English harbour,

Saveraux protested that he was a Breton and that both he and his ship were under the direct protection of Duke Francis of Brittany. He shouted how he would, as soon as he reached Nantes or La Rochelle, lodge the most serious complaint. Saveraux gabbled on, only to fall silent as Mauclerc lifted the point of his sword to only a few inches from the Breton's face.

'We need to see your muster rolls and other documentation,' Mauclerc insisted. 'What is your cargo, what does your manifest say? And I want them now. Come on, come on.' He snapped his fingers. 'Give me the muster roll. Better still, I want the entire ship's company here on the main deck. Christopher,' Mauclerc gestured at Saveraux, 'show him the reason for our visit.'

Urswicke sheathed his sword and dragged Ragwort and Henbane across the deck, holding each by the arm. He pushed these towards the Breton who just turned and neatly spat on the deck between them. He was about to turn away.

'This precious pair,' Urswicke declared, 'could lead to your arrest whilst your cog and all it holds would be impounded.'

Saveraux walked forward.

'Tell him!' Urswicke yelled, shaking both beggars vigorously. 'Tell him what you saw.'

Ragwort repeated their story. Saveraux would have lunged at him if Christopher and one of the men-at-arms had not intervened, pushing the two beggars out of the way. Saveraux just shook his head, spitting dangerously close to Urswicke's boots.

'I know of no such visitors,' he protested. 'No well-garbed young man has been brought onto this cog.' Again he spat. 'I carry bales of English wool to Dordrecht in Hainault and more for the Staple at Calais. Now search my ship, question my crew. I tell the truth.'

Christopher shoved the beggars away and watched his father and Mauclerc organise a most thorough search of the hold, its supplies, cargo and weapon store. Nothing was found. The ship's crew was mustered. Each man declared his name and origin, which the Recorder carefully compared with what was entered on the muster roll. At last the search and questioning drew to a close. Saveraux, now protesting his innocence, and quoting the trade treaties between Duke Francis and the English Crown, shouted that he would lodge the most serious complaint. He and his ship were Bretons. If this violation of their rights continued, Duke Francis would surely retaliate against English ships and merchants. Mauclerc and the Recorder had no choice but to agree. A trumpeter blew a blast whilst the herald shouted across the water to the captain of *The Morning Star* that *The Galicia* now had permission to sail.

'And what about these,' Saveraux pointed to Ragwort and Henbane, 'the source of all this nonsense?'

'Oh yes,' Christopher retorted swiftly, drawing a leather club out of his warbelt. He strode across the deck and began to beat both beggars until they fell to their knees, hands out, crying for mercy. Christopher ended his tirade by giving both unfortunates a vigorous kick and throwing the leather club down at Saveraux's feet.

'Take these two nithings down river, as far as you can. Leave them on a sandbank. The water there is shallow enough and, if they want, they can clamber ashore and walk back to whatever midden heap they crawled from.'

Saveraux needed no second bidding. He grasped both beggars, throwing them roughly down into the black, stinking hold, shouting how they would receive further beatings before they left his ship. Both Mauclerc and Urswicke's father had now lost interest in the proceedings and led their cohort back down the gangplank. Christopher followed and, without a backward glance, strode across the cobbles and into the tangle of alleyways which ran from Queenhithe up into the city.

Later that day, when the Vesper bells clanged across the city and the beacon lights flared in the church steeples, Christopher Urswicke sat in a flower arbour at The Lamb of God, a spacious, stately tavern overlooking Cheapside. Christopher watched the shadows of the massive oak trees creep across the well-tended grass, the first fingers of darkness beginning to curl around the flower beds and herb pots. A small fountain, carved in the shape of a pelican striking its breast, tinkled and glittered. Somewhere in the tavern a casement window hung open and the soft, sweet sound of a lutist playing a lullaby drifted out into the velvet darkness. Urswicke half closed his eyes as he stared into the gathering dark. He pretended he was in his father's garden and his mother, bright faced and busy, would come out through the kitchen door, humming some soft song, hurrying to sit by him on the turf seat. She would put an arm around him and talk about the little people, magical creatures who lived in a small cave at the far end of the garden. Urswicke blinked away the tears as he let himself go gently back into the past, well away from the terrors of the day with all its ever-present dangers. Tomorrow would be different. He must sleep well tonight and prepare. The news was all over the city. Edward of York was advancing in full splendour on London.

'Christopher, Christopher?' Urswicke startled, immediately stretching out for the warbelt on the bench beside him. 'Christopher, it's me.' Urswicke peered through the gathering murk at the Countess Margaret with her constant shadow Reginald Bray.

'Christopher?'

Bray gestured towards the tavern. 'You hired a chamber?'

'Aye.' Urswicke got to his feet. 'A well-sealed room furnished with all we need.'

'Good, good.' Margaret looked up at the sky. 'Thanks to you, Christopher, my son and my kinsman Jasper are now safely on the Narrow Seas.'

Christopher mockingly bowed.

'My Lady, they will be bruised and hurt after the beating I gave them. But those who hunted your son now believe that *The Galicia* simply carried away two beggars to be punished even further. I must admit,' Urswicke grinned, 'I prepared them well, blotched and stained, clad in ragged clothes. Lord Jasper is skilled in accents whilst young Henry simply had to act the sharp-eyed mute.'

'It was a risk,' Bray countered.

'A calculated one, I agree, but neither Mauclerc nor my father has ever seen Jasper Tudor or the young Henry. No accurate description of either of them is available. I set a trap and my father walked into it without a second thought. No one doubted my story, as I have been a constant source of good intelligence. Why should I be wrong about those two?' He paused, chewing the corner of his lip. 'Ah well, now they are out of harm's way. Saveraux will see they are safely delivered. Ours was a most cunning and subtle device. I have seen it used before to hide someone or something in full view. One day, not now but in the future, when Fickle Fortune gives her wheel another spin, I would love to tell my father the full truth behind what happened.'

'In the meantime,' Margaret declared, 'Edward of York is about to enter London and we must prepare, plot and plan. We must also use the old King's writ to move around this city – soon, I suspect, such a writ will be worth nothing!'

The Yorkist lords swept into London on the morning of 24 May. Edward met the mayor and leading citizens of the city in the meadowlands between Islington and Shoreditch. He received their assurances that his leading city was completely free of all rebels whilst those captured were now no more, their severed heads and steaming quarters being despatched to hang above the city gates or along the railings of London Bridge. The Yorkist King responded to such loyalty by knighting from horseback his fervent supporters in the city, including Thomas Urswicke. Once the ceremony was completed, the royal herald proclaimed they would now advance into London, processing to St Paul's, where His Grace the King could view the naked corpses of his enemies, Warwick and the others. Trumpets and clarions blew. Standards and banners were unfurled. Shouted proclamations issued as the cortège, including three dukes and all the leading barons of the kingdom, solemnly wound their way into the city. Marshalled behind the royal party were others, including Countess Margaret, since she was a Beaufort as well as the wife of a Yorkist lord. She had been summoned to trail behind the King's cortège, along with other leading ladies of the court.

During the initial ceremonies Margaret simply sat patiently on a palfrey. She had done her best to honour the occasion, being garbed in a gown of blue and gold and wearing a wimpled headdress of the same colour and texture. She had been informed that the procession would take hours so she wore elegant leather riding boots and grasped the reins of her gentle-eyed mount, her hands protected by the softest, doeskin gloves. All around her were others, including Bray and Urswicke, suitably apparelled and well horsed. Margaret did her best to steel herself against this show of Yorkist glory and triumph. She had to accept this was harvest time, the sowing had been bloody and so would the reaping. She had to remain impassive and act the part. As the

royal procession was organised, the countess became more
intrigued by Edward's principal captive, the fallen Queen
Margaret of Anjou. The Angevin, dressed in a simple red gown
which covered her from neck to bare, soiled feet, sat on the bench
of a prison cart pulled by two huge dray horses, their hogged
manes and plaited tails garlanded with purple ribbons. The
Angevin sat, hands on her knees, staring dully into the main
distance, her lips moving soundlessly. Margaret couldn't decide
if the fallen Queen was praying, talking to herself or humming
a tune: she looked a pathetic sight, her once-golden hair faded
and streaked with white; the former Queen seemed like some
felon being taken from Newgate to the gibbet over Tyburn Stream.
The prison cart stood alongside the royal cortège. Few gave the
former Queen a second glance, even the crowds who swirled in
a sea of colour and a mixture of smells, ignored this pathetic
relic of former glory. Margaret studied the Angevin and decided
to make good use of her presence in London.

The rest of that day Margaret played out the role assigned to
her. The royal procession swept through the city to be greeted
ecstatically. The citizens, encouraged by Edward of York's
agents and gang-leaders, welcomed the victor of Tewkesbury
back into London. White silk and linen cloths hung from the
open casement windows of the mansions along Cheapside.
Carpets, cloths of gold, sheets of Rennes linen, coverlets and
counterpanes of the richest material were draped over the various
city crosses and statues. Fountains and conduits disgorged free
wine, ale, beer and different kinds of fruit drinks. The stalls of
Cheapside groaned under great platters of food piled high. City
bailiffs, armed with clubs, stood on guard against the legion of
beggars who watched all this with glittering eyes and empty
bellies. At last the royal procession wound its way back into
the Tower, preceded by the fallen Queen who had acted stoic-
ally throughout this long and public humiliation. At the Lion
Gate, the yawning, hollowed entrance to the fortress, the procession broke up. Most of the courtiers streamed back into the city
to participate in the festivities, feasting and frivolities which
would last into the early hours.

Countess Margaret noticed how the King and his two brothers
ignored this; they seemed unwilling to leave immediately but

rode up the dark, sinister gullies which cut through that formidable fortress into the great bailey before the soaring White Tower,
freshly painted to welcome York's return. Countess Margaret
and her henchmen followed Edward and his brothers. Eventually
the royal party, together with chosen henchmen such as Mauclerc,
Hastings and others, adjourned to the King's apartments, close
to the chapel of St John on the second gallery of the White Tower.
The Angevin Queen was handed over to the constable, the
grim-faced John Dudley. He ignored her cry that once he had
fought for Lancaster, and ordered her to be taken across to
be lodged in the Wakefield, the same tower which housed her
husband.

Countess Margaret decided to bide her time. The evening was
warm and balmy. The setting sun, still strong, bathed the bailey
in a welcoming light. Margaret sat down on a stone bench close
to the Chapel of St Peter in Chains, watching the Tower people
streaming backwards and forwards, though she noticed they were
kept well away from the steps of the White Tower, closely guarded
by a phalanx of archers, men-at-arms and knight bannerets.
Margaret posed, all composed, listening to the cattle lowing and
the pigs screeching as they were herded up to slaughter pens.
She caught the tang of cooking from the Tower kitchens, which
mixed with the different smells from the stables and outhouses
around the bailey. She watched a group of women busy at the
wells, washing clothes as well as pots and pans from the buttery.
Margaret glanced over her shoulder at Bray and Urswicke who
stood deep in conversation. She invited them over to sit either
side of her.

'What now, Mistress?' Bray demanded.

'What now, sir?' She mocked back. 'What were you discussing?'

'The traitor, Mistress, we have a traitor in the household,' Bray
insisted. 'As you know, I suspected Christopher, I even began to
suspect myself. Had I made some hideous mistake? But now,'
he lowered his voice, 'I have reflected and so has my friend here.
Looking back at what has happened, reflecting on past events, there
is no doubt that our enemies, although they did not know for certain,
suspected something very important, crucial to our cause, was
happening. Our visits to The Wyvern's Nest were necessary but
our secret, even furtive movements in going backwards and

forwards from there deeply agitated our opponents. Christopher and I believe that someone in our household knew that we were fervently involved in a matter vital to the Lancastrian house. Such a traitor did not know the details but they conveyed their suspicions to the Recorder and the likes of Mauclerc.' Bray paused. 'In a word, Mistress, we suspect Owain and Oswina, it must be them . . .'

'Nonsense, nonsense!' Margaret leaned forward, peering through the gathering murk. 'Surely not, surely not,' she half whispered. 'I too had my suspicions, I too have reflected, yet Owain and Oswina are like kin. We have the blood-tie between us. Surely they would not play the Judas? No, no,' she shook her head, 'no,' she whispered, 'not with me, surely?' Margaret held up her hands, forefingers entwined. 'Owain and Oswina are twins; they are like that, bound together. If the sister goes out of our house, the brother always accompanies her. Yet when I made my own enquiries, I understand the twins never left Sir Humphrey's mansion, whilst no strangers were seen approaching them or, indeed, any of my household. So . . .' She paused as Sir John Dudley came down the steps out of the White Tower. Margaret rose and walked swiftly towards him.

'Sir John, a word?' She grasped the constable by the sleeve, taking him away from his escort.

'My Lady.' The constable leaned down. 'I have heard how your husband was sorely wounded at Barnet.'

'He lies grievously ill,' she agreed, and stared pleadingly up at him. 'Another widow to be, eh Sir John?' She shrugged prettily. 'Surely you must, as a widower, recognise how lonely it can be?' Dudley grasped her right hand, raised it and kissed her fingertips.

'In such circumstances, my Lady, I would hasten to give you any help and whatever comfort you needed.'

Margaret smiled brilliantly and moved a little closer. 'Lord John,' she murmured, 'times are changing. New alliances are being formed. The past is dead. Our King is triumphant and soon I must return to my manor and poor Sir Humphrey. So, Sir John, I would like to visit the Angevin queen and my royal kinsman.' She paused. 'Is that possible?'

Dudley pursed his, lips deep in thought. Margaret gently rested a gloved hand on his wrist. 'You know what is going to happen,' she whispered hoarsely, 'I am of the court party. My loyalty to Edward of York cannot be doubted, but these two prisoners, Sir John for pity's sake, for the mercy we all ask of the Lord, let me say my farewells before I leave London.' She dabbed the tears from her eyes then struck her breast. 'Sir John, Sir John, I beg you. What harm is there in saying farewell?'

Dudley quickly agreed. Margaret was taken over to the Wakefield and ushered into the chamber allocated to the fallen Queen. Dudley then left. The Angevin was sitting in a high-backed chair, the small table beside her had a platter of bread and cheese next to a jug of wine and a deep-bowled pewter goblet. Little had been done to prepare the cell, which was as gaunt and stark as any corpse chamber in a death house: a cot bed, a chest, some candles and a few stools. Cobwebs spanned the ceiling like nets. Mice scrabbled in a corner whilst the shutters across the lancet windows rattled in the strengthening night breeze. The Angevin peered at Margaret as the countess pulled up a stool in front of her.

'The little Beaufort woman,' she rasped, 'I remember you. The last of your family eh?' The Angevin put her face in her hands and sobbed quietly for a while. Margaret just watched the flame on the squat tallow candle which marked the passage of time in broad red rings. The usual noises of the Tower were now fading, but she heard the sound of revelry and she wondered if the Yorkist warlords were celebrating the annihilation of their foes, including this broken woman who had fought them for years. The Angevin took her hands away and frowned at Margaret. 'Night is gathering,' she whispered, 'and I am finished. My husband, I understand, lies imprisoned in this very tower. My son is murdered, as are all your family. The Beauforts are no more. So what do you want with me, little woman?'

'The "Titulus Regius" – what do you know?'

'I don't know anything and, if I did, why should I tell you? My cause is finished. You rode in the Yorkist triumph. I saw you watching me constantly.' The Angevin showed some of her old imperiousness, pulling herself up in the chair, shaking herself, staring around as if to summon servants. 'Why should I talk to you, Beaufort? Why should I tell you anything?'

'You should tell me,' Margaret countered, 'for a number of reasons. First, I may have ridden in the Yorkist entourage, but I had no choice. I am not their friend or ally, in fact the opposite. They wish to keep me close not because of any love but to mount careful guard over me, which they do constantly. Secondly, the Yorkist lords fear me because secretly they recognise me as a rival; and so I am – or at least my son is.'

'Where is he?'

'Safely spirited away. His existence, his survival, means our struggle goes on, the dream of winning recognition for the House of Lancaster. Our cause will not die this day; in fact, it may now move from strength to strength.'

'Edward and his siblings rejoice . . .'

'For today, but the tensions are there. Edward's wife is a Woodville, she and her family are truly hated by both of Edward's brothers. A great weakness, easy to exploit, as Scripture says, "A House divided against itself cannot stand." Oh, these halcyon days of York will end soon enough. Divisions, enmities and deep hostilities will emerge. None more powerful than the over-weaning ambition of George of Clarence. We know that he works on justifying his own claim to the throne. He and his most trusted confidants have a book, a manuscript, a chronicle called the "Titulus Regius". What if such a work became public knowledge? Would it seriously weaken the claims to the throne of both Clarence's brothers? My Lady,' Margaret urged, stretching forward to touch the former Queen's knee, 'I need to discover the truth about all this. I have learnt that the "Titulus Regius" is the creation of three clerks in Clarence's Secret Chancery. They work under the supervision of Mauclerc, Clarence's principal henchman.

'And so it is.' The Angevin relaxed, slumping further down in her chair. She picked up the goblet and drank noisily. 'And what do I get if I tell you what I know . . . which,' she waved the goblet, 'is not much?'

'You are a prisoner here,' Margaret replied. 'Now I do have some influence to make things a little easier, more comfortable for you. Edward of York has to be careful. You are a princess of Anjou, a former Queen of England, a noble woman of ancient lineage. True, the Yorkists wish to parade you through London;

however, from what I know of King Edward and his brother Richard, they have no great appetite for humiliating a captured lady who has suffered so much. I could persuade them that you could be lodged with your old friend the Duchess of Suffolk in much more luxurious quarters at Wallingford Castle . . .' Margaret paused. 'I also have some influence with Duke Francis of Brittany, as well as King Louis of France. Nor must you forget your father, René of Anjou. News travels fast. Your father will not be pleased at your plight. This kingdom depends on trade, on English cogs sailing wherever they wish. The powerful merchants, the men of real power, would not want foreign ports closed to their shipping. Of course, I cannot proclaim this all in a day but like water dripping onto a stone . . .'

'You would do that?' The Angevin's eyes narrowed.

'I would try my very best, I swear that on the life of my son. So, the "Titulus Regius"?'

'As you know,' the Angevin replied, 'during the civil war, Clarence deserted his family, full of his own ambition, he joined myself and Warwick in exile. Clarence is insufferable. He often insinuated that he was the only true Yorkist claimant to the throne. At first we ignored him, being involved in our own struggle. We then heard of Mauclerc and the Three Kings. Of course you know of them?' Margaret nodded. 'Believe me,' the Angevin held up a hand, 'those four are Clarence's creatures to the very marrow of their souls. We heard they were searching for evidence for this or that, God knows truly what, but Clarence seemed cock-sure of himself. Others in my party heard about this secret work, the "Titulus Regius" but we were unable to discover the manuscript, the actual text. Warwick's people even hired the most skilled picklocks to open the chest and coffers in Clarence's chancery.' She shook her head. 'Nothing came of that. And so there's the real mystery. What is the evidence Clarence is trying to collect? How is it preserved?'

'And only Mauclerc and the Three Kings know this?'

'No, I would say only the Three Kings themselves. From what we learnt, even Clarence and his leading henchman do not know. They have not yet received the full extent of the secrets that the Three Kings are digging up. There is one other, a parchment seller. I believe he trades under the sign of "The Red Keg" on Fleet Street. I do not know his name, but Clarence once referred to him as a fellow seeker of the truth. This parchment- or book-seller is a Rhinelander; he is also involved in searching for evidence to bolster Clarence's claims: be it parchment or person, anything or anyone to assist in the mischief they are brewing.' The Angevin sipped from her goblet. 'There is,' she sighed, 'no real secret about what Clarence truly intends. The real mystery is what have his clerks actually collected and, as I have said, where is it preserved?' The Angevin now became quite heated. 'I have told you this, little Beaufort, and I say it again: no one knows anything about the details, even though Clarence passed through the House of York to that of Lancaster and then back again. As I have said, his manuscripts were carefully scru- tinised not only by the likes of your kinsmen the Beauforts but even by his own brothers. Nothing! Nothing has ever been found!' The Angevin shook her head. 'I can say no more because I know no more.' She glanced pitifully at Margaret. 'A boon, a favour, my Lady?'

'If I can.'

'My saintly husband,' the Angevin's words dripped with sarcasm, 'is lodged above in the oratory chamber. Would you please take messages to him, assure my Lord of my love and my loyalty. Tell him . . .'

The Angevin bit her lip as tears welled in her eyes. 'Never mind. Never mind,' she whispered. 'All is done, all is lost, all is dark.'

Margaret realised the Angevin would tell her no more. She searched out Dudley who had been drinking in the royal quarters, a timber and plaster mansion close to the chapel of St Peter in Chains. Full of ale and benevolence, he agreed to Margaret visiting the imprisoned Henry.

'For a short while, for a short while,' Dudley slurred, 'and then Mistress, if it so pleases you, join me and my comrades at the table.'

Margaret smiled understandingly and allowed the constable, deep in his cups, to escort her up the stone spiral staircase of the Wakefield Tower. Two soldiers stood on guard outside the half-open door to the old King's prison chamber. Dudley pushed this open and waved Margaret in, closing the door quietly behind her. The light was poor. The room full of flitting shadows. Margaret glimpsed the streaks of light from the small oratory and heard the patter of a psalm: 'Out of the depths have I cried to you, oh Lord. Lord hear my voice.'

Margaret entered the small oratory shaped in a semi-circle, a narrow window high in the wall. Henry was kneeling on a prie-dieu, arms extended, staring up at the stark crucifix at the centre of the altar. Margaret coughed. Henry, however, continued to pray until he had finished the 'Gloria'. Once completed, he blessed himself and rose, shaking the shabby blue robe which covered him from neck to sandalled feet. A wooden crucifix hung around his neck, a friar's girdle with its three knots symbolising obedience, poverty and chastity about his slender waist. Ave beads wreathed his fingers. He looked gaunt, more hollow-eyed, and blood-encrusted spots peppered his mouth.

'Sister?' Henry stretched out his hands towards her. 'Angels have visited me here. Truly they did. Now I have one in the flesh.' He stepped into the pool of light thrown by a tallow candle, ushering Margaret out of the oratory.

'I bring messages, your Grace.'

Margaret paused at the sound of growing revelry; drunken men rejoicing in their victory, shouting the war cries of the House of York. Henry stood listening to the clamour, then he turned, lips murmuring as if he was talking to someone Margaret could not see. She felt the full pathos of this encounter: a shabby, former King standing in a dingy chamber with candle-flame flickering and shadows shifting, his mocking enemies only a short distance away. Margaret tensed. The cries and shouts were growing closer. The sound of spurred boots echoing on the hard flagstones of the tower staircase. Henry half turned as if listening more acutely. He then grabbed Margaret by the shoulder.

'Someone,' he hissed, his mouth close to her face, 'someone warned me that they would come.'

Margaret caught his alarm, his wild panic. The booted steps seemed to carry their own dreadful menace. The devils were closing in! Henry abruptly pushed Margaret back into the chamber and across to the lavarium, an enclave built into the wall with a carved water bowl and a jake's hole hidden behind a heavy latticed screen, its woven wood much decayed and crumbling.

Margaret stood there holding her breath as Henry pushed the screen as close as he could before hastening back into the oratory. From where she stood, Margaret could see him once again kneel on the prie-dieu, arms extended before the crucifix. The door to the prison chamber crashed open. Three figures entered the room. The foremost, Richard of Gloucester, carried a night lantern; its glow illuminated the cold features of Mauclerc and the drunken, slobbery menace of Clarence. All three were dressed in half-armour with mailed surcoats, each carried sword and club. They swept into the oratory where Henry continued to pray, his voice growing louder as he intoned the great mercy psalm.

'Have mercy on me oh God in your great kindness . . .'

Mauclerc stepped forward and shoved him in the shoulder. Margaret watched in deepening horror as the murderous mystery play began to unfold in that ancient chamber, with its oratory lit by dancing candle-flame. All around flitted shadows, as if the ghosts were gathering to watch this bloody masque unfold. The old King, tottering on his feet, rose to meet his visitors. Gloucester stepped forward, still holding sword and club. Henry stretched out his hands in greeting. Margaret caught his words of welcoming, 'to his dear, sweet cousins'. Gloucester sheathed his sword, dropped the club and walked out of the chamber. Henry now turned to Mauclerc and Clarence.

'What do you want with me? Shouldn't you,' Henry's voice rose, 'shouldn't you now kneel in the presence of your King as I now kneel in the presence of mine?' Henry then shrugged, flailing his hands, as if his visitors were of no importance. He went back to the prie-dieu. Margaret caught her breath as Clarence steeped forward, raised his club and brought it down time and time again on the old King's head. Henry slumped onto the prie-dieu then slipped to the floor, still mouthing the words of the mercy psalm. For a while he lay, arms and legs jerking. Mauclerc, at Clarence's invitation, stepped closer and delivered a final cracking blow. Henry lay still. Clarence kicked the body, grabbed Mauclerc by the arm and both men hurried out of the chamber. Margaret waited until they had gone. She slipped from behind the screen and hurried across into the oratory.

Henry was dead. He sprawled, head to one side, eyes half open, mouth gaping, the pool of blood widening, the back of his skull shattered like a broken pot. Margaret hastily crossed herself, murmured the requiem and left. The stairwell outside and the steps leading into the Wakefield Tower were now deserted. No sound except the screech of bats winging their way above her. All guards, officials and servants of the Tower appeared to have been withdrawn so the old King's execution could be swiftly carried through. Margaret stared around but she could see no one. Again she crossed herself and hurried across to the Tower kitchens where Bray and Urswicke were waiting for her.

Christopher Urswicke lounged against a pillar in the death house, which formed part of the ancient crypt beneath Chertsey Abbey. On a trestle table close by rested an open lead coffin containing the mortal remains of Henry VI, late King of England; cleaned and skilfully embalmed in the Tower mortuary by Cedrick Longspear, Keeper of the Dead in that dismal place: he was now being questioned and tortured by Mauclerc and the Three Kings. All four had paused to refresh themselves with more deep-bowled goblets of wine. Longspear sat retching and gasping after Mauclerc had loosened the cord bound tightly around his forehead. Urswicke stared round that macabre chamber, the stout, barrel-like pillars with their eerie ornamentation at top and bottom; carved satyrs, goats, monkeys and other *babewyns* and gargoyles glared stonily out through a tangle of briers and brambles. This was the death house, screened off from the rest of the crypt by a stout fence of intertwined elm-wood. Behind this rose mounds of bones, skulls and shards of skeletons, the macabre remains of monks buried centuries ago in the ancient graveyard and, when this became full, the bones were dug up and piled here, making room for fresh burials outside. Longspear whimpered and glanced pitifully at Urswicke, who hid his own guilt and glanced away. To distract himself from the prisoner, Urswicke walked over to the lead coffin resting in its oaken casket; he stared down at the pallid, narrow face of King Henry. Death was making its mark, the skin was turning slightly yellow, the eyes becoming even more sunken, the nose more sharp, whilst the bloodless lips were beginning to turn inwards. The late King's soul had definitely left on its journey to judgement but, even in death, Henry had provoked violence. The cause of all this were the deep, broad blotches of blood staining the gold velvet cushion beneath the royal head.

Henry's corpse had been embalmed and prepared for burial in the Tower before being moved to lie in the great nave of St Paul's, its face exposed for public view. The Yorkists were determined to demonstrate that the King was certainly dead. There would be no rumours of a possible escape or the opportunity for mischief-makers and malcontents to field an imposter. Londoners were now growing accustomed to viewing the enemy dead of those in power. Nevertheless, Henry's corpse drew large crowds, which surged through the old cemetery and into the nave. The body had lain in state for a day but on the second, just before the noonday Angelus, a near riot occurred when the corpse was seen to bleed from the mouth. A sure sign, so the soothsayers who gathered there proclaimed, that the King had been foully murdered. The gushing of blood from his cold, hard corpse was a public accusation of this, as well as providing the necessary proof. The Dean of St Paul's had come down all a-fluster. A cohort of royal archers was summoned to ring the corpse but the damage been done. Henry the King had been assassinated! The news spread through London. Henry was a saint! Henry was a martyr! And his killers were from the House of York who had been drunk and revelling in the Tower on the night the King had been murdered. Such rumours swept the city and the shires beyond. Margaret Beaufort, aided by Bray and Urswicke, had spent good coin secretly encouraging such gossip, fanning the flames into a real fire. Margaret used the likes of the tavern keeper Hempen and a host of other little people in Margaret's party throughout the city. The Countess of Richmond, however, genuinely mourned the death of poor Henry VI. She had confided in Bray and Urswicke the details of his murder, as well as her steely determination to exploit its consequences for her own gain.

Urswicke had played a prominent part in that and, as Henry's corpse lay bleeding in St Paul's, he had watched in quiet amusement the public consternation of their enemies. Eventually, escorted by hobelars carrying glaives, and archers bearing lighted torches and accompanied by friars of all the major orders, the royal corpse had been moved with lavish pomp and ceremony. Psalms were chanted. Thuribles smoked. Candles fluttered as the royal cortège moved upriver to the great abbey of Chertsey, founded by St Erconwald so many centuries earlier.

The funeral procession had been welcomed by Father Abbot. Once again the corpse lay exposed to public view and, to the fury of Clarence and Mauclerc, once again the corpse began to bleed from the mouth. The news, swifter than a swallow, swept through the abbey and beyond. A procession of monks appeared with cross, candle and thurifer to salute this new martyr in the heavenly court. Father Abbot was shrewd enough to realise he might receive little love from the King about what was happening, but he and his abbey could accrue great profit from the people by proclaiming how their church now housed a saint and martyr. Visions of Chertsey becoming a rival to Becket's shrine at Canterbury lured the abbot and his community not only to proclaim the great event, but to encourage the faithful who followed the funeral cortège to seek miracles. Soon the nave of the abbey church became packed with the crippled and blind, the legion of beggars who moved in a swarm from one shrine to another in search of a cure. Clarence, urged on by the King, insisted the crisis be settled and that Henry be buried both physically and as a source of future trouble.

Mauclerc demanded such matters move as swiftly as possible and he had his way. The late King's requiem mass was celebrated in a cloud of incense, the ringing of bells and the chanting of psalms. Once these were over, Henry's corpse, hidden in its lead coffin, was then placed in its elm-wood casket, to be buried with the minimum of fuss in the quiet of the church. The monastic community had been forced to agree. The royal remains were then moved down to the crypt. The Three Kings had taken Henry's corpse out of its casing and laid it on a trestle table. All clothing, shrouds and sheets were removed and the Three Kings had searched the cadaver, affording it little dignity or respect.

In the flickering candlelight, their shadows dancing against the wall, the three clerks reminded Urswicke of grey-hooded crows pecking at a corpse. During their examination, the Three Kings had been watched by a terrified Longspear, who had been summoned to accompany them from the Tower. The Keeper of the Dead had hoped that once the requiem was finished he could leave, but Mauclerc had detained him. Longspear had been hustled down here to be confronted with the evidence for the so-called miracle: miniature sponges soaked in blood had been cleverly inserted into the corpse's mouth, tightly wedged between the dead King's peg-like teeth. The sponges were of the highest quality and, due to the constant movement of the corpse from here to there, the blood would eventually drip, filling the mouth and trickling out through the lips.

Urswicke knew all about this. The plot had been concocted by the countess and himself. Urswicke, visored and cowled, had met Longspear in a desolate place near the Tower water-gate. Urswicke had offered six pure, freshly minted coins if the Keeper of the Dead agreed to take the sponges and insert them in the mouth of the royal corpse before it was moved to St Paul's. Longspear had agreed with alacrity, asserting it would cause no harm and simply proclaim the truth that the old King had been foully murdered. Longspear even offered, as official Keeper of the Corpse, to tend to Henry's face on his journey here and there. He would intervene to maintain the position of the royal head whilst, at the same time, gently squeeze the flesh either side of the mouth to help the blood seep out. He had done this successfully, but now Longspear was to pay the price for his meddling.

Henry's corpse had been sheeted and returned to its coffin. The Three Kings and Mauclerc finished slaking their thirst and returned to question Longspear. The suspect sat bound in a high-backed chair, his hands tied to its arms, his ankles lashed by coarse rope and a noose placed around his forehead with a steel rod inserted in the knot; this could be turned so tightly, the flesh ruptured and the pain intensified. Longspear's mouth was gagged with a filthy rag, the prisoner could only jerk in violent spasms, face all red, eyes bulging. Now and again the rag would be removed. Mauclerc would crouch before the prisoner, taunting him by slurping from a wine goblet before asking him the same question: 'Who hired you to do this?' Urswicke felt sorry for the Keeper of the Dead, but there was nothing he could do. Longspear could not answer except gabble that he had been enticed to a meeting with a shadowy figure, a man who hid in the darkness around the water-gate at the Tower. Mauclerc seized on this. If it was the Tower, he asked, then it must be somebody pretending to be of the House of York.

'What was his tongue?' Mauclerc demanded.

'I believe he was Welsh,' Longspear blurted out, 'but I can tell you no more. Perhaps if you free me . . .'

Mauclerc answered with a blow to the man's face; the gag was pushed back and the questioning continued. At last Clarence, who stood lounging against a pillar, arms crossed, stamped a spurred boot, the jingle echoing through the cavernous place.

'Finish it,' he barked.

Mauclerc slid behind Longspear; he jerked back the prisoner's head by the hair and slit the prisoner's throat from ear to ear, the razor-sharp blade glinting in the torchlight. Longspear shook, gargling on his own blood. He rocked violently in the chair as his lifeblood gushed out before him, then he hung still, head down. The sudden violence was followed by a deep, oppressive silence, broken only by the screech of a night bird hunting above God's Acre outside. Bats flitted through the lancet window, many of them nested in the crypt, though Urswicke, recalling stories from his childhood, wondered if they were the souls of the damned.

'It is done.' Clarence gestured at Longspear. 'Fetch a sack, some stones, bury him in the Thames. As for this . . .'

Urswicke watched as Clarence and Mauclerc pulled back the coffin sheets over Henry's corpse. They then fetched a shabby arrow chest and placed it alongside: lifting the royal corpse, they thrust it in, pushing down the lid.

'That,' Clarence declared, face all flushed, 'can join the other bastard in the Thames. In the meantime . . .' He snapped his fingers. The Three Kings, busy with Longspear's cadaver, hastened into the shadows and brought back a second arrow chest. They put this down in the pool of light and lifted the lid. Urswicke caught the foul stench and gagged. One of the Three Kings, Melchior, handed out scented pomanders, beckoning Urswicke across. Urswicke did so and stared down at the mangled remains of some unfortunate: the back of the severed head was smashed in; the rest of the limbs nothing more than a tangled bloody midden heap of human flesh. Urswicke realised that these must be the remains of someone whose head had been severed and his limbs quartered: he had suffered the full, horrific punishment for high treason.

'Edmund Quintain,' Mauclerc declared. 'One of Fauconberg's captains out of Kent, hanged, disembowelled and quartered: his corpse will replace that of the saintly King.'

And, without further ado, Urswicke was ordered to help him and the Three Kings lift the gruesome mess across to be tossed into the empty royal coffin, as if they were tipping some filthy lay stall into a city dung cart. Urswicke hid his revulsion at this blasphemous desecration, the vicious sacrilege being carried out. He concentrated on other matters. He recalled the precious Holland cloth, the pounds of spices, the pure beeswax used for the royal funeral. The pomp and liturgy surrounding Henry's corpse, the vigil set up by knights and friars. It had all been brought down to this: squalid desecration in a desolate, dirty crypt. Henry VI had once been crowned King of England and France, the lord of a great Empire. He had assumed the personal insignia of the graceful Swan and Antelope but all of that had been pecked to death by these crows of York. Clarence, in particular, seemed to revel deeply in the degradation being heaped on the dead former King. Urswicke decided he could not sustain this blasphemy and must bring it to an end. The mortal remains of Edmund Quintain were eventually sealed for burial in the royal casket: no one would even dream of the desecration being perpetrated.

'Why?' Urswicke demanded abruptly. 'Why all this?'

'So no miracles can be performed,' Mauclerc smirked, 'no special sign from heaven. Anyone who claims to have received such a grace must be an imposter, a rebel, a traitor. Think about it, Christopher. Some cripple who visits Chertsey here and throws away his crutches, dancing about like a fly on a hot plate screaming that he is cured. We'll know the filthy remains of Edmund Quintain cannot be the cause of such a miraculous event. We will arrest the cripple, put him to the question and discover more about those who lurk in the shadows and encourage such treasonable mummery.'

Urswicke nodded solemnly. He suspected that was the case and he would certainly inform the countess that this was not a path to follow: her agents in the city must not be drawn in and trapped.

'And the old King's corpse?' he asked.

'Oh, it will be sheeted in its shroud and buried in the Thames. Why?'

'I would advise against that, just in case.'

'In case of what?' Clarence retorted.

'Think, my Lord. Once the corpse goes into the Thames, we have no further control over it. Why not compromise? Bury it quietly, secretly, in God's Acre here at Chertsey. You never know when such information might be of use. Would you commit the sin of sacrilege? Let us honour the royal corpse and, if circumstances change, we can present ourselves as defenders of the old King's dignity, when others,' Urswicke waved a hand, 'might have wished Henry VI's mortal remains be scattered to the winds.' Urswicke held Clarence's gaze. He watched those cunning eyes, the full lips ever ready to pout in protest. Mauclerc whispered in Clarence's ear, the Yorkist lord nodded, still staring at Urswicke.

'I like that,' he whispered. 'On the one hand we create a false shrine and draw in our enemies like flies to a turd. On the other, if Fortune's wheel spins, we can blame those on my brother's council, who argued for the total destruction of Henry VI and all he represented. Christopher, you are within my love.' Clarence stepped forward and embraced Urswicke in a tang of rich Bordeaux. 'I accept you as my liege man, Christopher. Be assured of that.' Clarence then stepped back; snapping his fingers, he pointed at the arrow chest. 'Have that buried in some desolate part of God's Acre. Mark the place well so, if we have to, we can return to it. Get rid of the rest, for we are finished here . . .'

PART FOUR

'I trust to God that the two dukes of Clarence and Gloucester shall be settled as one by the word of the King.'
The Paston Letters

Christopher Urswicke sat on the cushioned stool. He studied the gold-blue and silver tapestry from Arras which adorned the wall above the mantled hearth in the countess's private chamber at her husband's mansion overlooking the Thames. No fire had been lit as the weather had turned decisively warm, although outside the light was fading as a rainstorm swept up the Thames. Urswicke stared at the tapestry, which depicted a pelican standing on a gilt-edged chalice, stabbing its breast to draw blood and so feed its young nestling in the bowl beneath: a well-known parable representing Christ giving himself under the appearance of bread and wine in the Eucharist. The four corners of the tapestry were decorated with silver-gold swans, the personal insignia of the House of Stafford. Urswicke heard Countess Margaret sigh and watched his mistress dab her eyes with a small hand cloth, which she then folded neatly and placed on the table beside her.

'Where is Reginald?' she asked.

'On some business or other,' Urswicke replied evasively. He had asked Bray to take over his watch whilst he stayed with the old King's corpse as it was moved from St Paul's to Chertsey.

'The Lord's Anointed.' Margaret pointed to the tapestry. 'Just as sacred as that emblem, Henry VI was our King, sealed with the holy chrism. He wore the crown of the Confessor, and yet what degradation Clarence and Mauclerc inflicted on his royal corpse.'

Urswicke nodded. He had reported what had happened at Chertsey, though he refused to divulge some of the more macabre details such as pig bones being mixed amongst the remains of

Quintain. Apparently the Kentish captain had been hanged, drawn and quartered on the great cobbled expanse before Newgate, where the slaughterers plied their trade. At the end of the execution, some of the offal lying around must have been mingled with Quintain's severed limbs.

'They will be punished for that,' Margaret murmured. 'Mauclerc, the Three Kings and, of course, that demon in human flesh, George of Clarence.' She paused. Urswicke was struck by the fierceness of her expression, which had transformed the countess's usual pale, narrow face into that of some warrior woman intent on battle. Urswicke turned at a knock at the door and Bray slipped into the chamber.

'Well?' Margaret asked. 'I know you have been busy on my behalf. You have hinted at that. You have been pursuing the traitor? Have we discovered the truth?'

'Yes, Mistress,' Bray replied. 'We have the truth and I have seen the evidence with my own eyes. You told us to hunt the Judas and we did. Mistress, you are confronted with a sea of woes, you pick your way carefully through a tangle of treason and deep deceit.' Bray pulled a face. 'All we are doing is making that less dangerous. We remove the lures, the traps and the snares primed to catch us all.'

'True, true.' Margaret crossed herself. 'We wage a secret war. Very well.' She straightened in her chair. 'Take care of what you have to. If it's to be done, then it is best done swiftly.'

Within the hour, Bray and Urswicke led Owain and Oswina out of the water-gate of Lord Humphrey's mansion. The evening was close and the threatened storm seemed imminent. The clouds hung dark and lowering whilst a stiff breeze chopped the water. They clambered into the stout, deep, well-tarred bum-boat tied to its post on the narrow jetty. They made themselves comfortable and cast off, Urswicke and Bray pulling at the oars. Owain and his sister, cloaked and cowled, sat next to each other in the stern. Urswicke glanced over his shoulder at the sack of rocks Bray had placed in the prow. They'd prepared everything before inviting both brother and sister to join what Urswicke called 'a most crucial task for their mistress, a matter of great secrecy'. Both Owain and Oswina had been only too eager to obey but now, with the boat out on the river, its swollen current swirling fast and strong, their mood changed.

'What is this task?' Oswina asked plaintively.

'Where in Southwark are we going?' her brother demanded. 'Who are we meeting at such a late hour?'

Urswicke just glanced over his shoulder and almost welcomed the rolling bank of river mist which enveloped them. 'Here,' he whispered. Both he and Bray rested on their oars. Urswicke bent down; he picked up the leather sack and placed it carefully between his feet. 'They are primed,' Bray whispered, 'all set, the bolts are ready.'

'What is this?' Owain would have sprung to his feet, but the boat rocked dangerously. The squire hurriedly sat down, staring fearfully at the arbalest, all primed, that Urswicke held ready to loose.

'What is happening?' Oswina pleaded, pulling back the hood of her gown. 'What have we done?'

'Treachery and treason towards a woman who took you in and mothered you better than any I know,' Bray retorted. 'You were granted a privileged place in her household by her late husband, Edmund Tudor of blessed memory. You were given dignity, high office and all the comforts of a good life. You rejected all that. You decided to act the Judas, crying all hail to the countess when you meant all harm. You were suborned, seduced by Clarence's henchman Mauclerc.'

'He probably informed you that Margaret of Richmond, the last of the Beauforts, would soon be for the dark.' Urswicke wiped the mist water from his face. 'He bribed you with good coin and even better prospects.' Urswicke challenged. 'He wanted to seize the countess's young son. You realised your mistress was nursing some great secret. You suspected that her boy was not hiding behind the fortress at Pembroke but probably here in London waiting to escape across the Narrow Seas. We witnessed first-hand the effects of your treachery. You worked with that wretch in Tewkesbury, the one who threw fire down into the courtyard as our mistress returned. You sheltered that assassin. You kept sharp watch on the countess's inevitable return. Who was it then? One of the Three Kings?' He stared at these two traitors who just sat, mouths gaping. 'What did you plot,' he continued, 'that our mistress might be hurt, killed? Certainly delayed in her return to London and, if she was, the hunt for her young son would be made all the easier. The attack failed but messages were despatched to the city. My father, the noble Recorder of London, pursued the countess like a hungry lurcher would a hare. You kept up your treasonable practices. One of you would slip out of Sir Humphrey's mansion, the other would stay in your chamber pretending that both of you were there.' Urswicke grasped the arbalest tighter. 'We discovered that. We also found a way of pursuing you from afar. Master Bray, here, has a number of street people in his pay. To cut to the quick, you visited a shabby tavern in Queenhithe, The Crutched Friar. Mauclerc would be there as he was early today. Yes Owain . . .?'

'The c-countess . . .' Owain stuttered.

'You betrayed her,' Urswicke replied. 'You know you did, both of you! We have seen you consort with her mortal enemies, men who would, at a spin of a coin, pay to see her die, her son murdered and those she trusts, such as ourselves, barbarously executed.'

'But the countess?' Oswina bleated.

'She bids you farewell.' Urswicke released the catch and the bolt sped out, smashing Owain's face to a bloody pulp. His sister half rose. Bray handed Urswicke the second arbalest; he released the catch even as Oswina leaned forward then fell back, hanging out of the boat as the barbed quarrel shattered her chest. Urswicke gingerly rose and pulled the two corpses together. Bray handed him the sack of rocks, then grasped the oars, holding the boat as steady as he could. Urswicke pushed the rocks amongst the clothing of his two victims then tossed both corpses into the river.

'A sad end,' Bray remarked as Urswicke took his seat on the bench.

'We did not cause their death,' Urswicke hissed. 'They did. They betrayed their loving mistress. They violated all faithfulness and fealty. They forsook their loyalty to her and to us. If they had been successful, Countess Margaret would have ended her days in some dingy cell in the Tower. Her son would be some battered corpse floating in this river whilst we would have suffered the full rigour of the punishment for treason.' Urswicke glanced at his companion. 'Reginald, my friend, we did not compose our sad world's music, yet, like everyone else, we have no choice but to dance to it.'

Three days after returning with Bray from their murderous journey across the Thames, Urswicke was roused by a servant who had been urgently despatched upstairs by the countess.

'Master,' the stable boy hissed, 'a stranger, cowled and cloaked, his face visored, waits for you in the stable yard. He claims to be sent by your father the Recorder on the most urgent business. He refuses to speak to any of us, nor will he come in. He says he will stay until you meet him.'

'In which case, I will.'

Urswicke climbed out of his cotbed, crossed to the lavarium and threw cold water over his face. He then hurriedly dressed, strapped on his warbelt, forced his feet into his boots and, throwing his cloak around his shoulders, hurried down past the countess, who simply nodded as he passed. The mysterious visitor was in the stable yard, one hand on the hilt of his sword, with the other he beckoned Urswicke closer before pulling down the visor, covering his nose and mouth. Urswicke immediately recognised Spysin, one of Clarence's squires, a sly-eyed fighting man, skilled with the dagger and garrotte, who also enjoyed the most unsavoury reputation of being a pimp for his betters. Urswicke noticed how Spysin was belted, spurred and booted, as if ready to leave on some errand.

'Master Christopher,' he murmured, 'my Lord Clarence and Mauclerc need you at The Sunne in Splendour – something has occurred.'

'What has my father got to do with that tavern?'

'Nothing at all – well, at least not yet. I simply concocted the message to stir your curiosity as well as to protect my master's business. But come,' Spysin urged, 'I am also busy. I must leave on the evening tide.'

Urswicke nodded his agreement and followed Spysin along the winding streets of Queenhithe. Morning mass at the different churches was just finishing, the lanterns in their steeples doused so the bells could toll, reminding the faithful to patter their morning prayers before the merchant horns sounded to start the business of the day. Already the crowds were thronging about, although everyone stood aside as a host of knight bannerets, their destriers caparisoned in emblazoned leather, moved down to the tiltyards and tourney grounds of Smithfield. The knights in half-armour, their jousting helmets ornate and crowned with mythical beasts, were carried along with their shields and lances by a noisy entourage of squires and pages. Urswicke was sure he glimpsed his father, who was already eager to prove his spurs during the great celebrations being planned for later in the summer.

Once the knights had passed, Spysin led him on. Although the city was celebrating, the effects of the recent fighting was still clear, with makeshift gallows standing at certain crossroads, each decorated with gibbeted corpses. Not even in death were these allowed to rest, their flesh being cut and scarred by the warlocks and wizards who regarded the grisly remains of a hanged man as possessing rich, magical properties. Urswicke recalled his execution of Owain and Oswina; he felt no guilt at their deaths. If they had had their way, his corpse and that of Bray would be gibbeted in iron cages.

At last they reached The Sunne in Splendour. Its courtyard and stable bailey were packed with men-at-arms wearing Clarence's livery, depicting the Black Bull or the Bear and Ragged Staff of Warwick. The tavern had been emptied. Minehost Master Tiptree and all his scullions and slatterns stood in a disconsolate group. Every entrance to the hostelry was closely guarded by men-at-arms with drawn swords. Urswicke and Spysin had to wait until Mauclerc came out. Urswicke stared across at Tiptree who was throwing his hands up in the air and wailing about the loss of business. Urswicke realised Tiptree was deeply agitated yet, behind all his bluster, was clearly terrified about what had happened in his opulent tavern. Urswicke wondered what had caused such a commotion and the secrecy cloaking it. Mauclerc strode out and greeted them. He told Spysin to wait and took Urswicke into the taproom, where Clarence sat crouched over a goblet of wine. He gazed drunkenly at Urswicke and flailed a hand towards the broad, open stairs leading to the upper chambers.

'All dead.' He slurred. 'Show him, Mauclerc.'

They climbed the stairs and along the narrow gallery to the chancery office Mauclerc had hired for the Three Kings. The door to it had been smashed from its hinges and now leaned against the wall. Mauclerc led Urswicke around this into the chamber. The shutters from the narrow window had been pulled back, lanterns and candles had been fired to cast light on the mayhem and bloody murder which had been perpetrated there against the Three Kings and one other, whom Mauclerc identified as the parchment-seller Oudenarde. The four corpses lay sprawled on the floor, the blood from their slit throats drenching the costly turkey rugs. The victims were grouped together, as if they had clustered close against their killer. Urswicke carefully picked his way around the murdered men. He noticed how their bodies were slightly twisted, but what was extraordinary was the lack of any sign of violence either to themselves, the chamber or any of its furnishings. He found it impossible to believe that these men had been led like lambs to the slaughter offering their throats to be cut. Apart from the gruesome death scene, everything else seemed in order: no destruction, no damage, nothing at all.

Urswicke approached the chancery table. Mauclerc edged up very close behind him, as if fearful at what Urswicke might discover. The clerk tried to ignore Mauclerc almost breathing in his ear as he sifted amongst the documents strewn there before picking up a book of hours, a bulky manuscript, freshly paged and neatly bound in gold twine held fast by a clasp. Urswicke opened this, turning the pages, admiring the miniature jewel-like paintings and the glorious decoration which marked the beginning of each prayer or psalm. He turned the pages then studied the front and back of the psalter.

'It is what it is,' Urswicke murmured, putting it down. 'A book of hours.' He gestured at the documents which covered the entire table. 'Nothing has been stolen?'

'No, no,' Mauclerc retorted.

Urswicke glanced sharply at him. For the first time since they had met at Tewkesbury, Clarence's henchman seemed genuinely puzzled, surprised as if caught off balance.

'Nothing has been stolen?' Urswicke repeated.

'No.'

'And there was nothing precious here to steal?'

'No.'

'So why did the Three Kings, together with Oudenarde, work so hard here in the chancery chamber of a splendid tavern, a room your three clerks closely guarded, so no one could spy on them? Now that's a mystery, Mauclerc! What was so valuable here to explain such secrecy or to account for their murders?'

'They were working on my claim.'

Urswicke spun round. Clarence lounged drunkenly in the doorway, arms crossed, staring fixedly at Urswicke. 'You,' Clarence pointed a finger, 'you have sharp wits and an even sharper mind, Christopher. You have proved invaluable. Find out who did this. Let me see them hang. You will receive my warrant commanding you. Act on it!'

'I will, my Lord. And so first, did you or Mauclerc visit this chamber yesterday, be it day or night? Or even earlier this morning?'

'No,' Clarence spat back. 'I should object to you, a low-born knave, questioning me so closely. But that has to be done, I suppose.'

Clarence pushed himself from the doorpost and turned drunkenly, balancing the wine goblet carefully in his hand.

'Mauclerc will take care of any questions.'

Once Clarence had gone, Mauclerc grasped Urswicke by the shoulder, his cold face hard, as if the deep malice which defined the man had returned. 'We have nothing to do with this,' he declared. 'My Lord Clarence and I were busy in the Jerusalem chambers at Westminster. Minehost Tiptree sent messages about what happened here? And as far as my Lord of Clarence's claim is concerned . . .' Mauclerc pointed at the parchments strewn across the chancery desk. 'As you know, Richard Neville, Earl of Warwick, the so-called King-maker and leader of the Lancastrian host, owned estates and manors the like of which have never been seen in this kingdom for many a day. According to those who know, Warwick was killed at Barnet by something flying.' He laughed sharply. 'A well-aimed war axe or crossbow bolt. Anyway,' he sighed, 'Warwick left no male heir and you must realise the implications?'

'Yes I do,' Urswicke agreed. 'Warwick had two daughters, Isobel and Anne. If the Warwick estates aren't seized by the King, and I doubt if they will be, they will be shared out amongst the two daughters, one of whom, Isobel, is married to our master, Lord Clarence. I heard rumours,' Urswicke lowered his voice, 'that Richard of Gloucester nourishes the most tender feelings towards Isobel's sister Anne, not to mention,' he added wryly, 'her estates. If Lord Richard marries the heiress, he will certainly demand a just division of the Neville inheritance.'

'My master,' Mauclerc interjected, 'is insistent that the entire Neville inheritance, its manors, estates and holdings, everything to be found there, are rightfully his. True, Richard of Gloucester challenges this, so our Lord builds a case to justify his God-given rights based on both law and fact.'

Urswicke suspected Mauclerc was lying for Clarence, but he nodded understandingly as if fully accepting what he said. He continued to survey the different parchments spread out across the table. Sharp-eyed and the swiftest of readers, Urswicke tried to make sense of what he saw. Most of the documents were bills, indentures, licences, lists and drafts of memoranda. One already laid out and sealed by Clarence caught his eye; a licence for 'Eudo Spysin, squire of my Lord Clarence, to leave the kingdom with important messages to be delivered by word of mouth to his Grace Duke Francis of Brittany.' Urswicke recalled Spysin all booted, buckled and belted, as well as the squire's self–important remark about being busy on some task and catching the evening tide. Urswicke studied the rest of the parchments, now aware of Mauclerc's impatience to distract him.

Urswicke realised he could do no more so he walked across to the window and stared out through the lancet opening. He had no illusion about what Spysin was intent on. The courier would be carrying messages, on Clarence's behalf, with the full support of the English Crown, graciously asking Duke Francis that if Henry Tudor arrived in Brittany he was to be seized immediately and despatched back to England. Clarence would offer lavish bribes and generous trade concessions to achieve this. Similar envoys would go to other kingdoms, though this did not concern Urswicke. Countess Margaret had confided how her son would shelter in no other place but Brittany, which enjoyed the closest ties with Wales and the Tudor family. Nevertheless, the danger was pressing. Would Duke Francis be suborned? Would members of his council, their purses bulging with English gold, argue that Tudor was not worth alienating the powerful Edward? And what would Clarence offer? Treasure? Trade? Treaties? Had Countess Margaret anticipated Clarence's next move? Somehow, perhaps because of the last treacherous act of that precious pair Owain and his sister, Clarence had come to realise that Henry Tudor was no longer in Pembroke but was probably on his way to Brittany or, perhaps, already there.

Urswicke stared down through the window; he made his decision. For a brief while he would have to stay in this chamber and act the part. But, before the tide turned that evening, he must kill Spysin. On that he was determined. Urswicke glanced sharply over his shoulder at the chancery table. He could detect no disturbance amongst the different parchments and documents. Was there something missing? Mauclerc didn't seem to think so. So why these murders in such mysterious circumstances? Mauclerc was now collecting the different manuscripts and placing them in the reinforced parchment chests.

'Why did my Lord Clarence choose me?' he asked.

Mauclerc brought the lid of the coffer sharply down. He snapped it shut, turning the key. 'We trust you Christopher. You have given us invaluable information and have been of great assistance to our Lord. Our master believes all this,' he gestured at the corpses, 'could even be the work of your redoubtable mistress or—'

'Or who?'

'Someone who is in bitter rivalry with our master.'

'Such as?'

Mauclerc walked towards him and pushed his face close to Urswicke's. 'Gloucester,' he whispered, 'and that little mountebank's claim to the Neville inheritance.'

Urswicke stared back in surprise.

'Oh yes,' Mauclerc hissed, 'there is more to this masque than meets the eye.'

'Yet you and our Lord,' Urswicke pointed to the corpses, 'do not seem too perturbed by the brutal murder of four chosen henchmen?'

'We have lost the same in battle, Urswicke. I have seen

comrades cruelly slaughtered or heard of their excruciating executions at the hands of our enemies. My Lord Clarence and I have been fighting for the last twelve years.' Mauclerc sucked on his teeth. 'Men live, men die. The Three Kings were faithful, shrewd and skilled. Oudenarde the parchment-seller equally so. They were all working on creating a book, a chronicle which would justify Clarence's claim to his inheritance.'

'What about Oudenarde's shop under the sign of "The Red Keg"?'

'Oh, don't worry about that. Our searchers will already be busy there seizing and securing whatever they find.' Mauclerc poked Urswicke in the chest. 'What you must do, like any scholar in the schools, is discover what truly happened here. Present a hypothesis which is logical and possible. If the hypothesis is probable, that would be even better.' Mauclerc's fingers fell to the hilt of his dagger. 'Once we know, then we can carry out the most bloody reprisal.'

Urswicke was left alone in the death chamber. At his request, some of Mauclerc's ruffians set up guard on the stairs to the chancery chamber and the room itself. Urswicke moved swiftly. He soon established there was no secret entrance to the chamber, only the doorway, and that had been battered, its lock twisted and the inside bolts shattered: the windows were too narrow for anyone to even try and break in. Moreover, they had been firmly shuttered because of the cold early summer night. Urswicke then scrutinised the food: scraps of chicken, pieces of fruit and a manchet loaf. The jug of Bordeaux was half full, with wine dregs in the four goblets. Urswicke sniffed at all of these but could detect nothing amiss. Moreover, the chamber, like many such tavern rooms, suffered from an infestation of mice. Urswicke discovered their droppings as well as scraps of food these rodents nibbled at. He cast about; if any of the food and drink had been poisoned, he would find the corpses of such vermin. But, there again, he could discover nothing.

Urswicke decided to be as thorough as possible. He took the deep bowl from the lavarium stand and scraped in the remnants of the food along with the wine from both the jug and the goblets. He mixed this together and ordered one of the guards to take it down to the tavern cellar and leave it for the rats. Urswicke then

turned to the four corpses and, for the first time since he had
entered that sinister death chamber, he felt a deep chill of fear.
Urswicke had viewed corpses on the battlefield, in lonely copses
of the wild, windswept north, as well as those left stabbed or
hacked along the dirty runnels and alleyways of London. He had
seen the dead piled high like stacks of wood before they were
tumbled into makeshift, common graves. This was eerily different.
The four victims sprawled as if they were asleep, except each of
them had drawn his dagger and held it in listless fingers. Four
corpses, eyes staring, mouths slightly open in shock at the savage
cut across each of their throats. Even more mysterious, there was
no sign of any struggle or violence, apart from those death wounds
and the blood floating out in great pools.

Urswicke crouched down and scrutinised the scene carefully.
'Impossible,' he whispered to himself. 'Impossible.' The clerk
hurriedly searched the pockets and wallets of the dead but he
could find nothing significant. He suspected Mauclerc had already
done this at Clarence's behest. Urswicke got to his feet and
crossed to the door, resting against its lintel, and carefully scrutinised how it had been violently broken. The bolts at top and
bottom had fractured the clasps whilst the key was still in the
now twisted lock. He asked the guards outside to move away
and stared around the stairwell, noticing the heavy yew log which
had been used as a ram against the door. Urswicke walked back
into the chamber. So far he had nothing to use, nothing he could
seize on to resolve these mysteries.

He ordered one of the guards to bring up Master Tiptree.
Minehost, sweaty-faced with a nervous twist to his mouth, came
hurrying up all a-fluster, wiping greasy hands on his thick, linen
apron. Behind him trotted two scullions and a slattern who,
Tiptree explained, 'had first raised the hue and cry ready to
shout "Harrow! Harrow!"' All four tavern people were nervous
at entering the death chamber, Tiptree in particular. He was
deeply agitated, lower lip trembling, teeth chattering. Urswicke
realised he would have no sense out of him. He ordered Tiptree
and the rest to go back downstairs into the small buttery which
adjoined the great kitchen before telling the guard to maintain
strict watch over the death chamber and allow no one in without
his permission.

Once gathered in the buttery, the landlord and his minions seemed more composed as they sat on the cushioned settle. Urswicke leaned across the table pointing at Tiptree.

'The truth,' he insisted, 'because if you lie it will be the press yard in Newgate. Now, you are a member of my Lord Clarence's household, or once were, yes?'

'I worked in his kitchen. I was a purveyor of food and his principal cook – a very good one.' Tiptree tried to hide his fear behind a blustering preening.

'I am sure you were, and my Lord Clarence used this tavern when he comes to London?' Tiptree nodded. 'And last night or this morning did you notice anything untoward?'

'No, no. Yesterday evening the four gentlemen assembled in the taproom, around a special table overlooking our garden which is well-stocked—'

'Yes, yes,' Urswicke intervened. 'They dined then adjourned?'

'Yes.'

'Did they receive any visitors?'

'No.' Tiptree shook his head. 'We left them be except, sometime after the Compline bell had rung for the lanterns to be lit, they ordered food, bread and chicken in a creamy sauce, along with a jug of my best Bordeaux. I took the tray up. I entered the chancery chamber. The four gentlemen, I thought them to be so because they were always courteous.' Tiptree shrugged.

'They were kindly to you?' Urswicke asked.

'Aye. And so was Oudenarde, but he was not always with them. Sometimes he'd come by himself. On other occasions he would bring people to see the clerks.'

'Which people?' Urswicke demanded, recalling what he'd glimpsed during his visits to The Sunne in Splendour.

'I don't know, sir. Always hooded and cloaked they were, even on a fine evening. Master, I am a tavern keeper,' Tiptree tapped the side of his nose, 'discretion is my main virtue. I see nothing wrong, I hear nothing wrong, I say nothing wrong.'

'Aye, and one stay in prison is bad enough,' one of the scullions scoffed, rubbing his mouth on the sleeve of his shabby jerkin. He opened his mouth to speak again but Tiptree glared at him.

'Tell the gentleman what happened this morning,' the landlord snapped.

'And who are you?' Urswicke turned to face the dirty scullion.

'I am Snotnose, or that's what they call me.' The boy wiped his face on his sleeve again. 'My first task of the day is to invite guests down to the taproom to break their fast. I knock on the bedchamber doors.' He paused at the change on Urswicke's face as the clerk realised he had overlooked the rooms where the Three Kings slept, but then comforted himself: as with the shop under the sign of 'The Red Keg', Mauclerc would have cleared the chambers of anything he did not want Urswicke to see.

The clerk glanced over his shoulder at the window; the hours were passing and he had not forgotten Spysin. He would love to return to the countess's house to consult with Bray, but time was of the essence and he did not wish to provoke any suspicion about his commitment to Clarence. He wondered about what Mauclerc had said? How the murders here could be the work of the countess? Urswicke chewed the corner of his lip. That was too fanciful! Nevertheless, it demonstrated that if Clarence and his coven could level accusations against his mistress and threaten her with the full rigour of the law, they would hasten to do so.

'Master?' Snotnose's voice was almost a screech.

'Continue.'

'I knocked then opened the door to all three chambers. They were empty, the beds not slept in. So I thought they must have spent the night in the chancery chamber. I hurried there and knocked on the door but no one answered. I tried again. I pushed hard but it was locked and bolted. I shouted and knocked again, nothing! I ran down to the taproom, into the kitchen garden and stared up. As you know, Master, the windows to the chancery chamber are narrow, but I could see the shutters had not been opened to greet the day . . .'

'By then,' Tiptree spoke up, 'we were all upset with Snotnose running around like a mad March hare. I knocked on the chancery chamber, shouted and yelled. No answer. Of course the entire tavern knew something was wrong. I sent Snotnose here to seek Lord Clarence and Mauclerc. Some of their,' Urswicke was sure Tiptree was going to say ruffians, 'some of their retainers,' the landlord corrected himself, 'lodged nearby. I decided to break down the door and, what you have seen, so did we.'

'The door was locked and bolted on the inside, the key turned?'

'Yes, we burst in. The chamber was dark. The candles had guttered out. The shutters were still pulled closed. I almost stumbled over the corpses. I called for light,' Tiptree spread his hands, 'and glimpsed the mayhem. I decided not to touch anything but left telling the others to stay well away.'

'Is there anything else?' Urswicke demanded. They all shook their heads. Urswicke stared at Tiptree; the landlord was still deeply agitated, terrified. Was there something else? Urswicke wondered. Did Tiptree fear punishment from a lord who was notorious for his vindictiveness?

'If you do recall anything,' Urswicke demanded, 'you will tell me.' He then rose, thanked them and returned to the death chamber. He sat in the principal chancery chair, trying to make sense of it. The guard returned to report that the rats had eaten the food but seemed as hale and hearty as ever. Urswicke smiled at the gentle sarcasm and asked the guard to remove the corpses to one of the outhouses. They were to be stripped and any valuables, Urswicke repeated his instruction, were to be collected, piled together and handed over to Master Mauclerc. Urswicke continued to reflect on what he'd seen and heard whilst the four corpses were sheeted, put on makeshift stretchers and taken away. Tiptree and his minions came up with mops and buckets to clear the bloody mess.

Urswicke watched them for a while and left the chamber ostensibly to view the four corpses. In truth, he was searching for Spysin, but Mauclerc's courier seemed to have completely disappeared. Urswicke recalled how Spysin had mentioned something about sailing on the evening tide. Urswicke wondered whether he should go straight down to Queenhithe quayside but decided to wait. He did not want to provoke suspicion: he knew he was being watched and it would be more logical to inspect the corpses and then return to his hunt for Spysin.

The stable outhouse had been turned into a makeshift mortuary. The four corpses, completely naked, lay stretched out on old sacking rolled across on the shit-strewn, soggy floor. A lanternhorn glowed beside each cadaver. One of the soldiers had inveigled a wandering Friar of the Sack to come into this filthy death house and administer extreme unction, a pattering of prayer above the dead with a cross of wet wax etched on each forehead. Urswicke waited until the friar had finished, taken his coin and left.

'Did you find anything untoward?' he asked the soldier, who'd organised the removal of the corpses and was now going through belts, purses and pockets.

'Nothing.' The soldier pointed across to an upturned barrel. 'Some coins, daggers which they'd drawn, rings and a bracelet. See for yourself.'

Urswicke walked over and began to sift through the tawdry items. He pushed aside the four blood-encrusted daggers, pulling across the belts and purses the soldier brought; they were now empty. Urswicke could see no coins but he didn't care if the soldiers had helped themselves. He recalled the Three Kings gleefully participating in the blasphemous desecration of the old King's corpse; in death they had been given more respect than they'd shown the Lord's Anointed.

Urswicke picked up one wallet, he shook this and a piece of parchment fell out. It was only a plain strip of writing, though Urswicke noticed the vellum was of the highest quality, used solely in the chanceries of the Crown and the great lords. The strip was quite long, its edges even, and Urswicke suspected that it had been expertly cut by a parchment knife from a page which had measured too long in comparison with the other pages in some folio or book. The writing was that of some very skilled calligrapher, the verse it bore was written in Latin.

'And the captain of archers,' Urswicke whispered the translation to himself, 'lay with the wife of Duke Uriah the Hittite and she conceived a son.' Urswicke noticed how certain words were written in a different-coloured ink. He was about to peer closer when he heard shouts outside and hastily hid the strip of parchment in his own wallet. The door to the outhouse was thrown open and Mauclerc stormed in.

'Master Urswicke, come, come now.'

Urswicke followed Mauclerc and a group of his ruffians out across the stable yard and into the narrow runnels of Queenhithe. Clarence's henchmen swept through the streets like a violent windstorm. Pedlars, tinkers and traders fled. Women grabbed

their children and retreated back into the shelter of shabby doorways. Dogs and cats scurried away. Carts and barrows were
hastily pulled aside. Here and there, protests and raucous shouts
echoed about the 'power of the great ones of the land'. A window
was thrown open and a chamber pot emptied, the slop narrowly
missing members of Mauclerc's retinue. This was followed by
shrieks of laughter. Clarence's retinue drew their swords. The
shutters slammed shut and silence descended. They entered the
quayside where the fish markets were closing down, the cobbles
littered with all the rubbish of a day's trading. The heads and
innards of the morning catch turned the cobbles slippery, though
the legion of beggars, hunting for scraps, moved nimbly enough,
filling their sacks with what they found. The air reeked of salt
and brine and other harsh smells.

Mauclerc's arrival brought everything to a standstill. People
became statues, frightened even to move or speak. Urswicke
glanced to his left; the tide was turning. The river moving
more swiftly. Mauclerc led them away from the quayside into a
large, shabby tavern, The Prospect of Grimsby. This had now
been emptied of all its customers. More of Mauclerc's men
gathered in the gloomy taproom, a dingy place with its floor
rushes turned to a mushy mess and its tawdry tables strewn
with the remains of food and drink. Mauclerc told his companions to wait and led Urswicke down a narrow, stone-paved
passageway which led out into the yard and its jakes, an enclave
built into the tavern wall and screened by a heavy door. Mauclerc
opened this and waved Urswicke forward. The murdered Spysin,
hose down around his ankles, lay back against the filthy wall,
eyes popping, mouth gaping. The front of his jerkin was
drenched by the blood which had poured from his cut throat,
a deep slice running from ear to ear.

'Sweet heaven.' Urswicke crouched down, desperate to hide
his own relief that at least this problem had been resolved.
'Robbery?' he asked, turning to Mauclerc.

'His money belt, wallet and weapons have been taken.'

'You do realise,' Urswicke got to his feet, 'Spysin's throat has
been cut; the wound is very similar to that of the four victims
at The Sunne in Splendour. I strongly suspect Spysin's murderer
was the same person except,' he held a hand up, 'nothing appears

to have been taken from the chancery chamber, whilst Spysin's possessions have been filched.' He turned to confront Mauclerc, and did not relish the look on that sinister man's face.

'Nothing was taken from the chancery room or any of the Three Kings' chambers?'

Mauclerc, still holding Urswicke's gaze, eyes and face as hard as stone, just shook his head.

'And here's a further problem,' Urswicke fought to remain calm, 'Spysin was a street fighter, a man of war, expert in dagger play, used to the cut and thrust, yes?' Again that cold, hard stare followed by a nod. 'So it would appear that Spysin left the tavern to relieve himself, comes in here, lowers his hose and squats on the jake stool. Now for someone to cut his throat like that, the assassin would have to be standing behind him, but,' Urswicke continued, 'that's impossible. It cannot be done. The killer must have struck from the front, yet Spysin offered no resistance. There is no evidence that any form of struggle took place. Now . . .' Urswicke broke off.

Mauclerc, resting his hand on his dagger hilt, leaned slightly forward. 'What is the matter Christopher?' he whispered.

'You know full well, you look accusingly at me. For God's sake, Mauclerc, your own henchmen will go on oath. I have been nowhere near this tavern or Spysin but busy elsewhere. You are not implying . . .'

'No, no.' Mauclerc relaxed and shrugged, as if his former mood was nothing at all. He pulled a face. 'As I have said, I did – we did – wonder if Margaret Countess of Richmond had a hand in the murders at The Sunne in Splendour. If my Lord of Clarence hates her, she certainly detests us.' Mauclerc poked Urswicke gently in the chest. 'Christopher, you talk about street fighters and you can brawl with the best of them. You are her dagger man but, of course, I concede that today you have been busy on our affairs. My own henchmen, as you say, will attest to that. Yet who, Christopher? Who is responsible?'

'Think, my friend,' Urswicke replied, 'who has the money, the power and the means to hire expert assassins?'

Urswicke gestured at Spysin's corpse. 'We are not dealing with footpads and felons but men of power and, of course,' he glanced swiftly at Mauclerc, 'you have not told me what Spysin was involved in. He did mention that he was about to take ship to foreign parts, sail on the evening tide.'

'He was taking messages abroad, our master's courier here and there.' Mauclerc scratched his stubbled cheek. 'He should have been more prudent. But I return to my question, Christopher, who is responsible for all this?'

Urswicke shook his head to hide his own relief. Mauclerc seemed genuinely mystified, his former hostility just a passing mood. Now he called him Christopher, almost suppliant in his search for answers that Clarence would certainly demand.

'So Spysin was to be despatched to foreign parts, but what was he doing here?'

'Spysin was a toper, a wine lover. He made a mistake and paid for it with his life. So never mind him. Let's return to The Sunne in Splendour.'

'No, no,' Urswicke pulled at Mauclerc's sleeve, 'Minehost here at The Prospect of Grimsby? Now is the moment to question him before time passes and memories grow dim.'

Mauclerc agreed and they gathered the landlord and his servants in the taproom. They could say little about Spysin, except that he'd swaggered into the tavern, ordered a goblet of the best Bordeaux and had gone and sat in the furthest window seat. He was cloaked and booted and they suspected he was waiting to board a ship at the nearby quayside. One of the scullions reported how he'd glimpsed someone approach Spysin; it could have been a Friar of the Sack begging for alms, as these good brothers were accustomed to moving from one riverside tavern to another. The same scullion, a sharp-eyed urchin, glimpsed Spysin leave rather hastily carrying his fardel, and guessed the courier had an urgent call to the jake's stool. Spysin hurried out into the yard and, as far as the scullion was concerned, that was the end of the matter. Urswicke repeated his questions, watching faces intently, but he could detect nothing suspicious and whispered the same to Mauclerc. They left The Prospect of Grimsby and returned to the closely guarded chancery chamber at The Sunne in Splendour.

Mauclerc ordered a jug of wine, two goblets and a platter of diced meat coated with a spicy sauce. Urswicke refused the food and only sipped at his wine. Mauclerc, looking deeply agitated, slurped his goblet, only pausing to ask Urswicke to describe his conclusions about the murder of the Three Kings and Oudenarde.

'Very little,' Urswicke replied. 'We have a chamber locked and bolted within. As for the windows, if the shutters were pulled back, they are still too narrow even for a cat to climb through. No secret passageway or enclave exists except for the narrow jake's room. But this is nothing much and useful for one thing only. The food and drink the victims consumed was untainted. I have established that as a fact beyond any doubt. Even more mysterious, the four victims were able-bodied men, used to violence on the battlefield, or elsewhere,' he added drily. 'They were armed, indeed all four had drawn their daggers, which is puzzling because the bodies were lying on the floor as if they were sleeping and there is not even a trace of a minor disturbance. Mystery twists the mystery even deeper. Four men, armed, giving up their throats to be cut without protest or cry, resistance or defence? And how can that happen in a room where the door was locked and bolted from inside? So how did the Angel of Death enter? How did the assassins cut the throats of four vigorous men so silently, so softly, and how many assassins were there? One? Two, or even more? Let us say there were five or six, yet no one in that tavern saw, heard or suspected anything amiss until a scullion knocked on that chancery door.'

Urswicke fell silent; the full effect of this murderous mystery was making itself felt and, as Urswicke conceded to himself, he could find little way forward.

'Who?' Mauclerc demanded. 'Who was responsible?'

'In God's name,' Urswicke snapped, 'I do not know.'

Margaret, Countess of Richmond, together with her steward Reginald Bray, sat in the Exchequer chamber of her husband's house in Queenhithe. The mansion lay silent, its servants and retainers resting after a day's work, eating and drinking in the well-furnished buttery. A time of peace and harmony. Once the noise and the clamour of the house subsided, all the servants would gather to taste the latest offerings of the countess's cooks, who had an enviable reputation for baking the juiciest venison pie and roasting the most succulent chicken and duck.

Margaret had dined alone in her own chamber. Once the meal

was over, she had adjourned to the Exchequer, eager to go through her household accounts and reports from her bailiffs. Bray had laid out all the necessary documentation on the long chancery table and was advising her on anomalies: these proved to be legion after the chaos of the last year when the quarterly returns to her Exchequer, as well as hers to the Crown, had been so severely disrupted. Margaret hoped to raise monies for the establishment of chantries where priests could sing requiems for the repose of all her kinsmen who had died during the recent wars. She was also fiercely determined to implement her plan to fund a new college or hall in Cambridge. Once she had secured a suitable building, the adjoining lands and outhouses, she would strive to attract the leading scholars of the day from both England and abroad. Margaret was particularly fascinated by the new scholarship emerging in Europe. She was also deeply intrigued by the developments in theology and was more than prepared to support direct study of the Scripture: indeed, one of her great dreams was to have the Bible translated into English.

Margaret was still engrossed in such details when her chamberlain knocked on the door and burst in, all flustered, to announce that Richard, Duke of Gloucester, together with his henchman Francis Lovel had arrived determined to speak to her. Margaret raised her eyes heavenwards at Bray but agreed. They found Gloucester and Lovel ensconced in high-back chairs before the solar's sculptured hearth. Both men had taken off their cloaks and bonnets; a servant was laying these out across a table whilst another served white wine and sweetmeats. Gloucester rose to greet Margaret with all the courtesy of a court gallant, Lovel likewise. Margaret remained wary. Both men were dressed in the dark brown-green leather jerkins of a royal verderer, and Gloucester explained how they had been hare coursing north of the city walls.

Margaret sat down on a chair, moving it to face both men, using the fussing of the servants to study this precious pair. Richard of Gloucester's narrow, long face looked paler than usual, his sharp, green eyes bright with excitement, his lower lip jutting out as if he was quietly rehearsing some speech. He carried gauntlets which he kept slapping against his thigh as he greeted Bray, turning to the blond-haired, bland-faced Lovel to confirm a certain

point about the recent hunt. At last the courtly courtesies ran their
course. Margaret could tell from Gloucester's peaked, pale face
and the way he kept playing with the silver medallion around his
neck, displaying the Fetlock and Portcullis of York, that he was
impatient to begin. Gloucester glanced at Bray, who had ushered
the servants out and came to stand beside the countess.

'Where's Urswicke?' Lovel, his bright blue eyes devoid of any
kindness, leaned forward, jabbing a finger at the countess. 'Where
is your dagger man?'

'Standing beside me,' Margaret retorted.

'No,' Lovel smirked, 'the one with the angel's face, even
though he crawls through the shadows.'

'Is that where he met you?' Margaret retorted.

'Come now,' Gloucester intervened. 'Let us be honest, Mistress,
Urswicke lurks in the twilight. I believe he is a man who serves
more than one master.'

'My Lord, who doesn't?'

Gloucester took a deep breath as if to calm himself. 'Let us
cut to the quick,' he snapped. 'I know, we know, you know.
Indeed, we all know that George of Clarence is involved, and
has been ever since he could think, in some devilish mischief.
We also know he fears and hates you and your son.' Gloucester
paused, eyes blinking. 'I have dreams,' he murmured, 'about your
boy. My brother, the King, believes young Henry is a real threat
to the House of York. What say you, Mistress?'

'His Grace has nothing to fear from either me or mine.'
Margaret quietly wondered where this conversation was leading.
Gloucester fell silent, rocking himself gently in his chair.

'Clarence certainly fears you,' he declared abruptly. 'My
beloved brother had spies in your household: two Welsh brats,
Owain and Oswina.' He paused. 'I have their corpses outside.'

Margaret felt Bray stiffen beside her. She held up a hand.
'Corpses?'

'Yes, Mistress, corpses drawn from the Thames by the
Harrower, a city official paid to pluck corpses out of the Thames
and give them Christian burial.' Gloucester's face was now
wreathed in mock concern. 'I mourn your loss, Mistress, but the
matter deeply puzzles me. Oh . . .' He rose to his feet, Lovel
also. 'You must want to view their corpses?'

And, without waiting, both he and Lovel left the solar. Margaret stared at Bray, lifting a finger to her lips as she followed the Yorkists out. She was tempted to protest heatedly against being summoned in such a fashion here in her own house, but decided that discretion was the better path to follow.

Gloucester swept down the stairs to the hallway where more of his henchmen gathered, gesturing at the door to be opened, leading Margaret and Bray onto the broad sweep of Fetter Lane. A cart pulled by two dray horses stood there. Gloucester clambered onto the side of the cart and pulled back the canvas sheeting. He then stepped down, gesturing at Margaret to stand on the footrest. Helped by Bray, she did so, grasping the side of the cart as she stared at the two corpses. Margaret tried to remain calm at this gruesome sight. The two cadavers displayed savage death wounds; their flesh was all puffy, bloated and discoloured from the river, the soft flesh pecked by the carrion birds. Margaret crossed herself and climbed down, Bray taking her place. He glanced at the corpses, cursed and stepped off the footrest.

'Mistress,' Bray totally ignored Gloucester and Lovel as he grasped Margaret by the arm, 'Mistress, it's best if you return.' And he gently led Margaret, who acted as if she was about to faint, back up into the solar. Once there, Margaret acted the lady in distress. Bray scurried about, ordering the servants to bring a hot posset for their mistress and a footstool for her feet, warm mittens for her hands which, she claimed, had become so cold. During these ministrations, Margaret kept a sharp, sly eye on Gloucester and Lovel. Her two unwelcome visitors had sauntered back into the solar and now slouched in their chairs, legs crossed, coolly picking at spots on their hose.

'Well, Mistress?' Lovel preened himself, his high-pitched voice harsh on the ear.

'I do not think,' Margaret retorted, 'that was at all necessary.'

'Oh, we think it is,' Lovel sniffed. 'My master here also has spies, and of course the corpses were searched by the Harrower. He found copies of your wax seal on both cadavers. Anyway, the Harrower was visited by one of my master's men, a skilled searcher – so experienced, he's called "The Lurcher". Now he recognised both the seals and the gruesome remains. You see, The Lurcher had been watching; he'd set up post close to the water-gate of this splendid mansion. He saw you, Master Bray, together with Urswicke, row these two unfortunates across the Thames. He watched you return but, of course, not with Oswina and Owain. They were gone; they'd disappeared until the Harrower found them. Apparently the rocks used to weigh the dead bodies fell out and, of course, the Thames always gives up its dead, including two corpses with crossbow quarrels which had been loosed so close they were embedded deep in the flesh. So . . .'

'All your spy saw, my Lord,' Margaret measured her words carefully, 'is this. Oswina and Owain left here in a boat rowed by my two principal henchmen.' She turned slightly in her chair. 'Yes, Reginald?'

'We took them on a special errand to Minehost at The Golden Hoop. You should know it, a splendid tavern close to the priory of St Mary Ovary in Southwark. On my mistress's instruction, the taverner was to give both Oswina and Owain good purveyance, food, horses and other necessities for their long journey to Woking and then on into Wales.'

'Yes, yes,' Gloucester murmured. 'And I am sure Minehost of The Golden Hoop, along with a packed choir of witnesses, will swear that Oswina and Owain were seen in his tavern, hale and hearty, very much alive and busy on their mistress's business. How they left but then disappeared until their corpses were found. Those unfortunate young things were attacked by wolfsheads who murdered them, plundered their possessions and then threw their corpses into the Thames.'

'You are very perceptive,' Margaret retorted, 'I think you have described what truly happened. I shall mourn for them, I shall pray for them, and I will petition your brother the King to take more rigorous steps to clear his highways and byways of such malefactors.' She held Gloucester's gaze. In truth, she didn't really care what he knew. 'Wouldn't you agree?' she demanded archly.

'I certainly do.' Gloucester's pale, narrow face broke into an infectious grin, making him more youth-like, the sinister threat he conveyed being replaced with a gentle, merry mockery. 'Margaret, Margaret Beaufort.' Gloucester dropped his gauntlets to the floor and leaned forward, hands outstretched. 'Margaret, let us ignore all this nonsense. The corpses outside will be swiftly and quietly buried in God's Acre at St Botolph's. Let us concern ourselves with the living. You know and I know this. Brother George has a manuscript, the "Titulus Regius", the work of the Three Kings and Oudenarde who now lie slaughtered in some Godforsaken death house.' Gloucester smiled again. 'Brother George is furious at their deaths, even more so because he does not know where the the "Titulus Regius" is.'

'What?' Margaret exclaimed. 'But all four worked for Lord Clarence, that is common knowledge. They were—'

'Not stupid.' Gloucester finished the sentence. 'Seemingly, they composed the manuscript, but kept its actual whereabouts a close secret amongst themselves, a guarantee for my good brother's faith – if he has any. Clarence is a turncoat. He betrayed his own family, joined the Lancastrians and, when they failed to show him what he considered to be his due, turned coat again to be welcomed back into the bosom of his loving family. The Three Kings wanted to finish the manuscript, then hand it over and be suitably rewarded, not just to be dismissed, or worse, at my perjured brother's whim.'

Margaret shifted in her chair, staring up at the pink-plastered ceiling. What Gloucester had told her was logical, given Clarence's talent for treachery. In the beginning the Three Kings would have been given the outline of what Clarence wanted and they, together with Oudenarde, had searched for the proof, creating a chronicle which they would only hand over when finished. By then they would know all the scandalous secrets about the House of York. Clarence would be in their debt and dare not move against them. Margaret wondered if the Three Kings had also created a copy. But where were these manuscripts which could do so much damage to Edward and his brothers? She herself would love to seize such evidence. Was Urswicke making any headway in discovering the true whereabouts of the 'Titulus Regius'?

'My Lady?'

Margaret smiled across at Gloucester. 'Just reflecting, my Lord, on what a tangled web is being spun here.'

'Even more tangled,' Lovel declared, 'are the murders at The Sunne in Splendour: the Three Kings and Oudenarde the book-seller?'

'Oh yes,' she replied, 'in the city, news flies faster than swallows. I do wonder,' she added, 'who could carry out such savage executions?'

'Perhaps someone else,' Gloucester declared, 'who is hunting for the "Titulus Regius".'

'Such as who?'

'My brother my King.'

'And what has this to do with us?' Bray demanded.

'Because everyone, especially my brother George, searches for the "Titulus Regius", and its authors the Three Kings, along with their fellow conspirator Oudenarde, have been murdered. It would seem they took their secrets to the grave. Let us be frank and honest. We all search for that document, as do you my Lady.' Gloucester swallowed hard and licked his lips. 'So here's my offer. If you find the "Titulus Regius" and hand it over to me, I shall personally guarantee that your son, who must now be sheltering in Brittany, will remain untroubled.' Gloucester paused.

'And secondly?' Margaret asked. 'There is always a second.'

'Your husband Sir Humphrey, Lady Margaret, is a very sickly man, greatly weakened by wounds inflicted at Barnet. I am not being malicious but, God bless him, Sir Humphrey might not survive the summer.' He held up a be-ringed hand. 'As I said, there's no malice intended. No insult being offered. I am speaking the truth, being as practical as possible. If Sir Humphrey dies, Lady Margaret, you become a widow, but you are also a Beaufort. The last of that name. You will be alone,' Gloucester waved a hand at Bray, 'except for your faithful henchman. In time you will become vulnerable to your enemies. Entire families like the Woodvilles detest your name and, if they can, will inflict great damage on you.'

'And we must not forget your brother, George of Clarence?'

'No my Lady, we must not.'

'So you are offering me protection?'

'I have already mentioned your son and, as for you, marriage to Lord William Stanley, a powerful baron, a bachelor, well-favoured by the King, with extensive estates and power in the north. A member of the royal council; in his own way a man of integrity, shrewd and redoubtable.'

'I have met and know of Sir William Stanley.'

'A good match, my Lady. He would prove a strong protector against the malice of your enemies. Anyway,' Gloucester rose to his feet. Margaret remained seated and stretched out her hand so Gloucester and Lovel had to bow to kiss it.

'We have an agreement?' Lovel demanded.

'We shall reflect,' Margaret replied. 'Now sirs,' she stood up, 'we have other matters to attend to. Master Bray will see you out.' She bowed and turned away, though listening intently as Bray deferentially led Gloucester and Lovel out of the solar and down the stairs to their waiting escort. Once they'd gone Bray returned, slamming the door shut behind him.

'Dangerous,' he murmured, as he poured both himself and his mistress goblets of chilled wine, 'a very dangerous man.'

'He offers some protection, Reginald and, at this moment of time, we need all we can get. As the poet says, peril presses on every side. Urswicke informed me about the slaughter at The Sunne in Splendour, as well as the execution of Spysin in the jakes of a riverside tavern. All a great mystery, eh Reginald?' She laughed, fingers fluttering to her lips. 'The work of a skilled craftsman, eh Master Bray? Do you not agree?'

'Talking of skill, I am thinking about those two corpses! We made a hideous mistake, we hurried their deaths. We should have taken more care. But, at the end of the day, we could not allow those two to live as daggers pointed at our hearts. They deserved to die.' He added morosely: 'They all deserved to die, didn't they?'

He broke off at a knock at the door and Urswicke slipped into the chamber. He crossed the room, bowed and kissed hands with Lady Margaret, who studied him from head to toe as he turned to greet Bray. She caught her breath and tried to remain composed. Christopher looked weary to the point of exhaustion. He had not shaved, whilst his doublet and hose were greatly stained, his boots scuffed and his cloak laced with mud from the streets. At her bidding, Urswicke took off his cloak and warbelt. Margaret made him sit down, serving him wine and a platter of honey-coated comfits a servant brought in. Urswicke just sat, watching the retainer gather the empty goblets and platters and, once the door closed behind him, Urswicke toasted both the countess and Bray with his cup.

'Let me tell you,' he began, 'how it is. First,' Urswicke held up a hand, 'no one really knows what the the "Titulus Regius" truly is, where it's hidden, or what form it takes. Such secrets died with the four men in that chancery chamber. Secondly, how the Three Kings and Oudenarde were murdered remains a complete mystery.' Urswicke sipped gratefully from the goblet. 'Four strong men, their throats slashed yet, apart from the blood and the fact they had drawn their weapons, no other sign of violence. Spysin died the same way, murdered while sitting on a jake's pot in a tavern garderobe. An almost impossible feat. A street-fighting man, Spysin's throat was cut from the front yet with no shred of evidence that the victim, who must have seen his attacker, resisted or retaliated.'

'Mauclerc and his master must be furious?' Bray could hardly conceal his glee as he glanced slyly at Margaret.

'Oh, and deeply apprehensive. From the little I have gathered, the "Titulus Regius" may never be found.'

'But,' Bray interrupted, 'Clarence and Mauclerc must have been apprised about what the Three Kings and Oudenarde were collecting? Be it a newsletter, a chronicle, or that's what we should think. However, we must remember that the "Titulus Regius" is not Clarence's work but the creation of those Three Kings, brothers, friars from the Rhineland. I believe they brought something to Clarence which he seized upon. A poisonous plant which they could nourish and nurse to full bloom. Mauclerc patronised those brothers and their assistant, Oudenarde. They insisted on working secretly in that chancery room at The Sunne in Splendour.'

'Yes, yes I see,' Margaret murmured, shaking her head. She reflected on what she had learnt about the 'Titulus Regius'. Clarence had saved those three brothers from the law. They must have responded by discovering something which Clarence seized on as a weapon to carve his own name in pride and so advance his ambitious schemes. In the end, Clarence didn't care about whom he hurt. On this issue the House of York and that of Lancaster were no different: they were simply obstacles Clarence had to remove. Margaret closed her eyes.

'Mistress?'

She glanced swiftly at Bray before turning back to Urswicke.

'But surely,' Margaret measured her words, 'once the Three Kings were dead, Mauclerc must have seized all the manuscripts in that chancery?'

'Of course, my Lady. But I don't think they found the "Titulus Regius". If they had, I am sure I would not be investigating that murderous mystery on their behalf. I play the part as I have told you, an ambitious clerk who will serve any master for profit. But on this, my service is not too good, for I am mystified about what really happened in that tavern. As God is my witness, I have made no progress at all.'

'Are you sure, none at all?' Margaret held her breath as she glanced quickly at Bray.

'None,' Urswicke agreed, 'except,' he lifted his head and grinned impishly at both the countess and Bray, 'the Barnabites.'

'Who?' Bray asked.

'Oh, I know about the Barnabites,' Margaret declared. 'I now recall them, a group of rather eccentric friars. A minor order with very few members. Their friary, if you can call it that, is a rather gloomy, shabby priest's house close to the ancient church of St Vedast; it stands between Hounds Ditch and the Moor. In fact, if I remember correctly, the Barnabites do not enjoy the most savoury reputation.' Margaret paused, staring at Urswicke.

'Mistress?'

'They have been in London for about two years. They come from the Rhineland, Germany, not far from Cologne.'

'The same place as the Three Kings?'

'Precisely,' Margaret agreed. 'I know about them because they petitioned Sir Humphrey and myself for a grant of monies. If you scrutinise the records . . .'

She went across to the chancery table and tapped the main household book, a heavy tome with the finest parchment pages all bound tight between silver-embossed calfskin covers. 'Anyway,' Margaret moved back to her chair, 'the Barnabites?'

'I made enquiries amongst the scullions and slatterns at The Sunne in Splendour. One of them told me a little more about the mysterious visitors to the Three Kings. I glimpsed the same being brought into the tavern, men and women, not many, five or six individuals in all. They were always hidden, shrouded in the distinctive blue and brown garb of the Barnabites who escorted them there.' Urswicke paused and walked across to the chancery table. He undid the clasps of the household book and began to leaf through its parchment pages, looking for the heading '*Expensae et Dona* – Expenses and Gifts'. He sifted through the different pages looking for the entry on the Barnabites when one item caught his eye. So surprised he glanced up. Countess Margaret and Bray were staring at him, so he returned to the household account, murmuring about the Barnabites. In fact he was making sure that he had read certain entries correctly.

'Christopher?'

'My Lady,' Urswicke kept studying the manuscript, 'I intend to refresh myself then pay these Barnabites a visit.'

Later that day, as the sun began to set and the shadows both deepened and lengthened, Christopher Urswicke crossed the stout wooden bridge over Hounds Ditch, that great wound in the land north of the city wall where the sewage of London was tipped by the huge gong carts. 'Hell's Pit', as some people called it, was a long line of steamy slime stretching across the heathland either side of the bridge. Here and there, bonfires flickered and burned, but even their acrid, pungent smoke could not disguise the rancid, foulsome odours. Like everyone who crossed the bridge, Urswicke brought a pomander heavily drenched in lavender to cover his mouth and nose whilst he averted his gaze from the swollen corpses of dogs, horses, cats and pigs, their bellies bloated to rupture and rip.

At last Urswicke was across, striding through the wild heathland, a blighted, neglected place with its scrawny bushes, copses of dark, stunted trees and a moving sea of coarse grass. The place was the haunt of felons and wolfsheads. Urswicke did not care; he walked with his cloak thrown back to display his warbelt furnished with sword, dagger and a squat leather case containing bolts for the hand-held arbalest he carried. Meagre light blinked and glowed through the gathering dark; Urswicke, however, knew his way. At last he breasted a small rise and St Vedast lay before him.

Once it must have been a bustling hamlet or village which had grown up around the ancient church with its rather majestic-looking priest's house built out of wood and plaster on a stone base. In the dying light, both church and house looked eerily deserted and much decayed. However, even from where he stood, Urswicke could glimpse the glow of candlelight which indicated habitation. Urswicke stared around and studied this isolated, ruined hamlet. He could make out the lines of former cottages and other buildings and concluded that this must have been one of those communities wiped out by the Angel of Death, the Great Plague which had swept the kingdom a hundred years earlier. A devastating onslaught which annihilated entire towns. This community must have died and the parish became nothing more than a lonely church and house.

Both buildings were circled by a high curtain wall. There were outhouses, storage sheds and stables, but most of the church estate was a sprawling cemetery, God's Acre, a truly desolate stretch of land to the north of the church. Urswicke took a deep breath, crossed himself and walked down the hill, along the wet, pebble-strewn path towards a main gate which looked as if it had been recently refurbished and strengthened. Urswicke glimpsed the bell rope to the side and pulled hard. The bell, under its coping, clanged noisily. Urswicke pulled again and heard the patter of sandalled feet. A voice demanded who he was and Urswicke shouted his name and how he was here on the specific orders of Lord Clarence and his most loyal henchman, Master Mauclerc. A small postern door in the main gate swung open and a cowled figure beckoned.

Urswicke stepped inside. Four figures awaited, their faces almost hidden by the deep capuchons pulled over their heads. One of these held a lantern, the rest were well-armed with swords and ugly-looking maces, morning stars, their cruel, sharp studs gleaming in the light. The lantern holder asked for proof and Urswicke handed over a copy of Clarence's seal. Mauclerc had given him a number of these to use on the duke's business.

'Come.'

The evident leader of the group who held the lantern and examined the seal, gave it back and beckoned Urswicke to follow him across the deserted cobbled bailey into the priest's house. Urswicke was immediately struck by how sinister and dingy this was: narrow with paved corridors, the ceiling and walls flaking, cobwebs spanned the corners whilst the squeak and squeal of scurrying vermin seemed constant. Urswicke was led into what he supposed to be the refectory, with a long board table down the middle. The smell of cooking fish and burnt oil hung heavy. The table top was littered with platters and goblets. Urswicke sat on a stool on one side of the table with the four Barnabites sitting opposite him. They pulled back their capuchons to reveal harsh, unshaven faces, heads shorn to a stubble, faces cruelly scarred. They reminded Urswicke of mercenaries rather than friars. Their leader introduced himself as Brother Cuthbert; he offered food and drink. Urswicke refused, pleading he'd taken his fill. The other three Barnabites introduced themselves as Brothers Alcuin, John and Luke.

Urswicke smiled and nodded as he tried to disguise his own growing apprehension. Were these four really friars or were they rifflers, dagger-men, street fighters masquerading as men of God? Such a practice was rife throughout the kingdom and Western Christendom, to the deepening fury and dismay of the Pope and other ecclesiastical and secular authorities. Time and again, the Papacy had fulminated against the practice of outlaws who joined some obscure, decaying order to hide both themselves and their villainy. Some of these malefactors simply donned the garb; others were admitted on the full understanding that they had no more interest in matters spiritual than a pig in its sty. Urswicke loved the poet Chaucer and recalled a phrase from one of his tales: 'Cucullus non facit monachum – the cowl doesn't make the monk.' The Barnabites facing him more than justified such a description. All four studied Urswicke before chattering amongst themselves. Urswicke did not understand what they said though he guessed that all of them, like the Three Kings, were from Germany, some city or province in the Rhineland.

'We know who you are – or think we do. We have studied the seal you carry.' Cuthbert's voice was harsh and grating. 'What do you want with us?'

'The Three Kings are dead,' Brother John spoke up, 'as is Oudenarde the parchment-seller, whilst another of my Lord Clarence's retainers, the courier Spysin,' Brother John grinned in a display of jagged, yellow teeth, 'was slain sitting on a tavern jake's.'

'And I am investigating their deaths.'

'So why are you here?' Cuthbert demanded.

'I understand from tavern chatter that you,' Urswicke gestured at them, 'or persons garbed like you, brought visitors, men and women, up to the Three Kings in their chancery chamber. Who were these and where are they now?'

All four Barnabites stared at Urswicke. Cuthbert, eyes narrowing, got to his feet, indicating that his comrades follow him to the far end of the refectory. Urswicke stared around as if curious about where he was. He noticed how truly filthy the refectory was: its walls were stained, the plaster flaking, the rushes on the floor a mushy mess. He also realised there were no triptychs, crucifixes, statues, or anything to reflect matters spiritual. Indeed, the only painting was a half-finished, faded wall fresco about the fall of Lucifer and his angels. A sombre painting, in which hideous-looking creatures roamed a gloomy landscape lit by flames from unseen fires. Urswicke glanced away, trying to soothe his own nervousness. He strove to keep calm despite the deepening fear that he may have made a mistake in coming to this evil place to meet such sinister men. He bent down, picked up the hand-held arbalest and slipped it onto the hook on his warbelt, covering it with his cloak. Cuthbert walked back, Brother John trailing behind him.

'We can answer your questions,' he declared, 'and show you the people we brought. Come.'

Urswicke followed Cuthbert out of the refectory, down a dank, smelly passageway which led out into God's Acre. Brother John, gasping about his sore leg, stumbled along behind him. The ancient cemetery was a forlorn wasteland; its crosses, headstones and plinths had long since crumbled. Cuthbert led him through this house of the dead, pushing aside trailing bramble and sharp gorse, which caught at Urswicke's cloak and boots. Darkness had fallen. The eerie silence was broken only by Brother John's gasping and the occasional screech of a night bird which set Urswicke's teeth on edge. He felt a creeping sense of danger, as he would threading through the treacherous runnels and dark alleys of London.

'We will soon be there,' Brother Cuthbert shouted over his shoulder as he walked on. 'Well, here we are.' Cuthbert raised the lantern, gesturing at the freshly dug graves. Urswicke abruptly stopped. Something was wrong. Brother John had fallen strangely silent. Urswicke whirled round as the Barnabite, no longer complaining about his leg, was ready to swing a morning star to shatter the back of Urswicke's head. The clerk, his dagger now drawn, danced swiftly to the left and drove his long Welsh stabbing blade deep into his opponent's belly. The Barnabite sank to his knees, choking on his own blood. Urswicke turned just in time, his weapon knocking down the sword Brother Cuthbert had concealed beneath his cloak. Urswicke backed away, drawing his sword, balancing both that and the dagger. Cuthbert, a poor swordsman, lunged forward, but he was nervous and stumbled, the point of his sword narrowly missing Urswicke's face. The Barnabite paid the penalty for such a mistake. Urswicke's sword cut deep into Cuthbert's exposed throat. He withdrew the blade. Cuthbert collapsed to his knees, eyes fluttering, his mouth gaping, his lifeblood drenching the front of his robe. The Barnabite gave a deep sigh and toppled lifelessly over.

Urswicke searched both men, removing their fat money purses yet, apart from the coins, there was nothing else. Urswicke then prepared himself. He charged the arbalest, slipping the ugly, barbed bolt into the groove, pulling back the twine over the lever so it was ready to loose. Sword and dagger sheathed, Urswicke crept back across the desolate cemetery and in through the postern door.

'Is it done?'

One of the Barnabites stepped out of the refectory, a clear target against the dim light, so Urswicke's bolt took him deep in the chest. The Barnabite staggered back and collapsed.

'It is done,' Urswicke breathed as he hurried round him into the refectory. The fourth Barnabite, Luke, was frantically trying to draw a sword from its sheath on a bench. Again Urswicke loosed, but this time his hand slipped and the bolt caught his opponent high in the shoulder, sending him crashing against the wall. Urswicke hurried across. The Barnabite had managed to draw a dagger from the pouch on his rope belt. Urswicke knocked this aside and crouched down. He studied his opponent; the man was moaning quietly, eyes half closed.

'Who are you really?' Urswicke demanded. The Barnabite just shook his head.

'Some wine,' he gasped. 'Something for the pain.'

Urswicke got to his feet and left the refectory. He searched the corpse of the Barnabite sprawled there. He found nothing except a well-filled purse. Ignoring the groans of the wounded Luke, Urswicke then ransacked both the house and church but he could find nothing significant. He returned to the refectory. The wounded Barnabite was still moaning so Urswicke took across a goblet of wine and helped him drink. The man gulped greedily. Urswicke left the pewter goblet with him and moved across to the table. He opened the small chancery coffer and emptied out the different pieces of parchment.

'Clever, clever,' he murmured, 'no manuscript. Nothing but licences for a group of Barnabites to travel through Dover, backwards and forwards across the Narrow Seas.' Urswicke was about to push these aside when he realised what he'd missed. He grabbed the licences and unrolled them. There were at least a dozen but they had one thing in common: they were all signed and sealed by no lesser person than Robert Stillington, Bishop of Bath and Wells, who'd been recently appointed as Chancellor of the Kingdom. Urswicke snatched these up, walked back and crouched before the wounded man who lay moaning, cradling the cup which he tried to pass to Urswicke.

'In a short while,' the clerk murmured, 'you will be beyond all pain.' He held up the licences. 'Why do you have these?'

'So we can travel.'

'Yes, yes I can see that. You have the Crown's permission to travel backwards and forwards to Dover. All royal officials are instructed to assist you in any way they can.'

'And?' the man gasped.

'All of them are signed and sealed by the most important man in the kingdom, the King's own chancellor, the Crown's chief clerk. Why was Robert Stillington, Bishop of Bath and Wells, interested in a group of ragged Barnabites travelling to and from this kingdom? Every one of these licences bears his name and seal, but I have worked in the royal chancery, this could have been done by some common clerk . . .'

'Wine,' the man moaned, 'give me wine.'

Urswicke could tell the man was weakening fast. He filled the goblet to the brim and helped the man drink.

'The licences?' Urswicke demanded.

'Where's Cuthbert?'

'He's dead, his throat cut, as yours will be soon. I will give you the mercy wound.'

The man tried to laugh. 'I know nothing,' he said. 'I followed orders. We would travel here and there, both in this kingdom and beyond, to take and bring certain individuals into London. I simply acted as a guard. Who these people were, what they knew and what they told the Three Kings . . .?' The man stopped, coughing violently, and Urswicke noticed the bloody froth seeping between the dried, cracked lips. 'I know nothing,' he gasped, 'Brother Cuthbert did. He once said Stillington was in his debt, that the bishop had promised to look after Brother Joachim.'

'Brother Joachim, who is he?'

'Once he belonged to our brotherhood, but then he fell sick, some evil humour of the mind. Cuthbert told me that Stillington had found comfortable quarters for Joachim at the hospital of St Mary Bethlehem here in London. Its inmates suffer from delusions, weakened wits, all forms of insanity. I will tell you something else,' the man spluttered, 'if you promise to give me the mercy cut and vow, on your own soul, that you'll hire a chantry priest to sing a requiem for mine.'

Urswicke nodded. 'I promise, what is it?'

'Oh, it's very simple. According to Cuthbert, he held Stillington in the palm of his hand. But how, why and what for, I do not know. I have spoken the truth.'

'Tell me,' Urswicke insisted, 'why did Cuthbert turn on me? After all, I carry Clarence's seal. I work for Mauclerc. Why?'

'You did not follow the protocol Cuthbert agreed with Mauclerc: you carried no specific letter. We knew about the killings at The Sunne in Splendour; you asked questions you shouldn't have. Cuthbert, who was a law unto himself, decided you were too dangerous to let go . . .'

Urswicke studied the man. He believed the Barnabite had told him all he could. He leaned forward, took the goblet, and forced the wine between the man's lips. The Barnabite drank greedily and lifted back his head so Urswicke could cut his throat from ear to ear. Urswicke crossed himself, returned to the table and sifted amongst the other scraps of parchment. Apart from the licences, there was nothing significant, and he realised the Barnabites had simply lived at St Vedast. In the main, all four men and any visitors had supped and dined in city taverns. They bought basic purveyance for the priest's house, a little food, some wine, candles and kindling, but nothing else.

Intrigued, Urswicke continued his searches. He recalled how the four Barnabites had been sitting in the refectory when he met them: a room where, he suspected, there'd been a constant presence, so he decided to concentrate on that gloomy chamber. His scrutiny proved successful. Urswicke noticed how one flagstone beneath the table was so loose it moved. Urswicke prised this open, thrust his hand into what he suspected was the old parish arca – a stronghold, a sealed pit where treasures could be stored. He searched around and felt a leather sack: he pulled this up, opened it and took out a book of hours; its calfskin cover held finely scrubbed parchment pages. Urswicke put this down, returned to the arca and drew out an elaborate chancery tray with quills, sheets of costly vellum, pots of coloured ink, pumice stones and parchment knives. He searched the pit again but there was nothing else.

He made himself comfortable, opened the book of hours and leafed through its pages. Some of these had small, jewel-like paintings which emphasised the first word or letter of a psalm or prayer. The writing was clerkly, in a range of red, blue and black inks. The book was almost full, only a few blank pages at the back. Urswicke closed the book of hours and wondered why it was so precious? He recalled a similar psalter he'd found in the chancery chamber at The Sunne in Splendour. Urswicke had now secreted this away with a goldsmith in Cheapside. 'The Barnabites feared neither God nor man,' he whispered to himself. 'I doubt very much whether they sang the Divine Office, pattered a prayer or even crossed themselves. So,' Urswicke stared down at the book of hours resting on his lap, 'why did they treasure you?'

Urswicke put the book on the table and stared at it. He carried the purses of the dead Barnabites in the deep pocket of his cloak. They certainly had good coin and the wherewithal to live high on the hog, though they seemed to own few possessions, nothing of value. So why did they treasure this psalter so much? Stored in the arca, kept well away from prying eyes? Did they intend to sell it?

Urswicke drew a deep breath and got to his feet. Taking a lantern, he combed both the priest's house and tiny church, but discovered nothing of interest. At last, with the chimes of midnight echoing faintly from the city, Urswicke declared himself satisfied. He dragged in the corpses from God's Acre and laid them alongside the other two killed in the priest's house. He then fetched the oil and kindling he'd glimpsed in his earlier searches. He piled wood over the corpses, drenched that and the rest of the furniture in oil. Once satisfied, he took a tinder, lit a torch and threw it into the refectory which, as he left the priest's house, burst into flames. Urswicke stood outside and watched the conflagration spread through that ancient mansion with its dust-dry woodwork and crumbling plaster.

Urswicke stood staring as the night wind fanned the flames even further, wafting them towards the nearby church. It was time to go. Urswicke picked up the leather sack containing the book of hours and the small pick and shovel he'd taken from an outhouse. He put these carefully in the leather sack, gripped the still flaming lanternhorn, and made his way back across God's Acre following the same path Brother Cuthbert had taken. At last he reached the place where the attack had occurred.

PART FIVE

'A quarrel rose between the King's two brothers which
proved difficult to settle.'

Crowland Chronicle

Urswicke picked his way carefully through the trailing
bramble and gorse. Immediately freezing as an owl, soft
and swift as a ghost, floated just above him. Urswicke
quickly crossed himself, watching the night-bird glide down
until it was skimming just above the gorse: it then disappeared
and Urswicke heard the screech of some creature caught in the
hunter's talons. The clerk put the lanternhorn down near one
of the freshly dug graves. He took off his cloak, draping it across
the sack, from which he took the pick and shovel.

'I need to disturb the dead,' he whispered. 'Eternal rest grant
to them, oh Lord, but not just for now.' Urswicke began to dig.
He soon realised the grave was very shallow, the corpse thrust
there treated with little dignity, bound up in tight, coarse sacking.
Urswicke cleared the dirt away, cut the sacking and stared in
disgust at the gruesome sight. The cadaver was that of an old
man with wispy-white hair, the face showing decay and corruption. The eyes had long sunk. The lips mere fragments of flesh
cut back to expose sharp, dog-like teeth. The head was slightly
tilted back to expose the great gash in the man's flesh. 'Brought
here for some purpose,' Urswicke whispered, 'and when that was
finished, so were you.'

Urswicke sketched a blessing over the corpse, kicked
back the dirt, grabbed his cloak and sack and strode off into the
darkness.

The following morning Urswicke, who had stayed at The
Sunne in Splendour to see if the destruction of the Barnabites
was reported, rose early, shaved, washed and changed his linen.
He then went down to the taproom and, bearing in mind what

he'd seen in the countess's household ledger, he decided to watch Minehost Tiptree, along with his family and servants, prepare for the day. The bakers had already filled a basket with soft, white manchet loaves, small rolls of bread with butter in the middle. Lamb chops had been roasted on a grill in the kitchen yard, and now Minehost, assisted by a bevy of sweaty spit-boys, was preparing a full side of hog to be roasted on the great spit in the taproom's majestic hearth. Urswicke savoured the delicious smells as he sipped his morning ale and slowly ate the porridge laced with honey prepared by Mistress Tiptree. Watching carefully, he asked questions of the different servants so he could clearly identify all members of the Tiptree family.

Once he was satisfied, Urswicke put on his boots, took his cloak and warbelt and left the tavern. So far he'd seen none of Clarence's household or any of Mauclerc's bully boys, nor had he even heard a rumour about the fire at St Vedast. Urswicke clasped his cloak more tightly and followed the twisting lanes up into Cheapside. The morning masses had finished with the tolling of the Jesus bell and the host of traders, tinkers and stall holders moved like a shoal of colourful fish into taverns, alehouses and cook-shops to break their fast. Market horns sounded above the crashing wheels of the dung carts. Half-naked children shrieked and yelled as they clambered over the slimy midden heaps.

The weather had changed, growing decidedly warmer, and the battles and storms of yesterday were now a fading memory. Merry Maytime had arrived! The season for welcoming the sun and rejoicing in a golden glow of summer. Maypoles, adorned with streamers, had been erected at crossroads and in every available free space. Minstrels, troubadours, travelling troupes of clowns and merrymen flooded into the city, hoping to be hired for this festivity or that masque. The days were growing longer and the light turning stronger. The great ones of the city would hold their lavish evening banquets, either in their gardens or on the paving in front of their fine mansions, so they were eager to hire whatever entertainment was available. May was also Mary's month, so decades of the Rosary, the aves ringing through the air, were recited on the steps of every church next to a statue of the Virgin wreathed in May-time flowers. All of this merriment, of course, was watched by the footpads, cunning men and felons who slunk like dogs, hungry for easy prey, even though the well-used stocks, pillories and gallows proclaimed stark warnings about where such villainy might end.

The criers and heralds were also busy: they proclaimed the news from the court and from the shires, as well as reminding the good citizens of the names of rebels who had taken up arms against the Crown during the recent troubles and had not been apprehended. Urswicke also noticed with grim amusement how other street criers, darting swiftly about to escape capture, spread news that the Lancastrian cause was not finished, for there was unrest here and disturbance there. Urswicke recognised most of this as the work of the fertile imaginations of the Countess Margaret and Reginald Bray.

Urswicke eventually reached the Guildhall, forcing his way through a highly excited baptismal party processing up to St Mary Magdalene Church in Milk Street. The beloved infant who was to be held over the font was bawling raucously, setting nerves on edge. Urswicke was glad to be away. He showed his warrants to the guards and was halfway across the cobbled bailey when he heard his name called. Urswicke turned as his father hurried across, his smooth face wreathed in a smile, two young women, garbed in the tightest of gowns, trailing behind.

'Christopher, Christopher, you have heard the news? I have been dubbed a knight, but now there's going to be a royal ceremony where my knighthood will be confirmed by no lesser person than his Grace the King. He will formally bestow the honour then kiss hands with me.'

'And when will this most magnificent ceremony take place?'

'On the feast of St John the Baptist in the Guildhall chapel. You will come?'

'Of course, and will they?'

Urswicke pointed to the two willowy figures standing so close behind his father.

'I can't answer that.' The Recorder patted his son on the shoulder. 'And why are you here?'

'To study the records, I am busy on my Lord Clarence's affairs.'

'And I am off to break my fast with my maids here before meeting with the sheriffs. You have heard about the fire at St

Vedast out on the moor?' Urswicke pulled a face and shook his head. 'The priest's house and the church were burnt to the ground. The fire started in the former but there was a powerful night breeze and the flames spread into the church. Nothing more than a charred ruin now.'

'And the perpetrators?'

'We found no coins, nothing of value, just four blackened, crumbling corpses. We believe it's the work of wolfsheads. Anyway,' the Recorder smiled falsely and gestured back at the Guildhall, 'the chancery chambers are over there. You will be given all the help you need.'

Within the hour Urswicke, using his name and warrants, ensconced himself in a small enclave on the gallery leading down to the great chancery office in the Guildhall. Urswicke was well served by two spindly shanked scriveners who, with their pointed noses, wispy hair and sunken cheeks, looked like gargoyles who'd clambered down from the stout, wooden pillars which ranged along the gallery. Both officials, however, were very skilled, and soon brought Urswicke all he needed: coroners' rolls, licences issued, a list of debtors, a schedule of committal to the prisons at Newgate and the Fleet, fines and penalties imposed, a fair reflection of the work at the Guildhall in keeping the money market of the city healthy and vigorous.

Urswicke, who was as skilled in chancery matters as any royal clerk, swiftly sifted through the different manuscripts. Now and again he would rise and stretch and sip from the jug of wine one of the scriveners kindly brought up. Time passed, marked by the tolling of city bells. When the Angelus rang, Urswicke went out to a nearby cook-shop for a soft, freshly baked pastry filled with spiced meat and mint. At last, late in the afternoon, Urswicke had finished his work; he found it difficult to accept the conclusions he'd reached. Nevertheless, those same conclusions rested on sound logic and hard evidence. For a while, Urswicke just sat staring at a carving on the wall as he plotted a possible resolution of the mysteries confronting him. He dearly wanted to return to the countess and question her but he dared not: his investigation was not complete because he was still deeply confused by the sequence of events over which he needed to impose order.

Urswicke eventually realised that he could do no more in the chancery office so he returned through the busy streets to The Sunne in Splendour. He passed an alehouse full of flickering lights and raucous noise. He paused, went in and stared round as he recalled The Wyvern's Nest and Master Hempen. An ale taster came up to him with an offer of drinks. Urswicke shook his head, deep in thought, as a possible solution emerged, an idea which took root in his mind, a possibility which could be turned into a reality. He left the tavern and, hand on sword, hurried through the darkening streets, avoiding the low-hung tavern signs, keeping a wary eye on the midden heaps and the piles of night soil. He reached The Wyvern's Nest and immediately demanded to meet Hempen. The landlord agreed, providing a secure chamber above the taproom. Once settled, Urswicke described the outlines of his plan. Hempen listened intently. When Urswicke was finished he shook his head.

'Master Christopher,' he whispered, 'to kidnap a fellow taverner and his entire family, I mean . . .'

'It is necessary,' Urswicke insisted. 'No violence, no theft. Tiptree and his family can take any moveables they wish. But they must all be removed from there and brought to comfortable but close confinement here before they are taken far away from the city. In the end, all will be well. This is for their own safety and for the enhancement of the countess's future plans, as well as protection against Clarence discovering the truth behind what happened to his henchmen in that murder chamber.' Urswicke undid his heavy money wallet and poured out the gold and silver coins taken from the Barnabites the previous evening. He pushed some of these across. 'That is for your troubles. So, to quote our mistress, if it's to be done, it's best done quickly. In the meantime . . .' Urswicke got to his feet.

'Where are you going, Christopher?'

'I deposited a book of hours with a goldsmith in Cheapside. I think it's best if I brought it here. You have a secure place?'

'Of course. An arca deep in the cellars.' Hempen grinned and ran a finger along the red rope mark which scorched his throat. 'Not even a rat could find it.'

'Good. I will not be long. Hire six veterans. Have them here, visored, cowled and armed with arbalests. However,' Urswicke went and stood over the landlord, 'no violence! They must act as if they are the masked retainers of Richard Duke of Gloucester. Two of them must also make loud reference to being involved in the destruction of the Barnabites out at St Vedast.'

'Oh yes, I've heard of that.'

'Never mind the details, gather your men. I must meet them cowled and visored here in this chamber.'

By the time Urswicke had returned to The Wyvern's Nest and placed the precious book of hours in the arca, Hempen had assembled six former soldiers skilled in dagger play and the use of both bow and arbalest. They gathered with head and faces hidden, dark shadows in the flickering light of the lanternhorn that Hempen placed at the centre of the table. Urswicke, his face also hidden, laid out some of the coins he had shown Hempen. He could tell from their sharp gasps that these men had never seen such wealth. Urswicke made them pledge their loyalty. After this was completed, he delivered his instructions, ensuring that they all understood.

Once the curfew bell had sounded and the belfry lights glowed from the city steeples, they would move to The Sunne in Splendour. Clarence had withdrawn his henchmen but Urswicke warned his coven they might have to deal with any guard or spy left to watch the tavern. Their first task was to assemble Tiptree and his entire household. They must also give the impression that they were Richard of Gloucester's men and let slip that they may have also been responsible for the destruction of St Vedast. On no account must they harm anyone, unless to defend themselves.

Once he had the confirmation of their agreement, Urswicke assured them they would be paid immediately on their return. The clerk left them in the chamber and went down to the arca; he wanted to make sure that the book of hours would remain safe and he'd glimpsed an entry on the inside of the front cover which had intrigued him. He was surprised that Mauclerc had left the book of hours in the chancery chamber but, there again, other items had been left and Mauclerc, hardly a man of prayer, would find nothing interesting in a psalter. Urswicke returned to Hempen and his party. They declared they were ready so Urswicke led them out into the street.

The night was dark, an ideal time for any ambuscade, the thin sliver of moon hidden by thick clouds. The city watch tramped the streets but they would have no quarrel with a group of well-armed men slipping through the dark. London was now occupied by the court and the city was accustomed to the great lords sending out their retainers to perform all sorts of tasks. Urswicke was confident that they would not be interfered with and they weren't. They reached The Sunne in Splendour and swiftly scaled the tavern wall, dropping down onto the cobbles. Of course the kennel dogs were aroused but, being fed juicy scraps of meat, were soon soothed and quietened. The men then hurried across to a narrow postern door leading to the kitchen and scraped on this. Urswicke held his breath as he heard stumbling footsteps. Again he scratched on the wood as if one of the kennel dogs had broken free and was clawing at the door. Bolts were drawn and a sleepy, heavy-eyed spit-boy. who slept beneath the kitchen table, opened the door and peered out.

Urswicke grabbed him, stifling his mouth and whispering that he would be safe as long as he kept quiet. The spit-boy nodded his agreement. Urswicke pushed him back into the kitchen, the others gathering around him. Urswicke swiftly established that there were no guests or any of Clarence's retainers present. He urged his followers, 'for the sake of their Lord Richard to be careful, as he did not wish a repetition of what had happened at St Vedast's'. At Urswicke's urging, Hempen and his men spread out through the tavern, securing the doors and bringing Minehost Tiptree, his family and servants down into the taproom. They huddled in a cowed, frightened group. Urswicke separated Tiptree and his family from the rest, who were taken to be held in the buttery. Once they had gone, Urswicke crouched before Tiptree, keeping both visor and hood covering his head and face.

'Listen Master Tiptree,' he urged, 'and heed my advice. If you do, you and your beloved,' he pointed at the landlord's wife who sat terrified beside her husband, 'I assure you,' Urswicke continued, 'will be taken to a place of safety. So first you must collect all your moveables, items you can easily carry: monies, precious objects. Go, do this now. We will look after your family until you return.'

Urswicke stretched out a hand and patted one of Tiptree's four children on his greasy head.

'Why?' Tiptree blurted out. 'Why all this? Who sent you?'

'I am your saviour, Master Tiptree,' Urswicke replied. 'You owe me your life and the lives of your family. You must accept that as God's own truth because, if my Lord of Clarence and his henchman Mauclerc discovered what you really did, you and your entire household would suffer the most excruciating deaths.'

Tiptree grew suitably frightened, very subdued. Urswicke realised he'd hit his mark. Tiptree did not bemoan his situation as he and his family were swiftly hustled out along the streets to The Wyvern's Nest. Indeed, over the next few days, the taverner fully reconciled himself to his fate. He soothed and comforted his family and fully cooperated with Urswicke and Hempen, even though he, his wife and children were confined to two chambers on the first gallery of The Wyvern's Nest. Urswicke suspected that Tiptree would become very aware that his captors knew the full truth about what had happened at The Sunne in Splendour. Tiptree would never plot to escape so Urswicke decided to leave Hempen in charge, instructing the landlord that Tiptree and his family must still be kept in close confinement; they must never see the faces of their captors or discover who was their principal abductor.

Satisfied and reassured, Urswicke returned to The Sunne in Splendour to find everything in confusion. The disappearance of Tiptree had caused the tavern to be closed, the servants being unable even to buy purveyance or, because of the rules of the guild, serve ales and wine. The tavern was barricaded up except for the side door through which Urswicke had entered on the night of the abduction. He went in along to the taproom. Mauclerc was there, his face mottled with fury.

'St Vedast has been razed to the ground,' he raged. 'The Barnabites who sheltered there are dead. God knows what happened to their possessions or what they hid away. The Three Kings lie murdered along with Oudenarde. Now Tiptree and his family have been abducted. I talked to the other servants and they claim my beloved brother, Richard of Gloucester's retainers were responsible,' he gestured around, 'for all this, as well as the destruction at St Vedast.'

'And the murders here.' Urswicke schooled his features into a frown, though in truth he was hiding his jubilation. The game had changed: this most sinister of henchmen was no longer its master, and neither was the dark-souled Clarence.

'I am sorry.' Mauclerc, one hand on the belt of his sword, the other on Urswicke's shoulder, almost dragged the clerk deeper into the taproom, away from the doorway and any eavesdropper, 'You have a suspect?' Mauclerc demanded.

'Of course, my Lord of Clarence's younger brother, it's obvious.'

Mauclerc let his hand fall away. 'Are you saying that Gloucester is behind everything?'

'Possibly.' Urswicke restrained the laughter bubbling within him, the sheer jubilation, so reminiscent of the excitement at his keenest games of hazard or his sharp debating as a scholar in the halls of Oxford.

'And you have proof of all this?' Mauclerc asked.

'Possibly, but I am gathering more as swiftly as I can.'

'Good, good.' Mauclerc patted Urswicke on the shoulder like some absent-minded magister would a not-so-bright scholar. 'My Lord of Clarence,' he continued, 'has moved to the King's palace at Sheen to discuss certain matters. Above all, the mischief being brewed by that holy dog the Lancastrian Archbishop Neville. There are also rumours of another traitor, De Vere of Oxford, leading a fleet of war cogs off the coast of Cornwall. So I must go there. To Sheen,' he joked, 'not Cornwall.' His smile faded. 'And you Christopher, you will resolve these mysteries?'

'You have my word.'

'Excellent. Well, until we meet again.'

Mauclerc was now in a better mood. He patted Urswicke on the shoulder and left the tavern, shouting for his retainers. Urswicke stood and heard them go. He felt pleased, confident that Clarence's henchman suspected nothing. He waited for a while then returned to The Wyvern's Nest. Hempen assured him that Tiptree and his family were isolated, safe and seemingly contented enough. Urswicke went up to his own garret where he took out that strip of parchment he'd found in one of the Three Kings' wallets. He sat down and studied this time and again. 'And the captain of archers,' Urswicke whispered to himself, 'lay

with the wife of Duke Uriah the Hittite and she conceived a son.'
Urswicke, who had studied the scriptures, recognised the reference was from the Old Testament. A story about King David
wishing to seduce Bathsheba, the wife of one of his principal
commanders, Uriah the Hittite. David became obsessed with the
woman. She became pregnant so David decided to remove Uriah,
instructing his general Joab to leave the Hittite exposed on the
field of battle. 'I know the story,' Urswicke murmured, 'but why
has it now changed? What could it mean?'

Urswicke returned to his scrutiny. He had graduated as a master
of the chancery, being closely instructed by the Dominican Albric
in secret ciphers and hidden writing. Albric had always insisted
on two principles. First, conceal what you want in public view
so clearly and precisely that people will never guess that what
they are looking at contains a whole wealth of hidden treasures.
Secondly, search for the pattern which should not really be a
pattern. For example, sentences will always begin with a certain
letter; their use is random depending on what's being written.
However, if certain letters are used to begin sentences time and
again, ask yourself why? 'So,' Urswicke whispered, studying the
script, 'what is being concealed here in public view and what
pattern can I detect?' He took out the book of hours and opened
it, turning the pages until his eyes grew heavy. He fell asleep for
at least an hour according to the flame on the red-ringed time
candle.

Urswicke roused himself and went downstairs to ensure all
was well. He took some food and drink and returned to his
studies. He examined once again the script containing the quota-
tion about Uriah. Holding it up to the light, the clerk noticed
how the beginning of certain passages in the book of hours, be
it psalms or prayers, had a different-coloured ink. For example,
'Pater Noster – Our Father' was written in red but the rest of the
script was in black. It was the same on the strip of parchment
where blue ink replaced black. Urswicke read the verse again
but, this time, moving from words written in black to the next
section written in black, so it read, 'And the captain of the archers
lay with the wife of the duke and she conceived a son.' That
made sense! Urswicke then applied the same technique to other
passages in both copies of the book of hours. Urswicke eventually

decided to write these out in his own abbreviated cipher. The more he transcribed, the more it made sense, and the secrets the Three Kings had disguised began to emerge. In a sense, it was very simple: the secrets were concealed in public view beneath a pattern of different-coloured inks. If certain sections were linked together, then the book of hours was no longer a psalter, a prayer book, but a treasury of scandalous stories about the House of York, King Edward in particular.

Urswicke felt deeply elated that he had stumbled onto such valuable findings. He now knew what Clarence was plotting. How that sinister prince had collected all the gossip, scandal and whispered secrets about his own house and handed these over to the Three Kings, who investigated them and discovered the evidence for a range of scurrilous allegations. 'Master Clarence,' Urswicke murmured, 'you have proven to be a foul son, a foul brother and a foul lord. A truly foulsome human being who will surely meet your death in a most violent way.'

Urswicke returned to the book of hours and re-read what he had glimpsed on the inside of the front cover of each psalter: the same inscription. Simple enough. '*Teste me*, Roberto Episcopo Bathoniense – witnessed by me Robert, Bishop of Bath and Wells.' Many psalters, prayer books and other devotional literature often contained such an inscription by the local bishop, which confirmed that the work in question contained no heresy or deviation from the liturgy of the church.

'But why,' Urswicke whispered, 'why is the name of Robert Stillington, Bishop of Bath and Wells, used here? According to canon law, such a declaration should be by the Ordinary, the bishop of the place where the book was created? In this case, the Bishop of London?'

Urswicke sat back in his chair. He was sure that the Three Kings and Oudenarde had no intention of handing the book of hours over to any bishop. So why use Stillington's name? Moreover, and Urswicke was sure of this, Stillington's name had been used without his permission. No, Urswicke concluded, the reason for Stillington's inclusion was that this bishop was connected to this mystery, Urswicke was certain of that. First, because of the location of Stillington's diocese, which was close to Shrewsbury, the ancestral home of the Talbots, whose kinswoman, Eleanor Butler, played – according to the secrets contained in the book of hours – such a prominent role in all these mysteries. Urswicke shook his head, marvelling at how the twisting path of life could be dictated by a dead woman. How a former lover of the great Edward of York could stretch from beyond the grave to cause deep dissent and the most dangerous rent in the body politic. If the secrets Urswicke had just read in the book of hours were proclaimed to the world, it would rock the throne and nullify Edward of York's recent triumph.

Secondly, Urswicke returned to the question of Stillington. He had allowed the Barnabites to travel in and out of the country on their own whim. Why? What did the Barnabites know about Stillington? And this business of Brother Joachim, the Barnabite sheltering in St Mary's Bethlehem? Why did Stillington agree to that, being prepared to pay all the expenses for such comfortable lodgings? Cuthbert must have threatened the good bishop. Urswicke wondered if he should use both his name and warrants to seek an interview with Stillington, but he concluded that would be too dangerous. God knows where Stillington's true loyalty lay and, for his own secret purposes, the good bishop would only lie, deceive and mislead. Moreover, Stillington must be aware of the destruction and deaths at St Vedast. Brother Cuthbert was now dead. Would Stillington continue to pay for Brother Joachim to be lodged at St Mary's? Stillington surely must have some idea, proof or evidence, that what Urswicke had discovered in the book of hours was true, hence the phrase 'Teste me – witnessed by me.' What form that evidence took would be difficult to establish. Urswicke made his decision. He must visit St Mary's Bethlehem, and the sooner the better.

Urswicke arrived before the main gate of St Mary's Bethlehem late in the afternoon, when the bells of its church were ringing out the summons to early evening prayer. A lay brother, garbed in a cream-coloured robe and black mantle, the hospital colours, scrutinised Urswicke's warrants and seals before admitting him through the postern gate. He led the clerk through the gardens and into the prior's parlour, which stood within the entrance to the main building. A comfortable, well-furnished chamber with its polished oak work, turkey rugs and vivid wall frescoes depicting scenes of healing from the Scriptures.

Urswicke sat down, savouring the pleasant smells after the stench of the busy city streets, where the air hung heavy with human sweat, ordure and all the reek of the middens. This was such a contrast, a veritable paradise; sweet cooking smells mingling with the fragrance of incense and beeswax. Urswicke closed his eyes and relaxed, only to be abruptly startled as the parlour door opened and closed with a slam. Urswicke rose to greet Prior Augustine; a tall, forbidding figure garbed in cream and black robes, his long, thin neck and sharp, bony face gave the impression of a bird; a likeness enhanced by his rather jerky movements as he allowed Urswicke to kiss his ring of office before sketching a hasty benediction above Urswicke's bowed head. He waved the clerk back to his chair as he sat down in the one opposite. Urswicke handed over his warrants and seals. The prior studied these, gave a half-smile and handed them back.

'Well, well, well,' the prior raised his head, 'no lesser person than the son of the great Recorder of London, the hero of the hour, a veritable Horatius who stood in the breach and defended the city against hordes of rebels.' Urswicke smiled at the gentle sarcasm in the prior's voice. 'You are also, apparently, a favoured henchman of my Lord of Clarence. Well,' the prior rubbed his hands together, 'you want my help and I am willing to assist. So what is your business, sir?'

'Joachim the Barnabite lodged here at the request, and probable expense, of Robert Stillington, Bishop of Bath and Wells and our present Lord Chancellor . . .'

The change in Prior Augustine's demeanour was startling. He leaned forward, mouth gaping, face full of fear. 'How do you know . . .?' He paused. 'That fire, those deaths out at St Vedast on the moor. You . . .'

'I know of them,' Urswicke retorted, 'but I was not involved. I was informed about Joachim from another source which will remain nameless. After all, as you say,' he bluffed, 'my redoubtable father is a Lord High Recorder of the city, whilst I am the Duke of Clarence's most trusted henchman.'

'And that of the Countess Margaret Beaufort?' Prior Augustine quickly recovered his poise, staring curiously at Urswicke. 'I have heard of you, and about you, Master Christopher. You live in a very dangerous world.'

'Oh yes,' Urswicke quipped, 'as the poet says, in the midst of life we are in death.'

'True, true,' Prior Augustine agreed.

'Joachim?' Urswicke pointed to the hour candle under its cap on a stand in the corner of the chamber. 'The hours are passing, darkness will soon be here.'

'If it's not already,' the prior murmured. He took a deep breath. 'Joachim was lodged here some time ago at the personal request and expense of Bishop Robert, who demanded that I keep the lodging confidential. He even asked me to take a vow promising I would.' The prior sniffed noisily. 'I refused. We lodge many unfortunates who suffer a collapse of the humours in both mind and soul. Men and women who are deeply disturbed. I informed the bishop that St Mary's was not a prison or a hiding place but a hospice for the sick. I accepted Brother Joachim because he was religious, a sick man and, I will be honest, the full expense of his stay here was to be met by Bishop Robert.'

'I need to meet Brother Joachim. I must speak to him. My visit here and my conversation must be kept confidential under the seal, yes?' Urswicke stretched out his hand, Prior Augustine clasped it and nodded. 'Is he lucid?'

'At times, but at others he becomes witless. He rambles, mumbling one nonsense after another. On a few occasions he claims to know great secrets, about the King and his court. He chatters about furtive alliances and illicit affiances. But,' Prior Augustine shrugged, 'we have patients who declare they really are the Holy Father or the great Cham of Tartary. Some of our inmates maintain that every night they fly to the far side of the moon and see the Hosts of Hell gather for a feast. Others confess to have seen battle fleets of demons cluster to the north of Bishopsgate. Indeed, Brother Joachim is, perhaps, one of the more lucid amongst our congregation.'

'Do you know why Bishop Stillington should care for a poor Barnabite?'

'Of course not, but I can speculate. Stillington is a shepherd who cares more for the fleece than his flock. A man of power, of wealth and status. He claimed that Brother Joachim was a very distant relative, I doubt that. So, to answer your question, Master Christopher, logic dictates that our poor Barnabite knows something highly embarrassing and possibly very dangerous to our good bishop. He has been lodged here not because of any compassion but due to the insistence of Joachim's superior, or so he calls himself, Brother Cuthbert. Master Christopher,' Prior Augustine pulled a face, 'I haven't the faintest idea what is behind all this and, to be honest, I don't really care. Such knowledge can be highly perilous. I do not wish to become involved in the filthy politics of the court or the city.'

'Does Joachim have many visitors?'

'Very few. Bishop Stillington rarely, a fleeting visit to ensure all is well.'

'Anyone else?'

'Brother Cuthbert, of course, the self-styled leader of the Barnabites.' Prior Augustine swallowed hard. 'Cuthbert was a Rhinelander. I suspect that he was a former mercenary who served on the Eastern March, the antechamber of Hell. He would come here with his hard-faced companions. He would leave these in our guesthouse so he could converse in confidence with his old friend and comrade Brother Joachim. I did not like Cuthbert at all. He had an aura of fear about him, a midnight soul; dark, sinister and secretive. All a great mystery then?'

'Aye and at the heart of it, Prior, is this question. Why should Bishop Stillington dance attendance on a poor Barnabite? After all, our good bishop has the power and the means to arrange some sort of mishap, an accident. Prior Augustine, this is London. Corpses float in the Thames, cadavers are to be found in lay stalls or at the mouth of some stinking alleyway. I would wager at least a dozen have been killed today in some sort of accident.'

'The answer to your question is simple,' Prior Augustine retorted. 'Joachim may hold secrets but he undoubtedly shared these with Brother Cuthbert who, in turn, has made it very clear to Bishop Stillington that he is also privy to highly contentious information which will remain secret as long as our bishop cares for Brother Joachim, Cuthbert and his ilk.'

Urswicke nodded in agreement. He had to be more prudent: he had almost stumbled into mentioning the licences and bulging purses he'd found out at St Vedast. He now knew the source of these: Cuthbert was a blackmailer and Stillington was his victim.

'As I said, Master Christopher,' the prior spoke up, 'it's a dangerous world. The psalmist is correct, nothing lasts under the sun. Life changes. The great fire at St Vedast is well known throughout the city and Fickle Fortune has given her wheel another spin. Yesterday evening the bishop's courier arrived to announce that tomorrow the bishop intends to return to his diocese. He has decided to take Brother Joachim with him to what he called "even more comfortable lodgings". In a sense, the courier was speaking the truth. You and I, Master Christopher, know that Joachim is being taken away to be silenced and swiftly despatched to the mansions of eternity.' The prior rose to his feet. 'I doubt very much whether our poor Barnabite will live to welcome midsummer.' The prior stared down at Urswicke. 'You may talk to him. Oh, by the way, Joachim has a passion for the creamiest cheese. Remember that.' He extended his hand for Christopher to kiss his ring. Again the prior blessed him. 'Brother Joachim,' he murmured, 'will also need all the prayers we can say for him. Two lay brothers will bring him here and stand on guard outside. Speak, have your words and then be gone.'

Urswicke was surprised at the appearance of Brother Joachim, who strode manfully into the parlour and jerked a bow at Urswicke before thanking the two lay brothers who had escorted him in. Once they'd left, Joachim, all bustling and friendly, sat down on the chair that Prior Augustine had vacated and beamed at Urswicke.

'Very rare to have visitors,' the Barnabite whispered. 'Prior Augustine told me who you are.' He extended a hand for Urswicke to clasp. The clerk did so, feeling the calluses on the Barnabite's coarse skin. 'I was a ploughboy once,' Joachim exclaimed, 'I could dig the straightest furrow and harrow the coarsest ground.' He withdrew his hand and stared at it. 'Came from south Yorkshire I did. A village close to Pontefract. Served as a soldier beyond the Narrow Seas where I met Cuthbert and the rest. We grew tired of fighting, so we followed Cuthbert into the Barnabite order.' Joachim tapped the cream robe and black mantle. 'These are the colours of St Mary's. I really should be wearing brown and blue.'

Urswicke nodded smilingly, studying Joachim, his thin, greying hair neatly tonsured, his ploughboy features, round and red-cheeked, his pointed chin unshaven. The Barnabite seemed clear-eyed enough, though Urswicke noticed how Joachim's face grew momentarily slack, mouth gaping, eyes fluttering, as if he was confused by where he was. He sat, hands on knees, smiling at Urswicke before glancing around the parlour. He pointed to a triptych celebrating the life of St Martin. 'That's beautiful!' he exclaimed. He was about to point at another painting but paused and turned to Urswicke. 'You want to see me, sir?'

'Yes, yes I do.' Urswicke dug into his wallet and took out a silver coin, pleased at Joachim's reaction. The Barnabite leaned forward, hands extended, but Urswicke shook his head. 'Not yet, but I could leave this with Prior Augustine. I could ask him to buy you the creamiest cheese, freshly baked manchet thickly buttered and a deep-bowled goblet of Bordeaux.' Joachim licked his lips, one hand going out towards the coin which Urswicke placed on the table beside him.

'Why do you offer that?'

'For what you know. Why are you here, Joachim? Why does the Bishop of Bath and Wells protect and cherish you here in such comfortable quarters?'

'Aye, and he has promised to take me to more suitable accommodation.'

'But why should he do that?'

The Barnabite's head went down.

'Cheese,' Urswicke whispered, 'the richest you have ever eaten?'

The Barnabite swiftly crossed himself and glanced up.

'Because I saw it.' Joachim was almost gabbling. 'I was there, about five summers ago in the chapel of Shrewsbury Castle. Bishop Stillington summoned me. At the time I was a wandering friar, a hedge priest begging for alms on behalf of my brothers, despatched by Cuthbert, our Father Guardian. I sheltered in the castle. Bishop Stillington got to know I was there. Oh yes, I was sitting in the refectory. The cook had cut me some cheese. The bishop's retainers arrived. They had made enquiries amongst those flocking into the castle. Anyway, they called my name and I was taken up to the chapel.'

'In Shrewsbury Castle?'

'That's what I said. I will be given the cheese?'

'Of course, but you must fulfil your part of the bargain.'

'I was taken to the castle chapel, the King was there.'

'Henry of Lancaster?'

'No, no not him. The young blond-haired sprig of York. I've seen him as he has passed through the city.'

'King Edward?'

'The same. He was in the chapel with the young woman, standing at the foot of the steps leading up into the sanctuary.'

'And who else was there?'

'King Edward and Bishop Stillington and, of course, the young woman. Fair she was, fresh and wholesome, like the dawn. Edward pledged his troth to her and she to him.'

'Surely,' Urswicke urged, though he already suspected the truth, 'that must have been Elizabeth Woodville: there are stories that Edward of York met her secretly?'

'No, no. This was Eleanor Butler. You see, I had to ask her name. Bishop Stillington made me officiate at the troth pledge. Oh yes he did. Can I have the cheese?'

'Soon.' Urswicke picked up the coin and twirled it through his fingers. 'You blessed both the King and this woman, then sanctified the troth pledge? Were there any records kept? Did you have to sign a document?'

'Yes, yes there was, on a green baize-coloured table to the right of the King. I am not too sure what it said but I scrawled my mark. Bishop Stillington wrote in the rest.'

'And?' Urswicke insisted.

'I was dismissed.' Joachim's face went slack, lips gaping, eyelids fluttering.

'And what happened then?'

'I returned to my wandering. I fell sick and Cuthbert looked after me. Strange, you see, I felt guilty about the troth pledge.'

'Did the King say anything to you?'

'No, both he and the lady acted as if they could not even see me. Master, I am one of the little ones. To the great lords I am nothing but a speck of dust, yet I know what I witnessed. I later realised that Edward of York did not honour his vow, becoming hand-fast with the Woodville woman, as Cuthbert calls her.' Joachim paused, eyes half closed. 'I wonder when Cuthbert will visit me again. I am not too sure whether he will be pleased at me being taken to fresh lodgings.'

'Ah yes, Cuthbert – does he often visit you here?'

'Of course. I confessed to Cuthbert all that I had seen in Shrewsbury Castle. Cuthbert is a good father to me. True, he could be violent, but he was the only person who cared for me. He was astonished at what I told him. He insisted that we travel to Bishop Stillington's manor outside Wells. Cuthbert told him what I had witnessed. The bishop was angry and surprised but Cuthbert said he would lodge this mystery elsewhere in case anything happened to him or to me. He insisted that the bishop look after me. He repeated that if any harm befell him or me, he would publish what he knew. The good bishop agreed. I was sent here and Cuthbert rejoined his other brothers, Rhinelanders like himself. I was the only English-born amongst them. I later learnt that Cuthbert was assisting others in some great enterprise. He talked of clerks and a book-seller.'

'The Three Kings and their associate Oudenarde?'

'Yes, yes that's it but,' Joachim's voice turned to a whine, 'I know nothing of their business.' He held out a hand. 'Master, the coin . . .'

Urswicke rose and went across. 'You can tell me nothing else?'

'No, Master, and I am becoming confused.' Joachim stared fearfully around. 'I would like to buy some cheese, I need wine.'

Urswicke pressed the coin into Joachim's hand. He then leaned down and gently kissed the Barnabite on the brow. 'God save you,' he whispered, 'God bless you on your journey.'

'And you be safe on yours. Be wary of the Watchers.'

Urswicke spun round and came back. Joachim held up the coin. 'You are so kind,' he murmured, 'you gave poor Joachim this for creamy cheese . . .'

'The Watchers?' Urswicke declared.

'Two brothers,' Joachim half smiled, 'fellow Barnabites, Rhinelanders, Odo and Bruno. Two of Cuthbert's most trusted henchmen. He informed me how they would keep close guard on St Mary's Bethlehem. They would keep sharp watch over those who came to see me, if anyone did. They are what they appear to be, begging friars, well known to those who live here. They do occasional work as lay brothers, gardeners, cleaning latrines and other such tasks.' Joachim pulled a face and stared greedily at the coin which he balanced in the palm of his hand. 'So God keep you safe, Master.'

Urswicke left St Mary's to make his way back to The Sunne in Splendour. He moved purposefully through the gathering dark, aware of the shadow-dwellers and night-walkers who clustered in the narrow doorways either side. Urswicke drew his sword and the sinister figures melted away. Now and again Urswicke would pause and stare back. He would linger in the entrances of shadowy alehouses. At first he could detect nothing amiss but, on one occasion, he glimpsed a darting figure, a shape of a man who moved swiftly back into the darkness. Urswicke walked on. He paused at the mouth of an alleyway, a thin ribbon of blackness with only one lanternhorn further down, glinting through the murk. Urswicke turned into this and ran as fast as he could before darting into a narrow enclave where he stood, sword and dagger at the ready. He heard footsteps, muttered curses. He tensed, sword and dagger at the ready. Two shadows passed the enclave. Urswicke slipped out, tapping his sword against the ground.

'Good evening, gentlemen, can I help you?'

His pursuers turned; one carried a club, the other a sword and dagger. One assailant didn't wait but lunged forward. Urswicke sidestepped, his assailant was no skilled street fighter but a lumbering oaf who paid for his mistake as Urswicke pierced his throat. The man fell to his knees, gargling. Urswicke kicked him over as he turned, dancing towards his second attacker, moving sword and dagger which caught the light of the distant lanternhorn, a shimmer of glittering steel in the darkness. Urswicke drove his opponent back. The man stumbled, dropped his club and held up his hands.

'Mercy,' he whispered hoarsely. 'Mercy indeed. I do not know who you are. Odo and I,' he gestured at the man who now lay sprawled in a pool of his own heart's blood, 'we worked at St Mary's as labourers, gardeners, we earned a penny and were given a crust. No one was interested in us. We heard you had visited Joachim, so we followed: that's what Cuthbert ordered us to do.' Again he flapped his hands. 'I ask for mercy; we were only following orders, even though Cuthbert is dead. Were you involved in that?'

Urswicke lowered both sword and dagger then sheathed his weapons. 'Your name is Bruno?'

'It is. I am a Barnabite. Will you not show me mercy, sir?'

Urswicke stepped closer, peering through the murk. 'I will grant you mercy,' he said, 'on two conditions. First, you return to St Mary's. Tell Prior Augustine I sent you.' Urswicke felt in his purse, took out two coins and handed them over. 'Take this and whatever you can find on your fallen comrade here. Fetch Joachim out of St Mary's and flee the kingdom. I am certain you are skilled enough in that already.'

'We have monies hidden away.'

'I am sure you have. However, for your sake and that of Joachim, put as much distance as you can between yourselves and this city. Be especially wary of anyone sent by the Bishop of Bath and Wells. Repeat that title.' The Barnabite did so. 'If you linger,' Urswicke warned, 'both you and Joachim will surely die. Now be gone. So,' Urswicke gestured at the fallen man, 'take what you need.'

The Barnabite hastily complied and, muttering his thanks, fled back down the runnel. Urswicke watched him go. He knew Prior Augustine would help both Barnabites. Bruno would take Joachim into his care and immediately secure passage on some cog across the Narrow Seas. Sooner or later, he reasoned, Joachim, in a period of lucidity, would tell Bruno the same he learnt earlier that day. Urswicke didn't care. He hadn't the heart to kill such an unfortunate, whilst Bruno and Joachim would eventually sell what they knew to someone abroad and, if scandal about the House of York began to seep through the courts of Europe, then all to the good.

Urswicke returned to The Wyvern's Nest, making sure he wasn't followed. He ate and drank, washed, shaved and changed into fresh linen, constantly reflecting on what he should do. He had scrutinised both copies of the book of hours so he decided he would carry out a thorough transcription of the secret chronicle concealed within its lines. In the end, it took him four days, during which Countess Margaret and Bray sent him cryptic messages. Urswicke ignored these until he had finished completely; he then replied, inviting the countess and Bray to the solar in the house opposite The Wyvern's Nest. He also issued instructions that Hempen make ready to bring Minehost Tiptree across when Urswicke asked for him. Hempen was mystified by what was happening; however he was also very aware of Urswicke's standing with the countess, not to mention the clerk's largesse with the few remaining coins taken from the Barnabites, so he heartily agreed.

Once Countess Margaret and Bray arrived and were ensconced in comfortable chairs, Urswicke poured pots of light ale and joined them around the table. For a while the conversation was desultory, until there was a knock on the door and Hempen, who'd received Urswicke's instruction, brought Tiptree into the chamber. The former landlord, pale-faced and trembling, took the other chair; he sat down, hands on knees, staring at the floor. He then looked beseechingly up at Urswicke.

'Master Hempen,' he murmured, 'told me all about the abduction at my tavern . . .'

'Yes, yes. I asked him to.'

Urswicke glanced swiftly at Countess Margaret; she continued to act composed, a slight smile on her face, her eyes holding that mischievous look which made her seem so much younger. Bray, however, was clearly discomforted, staring into his tankard as he tried to avoid Urswicke's gaze. The silence deepened until Urswicke believed he had the full attention of everyone sitting around that table.

'Master Thomas Tiptree,' Urswicke began, 'taverner, landlord, mine generous host, formerly of Lord Clarence's household, a man of deep and wide experience in the bakery, brewery, buttery and kitchen of that so-called nobleman. Master Tiptree, you eventually left Clarence's service and, with the monies you'd earned and lodged with a Cheapside merchant, you bought The Sunne in Splendour. The tavern sign is a sop to the House of York which has the sun amongst its many family emblems and insignia. You began with high expectations but times were very hard. The unrest in the shires spread into London. Foreigners decided to stay away. Domestic merchants did not regard lodgings in the city as safe. In brief, you did not make the profits you hoped for and you swiftly sank into a quagmire of debt. Your creditors, the powerful city merchants, forced closure and you were placed into the debtors' side of the Fleet Prison. Your tavern was sealed shut, no Tiptree, no servants, nothing. God knows what happened to your poor family.'

'Relations,' Tiptree murmured, 'my wife has kin in the shires.'

'Wretched people,' Urswicke continued, 'certainly no one to help debt-stricken Tiptree languishing along the filthy corridors and cells of the Fleet. A place of deep darkness, brutality and the most hideous conditions. Imprisoned there, you spent precious pennies writing letters begging for help, redress to the Guildhall. I have seen such documentation. You pleaded for your petition to be forwarded to your former lord and master, George of Clarence. No one replied, at least nobody I could discover. Clarence certainly didn't. He never came to your help; he ignored you, didn't he? Didn't he?' Urswicke repeated. 'True or false?'

'True.'

'Hapless Tiptree, deserted by all, forsaken by your former lord. You then petitioned Sir Humphrey Stafford, my Lady's husband, a man noted for his dedication to the poor, the leader of a group of city notables committed to helping those in debt – yes, my Lady?' Margaret just smiled, a look of pride, as if Urswicke was proving the trust and confidence she had placed in him. 'You, Mistress, took up Tiptree's cause. You saw him as a possible path into the councils of your sworn enemy Clarence. Tiptree's debts were paid and cancelled. More followed. Grants of money to reopen, refurbish and replenish The Sunne in Splendour, all quietly done. I have personally seen the evidence for this in your accounts, Master Bray, and you know the reason why. Due to our mistress's help, Tiptree emerged as a prosperous landlord, the owner of a magnificent hostelry at the very heart of the city. He offered its services to you, my Lady, but you quietly insisted that Tiptree show such generosity to his former master Clarence.'

Urswicke sipped at his ale. 'Now that lord is as arrogant as Lucifer. He would forget his former neglect of you and take such an offer as if it was his birthright, his God-given due. He would use such a place as yours as his own personal hostelry. Of course, he would never offer even a farthing in return. Yes?' Tiptree nodded mournfully. 'But you, my Lady,' Urswicke turned to Margaret, 'continued to secretly subsidise The Sunne in Splendour. You saw it as a squint-hold, a gap in the defences of your mortal enemy. Tiptree here would pour the wine and ale, have the tables groaning under platters of delicious food. Of course, when the drink flows, so does the conversation. Hence the well-known saying "*in vino veritas* – wine always brings out the truth". Tiptree, of course, would faithfully report whatever he saw or heard. He would have to do it discreetly. Clarence may be arrogant, but Mauclerc is as cunning and as vicious as a weasel.'

'I didn't learn very much,' Tiptree broke in. He gestured at Lady Margaret. 'You know, indeed we all do, how secretive Mauclerc is, whilst those other demons the Three Kings were no better. I tried to discover why they were so close, so mysterious in all their comings and goings. Those strangers who visited them wrapped like friars in cloaks and cowls. I wanted to eavesdrop but, Master Christopher, you have seen my tavern, the doors are thick wedges of wood. One time I did listen when the door was off the latch but, of course, they were speaking in their native tongue which, I suspect, they did all the time.'

'I agree,' Urswicke declared. 'You made little progress, which is why you were drawn into a much more devious and dangerous plot. The complete destruction of the Three Kings and Oudenarde, their associate. You were partial to that weren't you? You took up the drugged wine and you set the stage for the bloody masque which followed. You carefully plotted so that the chancery chamber become a murder room – not that you were actively involved in their deaths, only in their preparation. You see,' Urswicke shifted in his chair and held Tiptree's gaze, ignoring Lady Margaret's smile, 'the chief perpetrator was no less a person than my good friend and colleague, Master Reginald Bray: a man who acts as a clerk, a steward, a quiet household man. However, appearances can be deceptive. I began to recall Master Bray's history, snatches of gossip and comments by himself and others. A true dagger man Master Bray.' Urswicke paused.

'Christopher, Christopher,' Countess Margaret stretched out a hand, 'you are sharp and swift. I wagered you would plumb this mystery.' She glanced at Bray who wanted to speak. 'No, Reginald, let Christopher tell us how he reached his conclusions. We must know what they are and so judge if Clarence and Mauclerc, who also possess considerable cunning, have not reached a similar solution. I pray to God they have not. Christopher, continue.'

'From the very start,' Urswicke returned to his account, 'I did wonder. The destruction of the Three Kings and Oudenarde was a most deadly body blow to Clarence and his schemes: his Secret Chancery was annihilated; it would take months, if not years, for him to reassemble it. If we regard Clarence as a wheel, the Three Kings were the hub. Consequently, I am also certain that the murder of the Three Kings at The Sunne in Splendour proved to be a source of great comfort to his brothers and, indeed, many members of the court who hate or resent Clarence. I doubt very much if anyone, apart from their master, will mourn their passing.' Urswicke lifted his tankard and silently toasted Tiptree.

'And so I turn to the actual circumstances of their deaths. First, I thought it was singular that the evening chosen for their execution was also the evening they were visited by the parchment-seller Oudenarde. Few people would know about such a guest, only Mauclerc, the Three Kings, and of course the tavern master, who would be informed as a matter of routine. In addition, Clarence and Mauclerc's absence from the city meant there was no danger of their involvement, though I am certain that you would have ensured that any unexpected change could be managed. Nevertheless, while the cat's away, the mice do play and, as I will demonstrate, there was a considerable gap in time between the fate of the Three Kings being known and that news being communicated to Clarence and Mauclerc, dancing attendance on their King at Westminster. So, we have the Three Kings and Oudenarde in one place at the one time. Clarence's Secret Chancery was to be totally annihilated. No survivors, just bloody mayhem to create complete chaos, deepen the confusion, and so prevent Clarence from continuing to plot silently and smoothly. Secondly, the deaths themselves in that sealed chamber? Its door, the only possible entrance, was locked and bolted from the inside with no sign of disturbance, even though the four victims had drawn their daggers, nothing else.' Urswicke gave a sharp bark of laughter. 'Think of it, four men with their throats neatly slit in such a place in such a way? No, no, the only conclusion I could reach was that the truth behind this mystery play had been cleverly concealed. I don't believe that the door's locks and bolts were all ruptured when the chamber was broken into. Nor did those four men willingly offer their throats to be cut.'

Urswicke paused. 'This is what really happened. Master Bray and you, Tiptree, plotted to kill all four. You chose an evening when Oudenarde would be with the Three Kings, and their masters some distance away. Minehost, here, took up a jug of his best claret and four goblets. He wanted to give his guests something special to drink, the finest Bordeaux, albeit heavily laced with a powerful sleeping potion.'

'And how was that done?' the countess demanded.

'Master Bray entered the tavern kitchens and buttery in disguise, dressed as a scullion, hired cheaply to perform menial tasks around the hostelry. A common enough occurrence. In your busy kitchens and buttery, Master Tiptree, Bray would hardly be given a second thought or glance. Anyway, to return to the chancery chamber. You poured the claret and invited all four to sip and taste. Hungry and thirsty, they do so, looking forward to the delicacies you promised to bring up. You leave and your victims sup deeply on the rich, red wine. You hurry down to the kitchen and fill a platter with the remains of bread and chicken, a jug of ordinary Bordeaux and four fresh goblets into which you pour some of the wine from the jug. You and the disguised Master Bray now return to the chancery chamber. All four men have fallen into a deep, drugged sleep. You exchange both the goblets and jug, leaving the fresh wine and scraps of food so it would appear that the Three Kings and their visitor had eaten and drank but nothing to provoke any suspicion. Am I not correct, Master Tiptree?'

'Oh you are so right,' the taverner blurted back; anger had now replaced his mournful look. 'Believe me, Master Christopher, I rejoiced in their deaths. I served Clarence for a year and many a day. I was a faithful retainer. I created delicacies for his table and did my very best to ensure all was good. I saved my monies, lodged them with a goldsmith. I left Clarence's household with high hopes. But, as you said, times were hard.' Tiptree shook off Bray's restraining hand. 'No, it's important. I want to tell the truth because they deserved to die. I did petition Clarence for help and assistance. He did not reply. He did not help. Later I found out that the Three Kings used to mock my letters as if they were mummery, the stories of a jester.' He shook his head. 'Rest assured, Master Christopher, it was no mummery. I was lodged in the debtors' side of the Fleet where you daren't even sleep. The rats are as large as cats, filthy food, rancid meat, brackish water. Violence and terror stalk you on every side. Master Urswicke, I am a cook not a felon. But there was worse. My wife and children were terrified, forced to beg for help from flint-hearted relatives. My wife was big with child. We lost it. The fear and hardship tipped her wits for a while.' He crossed himself and gestured at Countess Margaret. 'She saved me. In fact she redeemed us all. I tried to perform good service for her but the Three Kings proved to be a quarry impossible to pursue. Do you know, now and again, they would rub salt in the wounds, make sarcastic references about my letters begging for help from their master? So when Master Bray asked to meet me in some lonely tavern down by the quayside, I accepted. And, when he told me what he plotted, I heartily agreed. It was I who discovered the best day for our vengeance. Mauclerc and Clarence were at Westminster and Oudenarde was about to visit The Sunne in Splendour. I served the food and the drink as you say.' Tiptree paused, lips still moving, as if still talking to himself.

'You served the drugged wine,' Urswicke agreed. 'Master Bray then carried out what you,' he pointed at the steward, 'and our mistress,' Urswicke emphasised the last words, 'regarded as lawful execution. To deepen the mystery and widen the confusion, you, Master Bray, drew the daggers of all four men and slit their throats as swiftly and as soundlessly as Master Tiptree would a chicken breast. Once completed, you surveyed the room. You are looking for anything suspicious. You hoped to find the "Titulus Regius", but of course you didn't. You scrutinised the documents on the chancery table. You did not discover anything of real importance, except for that licence issued to Spysin, authorising him on behalf of Clarence to travel to Duke Francis of Brittany. You realise what mischief was brewing. Clarence was determined to suborn Duke Francis and arrange for the forced return of Henry Tudor, the claimant to the Crown. You, Master Reginald, realised what was being plotted. You and Tiptree then left that chamber, but not before buckling and rupturing the lock as well as the bolts at the top and bottom of the door so it would look as if they had been forced. Any further work on them could take place on the morrow when you, Master Tiptree, returned ostensibly to discover what was wrong. On that evening, however, you simply locked the door from the outside and went down to the taproom. During the night, you'd keep a sharp eye on those stairs, as well as tell your porter to alert you if any unexpected visitors arrive. Nothing alarming occurred. The next morning – well, you know what happened. The doorway was forced, the key slipped back into the lock, the corpses were viewed and urgent messages despatched to Clarence and Mauclerc. Of course, you'd realise it would take time for such news to reach them and for them to return.' Urswicke smiled. 'Very clever. You were given fresh opportunity to deepen the mystery and cloud the truth. True?'

'True,' Tiptree agreed. 'I advised Master Bray to stay well away from the tavern. When we did force the chamber, I ushered those who had helped me out and studied the room most carefully. There was nothing amiss; nothing which would point the finger of suspicion at either me or mine. Before Master Bray left, he asked about Spysin and I provided him with a clear description of Clarence's courier.'

'Of course you did,' Urswicke exclaimed. 'Master Bray, you had Spysin marked down for death. He was a bully boy, puffed up with arrogance, walking about all buckled and prepared for his so-called important mission. Reginald, you followed Spysin down to that dingy tavern on the quayside. You approached him and poured a potion into his drink. God knows how you did, but you are skilled enough, right? Spysin felt unwell. He hurried out to the jake's cupboard and slumped on the latrine. He was weak, perhaps even asleep, but he could offer no defence when you opened the latrine door, cut his throat and took whatever he carried in his wallet. Spysin would not be boarding any ship to carry out a Yorkist enterprise against Henry Tudor. In a sense, a good day's work. Clarence's Secret Chancery utterly destroyed and the mischief he intended in Brittany brought to nothing. Am I correct, Mistress?'

'Christopher, you are. You have spoken the truth but it must be put within the context of my world. First.' Margaret folded back the cuffs of her gown, a mannerism she always adopted when describing something important. 'First, I, we, are dedicated to opposing this usurpation of the Crown by the House of York and, in particular, the personal malice of Clarence. We will weaken them by each and every way possible. There are no exceptions. You personally witnessed the bloodshed after Tewkesbury. Edward of York intends to annihilate all opposition and we must defend ourselves as well as weaken our opponents by any means. This is not just a matter of a cause. Edward and his brothers are a direct threat to me as well as the life and legitimate ambitions of my darling son.' Margaret's face grew tight with anger. 'We all know Clarence, if given the slightest opportunity, will kill my Henry.' Margaret's head went down. She drew out a set of ave beads from her belt purse, lacing them around her fingers. 'Secondly, I was horrified to hear how the so-called Three Kings treated the sacred corpse of a truly anointed, saintly monarch, as if he was nothing more than offal on a flesher's stall outside Newgate. They committed the most heinous treason and abominable sacrilege. They deserved to die, as do Clarence and Mauclerc. Judgement against them has only been postponed, not cancelled. They perpetrated the most sordid sacrilege.' Margaret paused and used the small napkin Bray offered to wipe the spittle from the corner of her mouth.

'You are correct, my friend.' Bray had now broken from his reverie; he got to his feet and extended his hand. Urswicke rose to clasp it. Bray beat his breast in mock contrition. 'I was responsible. Spysin entered that tavern. I managed to slip a potion into his wine. He felt unwell and stumbled out to the jakes. I followed and pulled open the door. Spysin was fast asleep. He hardly moved as I slit his throat. I took his warrants, licences, money, and left. Clarence will be wary of sending further messages to Brittany.'

'The cracks in the Yorkist supremacy are beginning to widen.' Margaret spoke up. 'I have news for you, Christopher, on this very issue. Gloucester has promised that if we help him with the "Titulus Regius", he will use his influence with Edward so that my beloved son will be allowed to reside safely in exile in Brittany. Now,' Margaret crossed herself, 'my poor husband, Sir Humphrey, lies ill. I must leave soon to visit him as the messages

I have received indicate he will not recover.' She shook her head. 'I know it sounds cold and unloving, but that is the truth. I have tried to be a good, faithful and supportive wife to Sir Humphrey. I have tended to all his ailments and done my very best to make him as comfortable as possible.' Margaret shook her head. 'God bless him and me, but I married Sir Humphrey not just because of any feeling for him but because of the world I live in. To put it bluntly, I married Sir Humphrey Stafford for protection. When he dies, I will be bereft of that protection. I shall be regarded as the widowed Beaufort woman. I have to defend myself,' she gestured around, 'and those I love, especially my son.' She took a deep breath. 'And so I come to the second part of Gloucester's proposal. If we succeed in handing over the "Titulus Regius" to him, after Sir Humphrey dies, Gloucester will press his brother the King that I be allowed to marry Lord William Stanley, a powerful northern lord who would certainly provide protection against Clarence's malice.' She paused as Urswicke whistled softly.

'That fits well,' he murmured, 'with the tapestry we weave.'

'Now, back to the present matters. What else, Christopher?'

'You,' Urswicke pointed at Tiptree, 'will have to disappear, along with your family.'

'I will help.' Margaret stretched out and grasped Tiptree's hand. 'I shall, through merchant friends in the city, arrange for The Sunne in Splendour to be sold back to the Guild of Vintners.'

'Wouldn't the Yorkist lords discover that?' Bray demanded.

'No, no. Sir Humphrey Stafford's people will make all the arrangements. It's well known that Sir Humphrey helped Master Tiptree here.'

'And if he's questioned on this?'

'Why Reginald, Sir Humphrey is a member of the Vintners' Guild, it's not the first time he has bought property in the city. The Guild will take the deeds of the tavern and offer that hostelry on the open market. Clarence may well suspect that Tiptree was involved in the destruction of the Three Kings and Oudenarde, but he can't really prove it and he knows that Tiptree will flee well beyond his reach. You, my friend,' Margaret pointed at the taverner, 'and your family will change your name and, with my help, buy a hostelry on my estates at Woking.'

'But, but . . .' Tiptree stammered. 'Clarence will see my disappearance as complicity in the murder of his henchmen. He will send Mauclerc and his ruffians to hunt me down.'

'No, no,' Urswicke intervened. 'Remember the night you were abducted, my men made it very clear that they were the retainers of Richard of Gloucester. I peddle the same nonsense to Clarence and Mauclerc. How I believe, Master Tiptree, that you're part of Gloucester's plot, and assisted those assassins to enter that chancery chamber. I will explain my reasoning as I have done here, except I will blame assassins, their names unknown, despatched by Duke Richard. You helped them and I shall hint that you, together with your family, have been despatched, God knows where! To some desolate part of the north, perhaps abroad – or even,' he grinned, 'to life eternal. Clarence has a large pot to stir. He will not waste time, energy and good coin hunting you down. Nor will he, at this moment in time, having seen the destruction of his Secret Chancery, be willing to deepen the rift with his powerful younger brother. Master Tiptree, do not worry. Clarence will be busy enough.'

'You will leave in a covered cart tonight,' Margaret declared. 'You have brought from The Sunne in Splendour all your moveables?' Tiptree nodded in agreement. Bray then left and fetched Hempen, who promised to keep strict watch over his fellow taverner until nightfall. Under the cover of dark and, furnished with letters from the countess, Hempen would take Tiptree, his household and all his treasure out of the city.

Once the taverners had left, Margaret beckoned her two henchmen to draw their seats close.

'Before you continue, Christopher.'

'You can read my mind, my Lady. I have a question.'

'And I know what it is,' Margaret exclaimed. 'Yes, Reginald?' Bray just nodded, fingers tapping the table. 'Why did we not tell you from the start?'

'Of course, but now I suspect the truth.'

'Of course you do.' Margaret rose and gently kissed Urswicke on each cheek before sitting down again. 'You are, Christopher,' she continued, 'a most cunning clerk who, on my behalf, can perpetrate the most subtle deceits. If you had been brought into this game from the start, you might have been exposed to great

danger. Mauclerc is no fool. If you made a mistake, a slip of
the tongue, of knowing something you really should not, that
would have placed you, indeed all of us, in the greatest danger.
Keeping you in the dark preserved you. At the same time, we
realised that with your keen wit and sharp mind you would
eventually discover the truth. Even though you might not find
any evidence to corroborate it. Of course you proved us wrong.
You reached the only logical conclusion possible and produced
the evidence for it. The assassins, whoever they were, must have
had some inside help, and the only real source for that was
Master Tiptree. You very successfully proved that he was
involved and why. You discovered the evidence in my accounts
as well as documents at the Guildhall. Once you'd pieced that
together, you realised that Master Bray and I were the true
architects of the devious plot carried out in that chancery
chamber. You then established my motives, clear enough in the
circumstances. I wanted them to die. I believed they should. The
Three Kings committed the most appalling sacrilege against
Henry's corpse and you realised the full extent of Clarence's
malice towards me. And now,' she stretched out a hand to caress
Urswicke's cheek, 'you have not only discovered the truth but
refashioned it so cleverly that the blame for all of it can be
placed at Gloucester's door.'

'On another matter,' Urswicke responded, conscious of Bray
staring curiously at him, 'you claim that Mauclerc is deserving
of judgement; now that is a twist in the game I must deal with
piece by piece, moving the figures across the board so that
Mauclerc's day of retribution, and that of his master, crawls like
some monster out of the dark to devour them. Mistress, that is
what you wish, isn't it?'

'Of course,' she whispered. 'I want the total destruction of
Clarence and his creature Mauclerc. Seek a path forward on this
and we will follow it.'

'And so we come to "Titulus Regius"?' Bray demanded. 'When
I was in that chancery chamber, I searched, albeit hastily, and
could find nothing of interest except Spysin's letter giving him
licence to go abroad.'

'Oh it was there Reginald, before your very eyes – and mine,'
Urswicke added hastily. 'How true,' he exclaimed, 'is the saying

of a certain cunning man who argued that the best concealment is most effective when it is conspicuous.'

'Meaning?' Bray snapped. 'Christopher, we are not involved in some Twelfth Night game, merry dancing around the maypole, or bobbing the apple on the village green or tethering the donkey against the door of the village church.'

Urswicke spread his hands. 'Reginald, I apologise, but let me show you what I mean. The Three Kings were very, very cunning.'

The clerk placed his chancery bag on the table, opened it and took out the two copies of the book of hours he had picked up in the chancery room and from the arca at St Vedast. He opened the pages of one of the psalters and gently tapped them. 'This, my Lady, is the "Titulus Regius", the Title of the King – what Clarence dreams of. It's a creation of the Three Kings and Oudenarde. All four searched out stories about Clarence's parents as well as the emergence of the Woodvilles. They wanted to create a chronicle or indictment which Clarence could use to bolster his claim to be the legitimate King of England. The Titulus lies here and can be divided into two parts. The first is about the origins of his eldest brother Edward the King, the first begotten son of Richard Duke of York and his wife the Duchess Cecily Neville, the so-called Rose of Raby. So let us begin there. Edward was born in Rouen on 28 April 1442. To cut to the quick, rumour has it that Duke Richard was not his true father but a certain captain of archers called Blackburn, Blackybourne or some such name. The rumours are persistent, pointing out that Edward's appearance, his extraordinary handsome looks and height, being well over two yards high, are very different from the physical appearance of both his father and his brothers, especially Gloucester. Now, of course, relations between the arrogant Duke of York and the passionate, vain, hot-tempered Rose of Raby could be extremely tempestuous. They clashed in the bedchamber and were quite happy to continue their arguments in the hall in full view of everyone. Moreover, Duke Richard was often absent from court, whilst his wife was very fond of dalliance with attractive young men, aping the tales of Arthur, Lancelot and Guinevere, of Tristan and Isolde. My Lady, you've seen this often enough, some great lady of the court playing cat's cradle with a handsome young fop or arrogant knight, be it in a window embrasure or flower-shrouded arbour.'

'Yes, yes I have, and I've also heard rumours about York and his proud, vain wife. She was a woman I stayed well clear of, her tempers were notorious. She could lash with her tongue as well as with a cane, or anything else she could lay her hands on.'

'The passionate arguments between Duke Richard and his wife,' Bray agreed, 'were well known. They say Clarence inherited his mother's vile temper and arrogance. Again, Edward of York is markedly different in character from both his parents and Clarence. Richard of Gloucester is a much more difficult character to read. Yet I must be honest. Edward, free of the malicious advice and the evil counsel of his henchmen, can be merciful, humorous and, on occasion, even magnanimous. Qualities,' Bray added bitterly, 'neither of his parents possessed.'

'Now I admit,' Urswicke tapped the book of hours, 'rumour often walks hand in hand with the most lurid scandal when it comes to the great ones of the land, be it bishop, lord or prince. The House of York is no different from that of Lancaster, where similar scandals lurk. Indeed the gossipers claim the late Prince Edward was not the son of the saintly Henry, God rest them both, but the offspring of De La Pole or some other favourite of the Angevin queen. Such stories of illegitimacy did nothing to enhance that prince or his mother. As you know, she was dismissed as a French whore and her only son a bastard. Indeed, when the late King Henry heard how his wife had conceived, he openly mocked the news, saying it was the work of the Holy Spirit, for he had certainly not lain with her.'

'I agree,' Margaret declared. 'The Beauforts also have their dark corners, and the gossipers have made great play of this affair and that. But chatter is one thing, proof is another.'

'True. And so we come to the second part of the "Titulus Regius" – the marriage of Edward of York to Elizabeth Woodville. Now, as you know, at the time of their secret marriage, Neville Earl of Warwick was King Edward's chief minister and plenipotentiary. Warwick wanted our Yorkist King to marry some foreign princess such as Bona of Savoy. Edward thought differently. He met and fell in love with the widow Elizabeth Woodville, a passionate, secret affair which, because of its passion, did not remain secret for long. The Woodvilles were, and still are, regarded as upstarts: petty-shire nobility with no right to be at court. They are grasping, avaricious and ruthless. Elizabeth looks as if butter wouldn't melt in her mouth, but many at court regard her as officious, a vindictive vixen who has ensnared Edward of York with her coy ways and bedchamber skills. Edward was, and still is, besotted with her. He may frequent the likes of Jane Shore and others, but Elizabeth always draws him back. Now, when Edward's mother, the Duchess of York, learnt that her son had secretly married "The Woodville widow", as she was then called, Duchess Cecily fell into such a frenzy. She ranted and raved. She even offered to submit in open court how her son Edward was not the offspring of Richard Duke of York but was conceived in adultery: illegitimate and therefore not worthy of the honour of kingship.'

'In God's name,' Margaret interrupted, 'and she said that?'

'Ah,' Christopher smiled, 'worse is to come. Duchess Cecily's hatred for the Woodvilles is public and very well known. However, a greater secret lurks beneath the surface, a rumour which is much more dangerous . . .'

'Which is?' Bray demanded.

'That Edward of York's marriage to Elizabeth Woodville is invalid.'

'*What?*' Margaret and Bray chorused.

'Edward's lust for older women is clear to everyone. He has from his early youth always had a penchant for the more mature ladies of his court. Now the Three Kings investigated this and uncovered a great secret: namely, that at the time of his marriage to Woodville, Edward was secretly committed by troth-plight to the Lady Eleanor Butler, widow of Sir Thomas Butler. Eleanor was the daughter of the redoubtable warrior, Talbot Earl of Shrewsbury. Eleanor died some years ago but she was very much alive when Edward married Elizabeth Woodville.'

'And the source of all this?' Margaret's voice was hoarse.

'Well, it is not mere gossip. This is a secret cherished by our present Lord Chancellor, appointed so by Edward himself.'

'In God's name, Robert Stillington, Bishop of Bath and Wells?'

'The same,' Urswicke agreed, and quickly gave both the

countess and Bray all he had learnt from Brother Joachim, the last remaining Barnabite. He explained how Stillington's name on the inside of the front cover of each copy of the book of hours was a clue to this, though in the text both he and Joachim were simply described as '*Presbyteri* – Priests.' Urswicke also described how he himself had stumbled on this when he'd studied the different licences given by Stillington time and again to Brother Cuthbert and his companions.

'Now.' Urswicke took a deep drink from the tankard of ale. 'There is no doubt that the Three Kings and Oudenarde acquired this knowledge. I doubt if they handed it over to Clarence but they certainly intended to. What we do know is that Stillington and that hedge priest Joachim witnessed the betrothal between Edward of York and Eleanor Butler. Such a holy vow is, according to canon law, valid and supported with the full force of church law. Edward of York was already affianced to someone else when he exchanged vows at the church door with the Woodville widow. Consequently such an exchange was not legal, and can never be so.'

'Saints be my witness,' Margaret breathed, 'the heirs of such a union are illegitimate and cannot succeed to the throne. If Clarence fully grasps this, he will argue that his nephews are bastards and therefore, by the law of succession, he is the next rightful King of England.' Margaret fell silent, staring down at the table top. She lifted her head. 'Do you think Clarence knows the full revelation?'

'No, Mistress, I do not. The Three Kings were extremely diligent and very cunning. Their discoveries and their secret writing were their preserve. They kept the full content of the "Titulus Regius" to themselves. They probably promised Clarence and Mauclerc a finished document, something which would delight them. They might make allusions, hint and whet their master's appetites, but not provide full disclosure. Eventually they would lead Clarence to the glorious conclusion of their work, which would win the Three Kings and Oudenarde even greater favours for the lord they served.' Urswicke paused. 'They collected the evidence. They searched out and brought into that chancery room individuals who might attest to what they wrote.'

'Such as?' Bray asked.

'Oh, former minions of the different Yorkist households; those who had served Duke Richard, his wife Cecily and their children, men and women, mere scullions who might provide juicy scandal. All servants like to gossip about their masters.'

'Yes, yes, I know what you are going to say,' Margaret interrupted. 'Richard and Cecily of York would not be the easiest lords to serve. Cecily in particular would make her presence felt; she'd cruelly punish those who disobeyed or failed her. The Three Kings would have a great deal to harvest.'

'And that's why the Barnabites were brought in. They would sift the wheat from the chaff. They would look for individuals who could substantiate their story and reject those who indulged in fanciful tales. They would do this quietly, secretly, and fear no reprisals.'

'Yes, yes. To cast aspersions on the King's legitimacy could be construed as treason!'

'Of course,' Urswicke agreed, 'Brother Cuthbert and his ruffians would tell all those they questioned not to repeat their conversation or they might find themselves indicted. He and his fellow mercenaries would select those they wanted and bring them to The Sunne in Splendour. They probobly came from far afield as well as the shires: Normandy, Hainault and Flanders; countries where Richard and Cecily of York stayed during their different sojourns abroad. Others, such as Stillington, would be warned to cooperate or face the consequences. After all, what could Stillington do? If he confessed, then both Church and Crown would turn on him, so he remained silent.'

'And what happened to the others?'

Urswicke crossed himself. 'My Lady, I went out to St Vedast where the Barnabites sheltered. They were nothing more than a group of ruthless, foreign mercenaries who hid beneath the guise of being members of some obscure order of friars. They were murderers, assassins. I visited the Godforsaken, dismal cemetery near that church. I believe that the lesser people, mere minions to the likes of Mauclerc, were silenced for good. Once they had given their evidence, these unfortunates were deceived into going to receive their reward, only to be brutally murdered and their corpses hurriedly buried in that desolate graveyard.'

'Of course,' Bray declared, 'lest they take their story or their meeting with the Three Kings to any other interested party.'

'Precisely,' Urswicke retorted. Urswicke crossed his arms and stared up at the ceiling.

'Christopher?'

'Further mischief, Mistress. The Three Kings were unable to finish their task but they were very close to it. I believe they were to propose one final masque which, if Clarence was arrogant and stupid enough to implement, and I think he is, would have caused a grievous rift between himself and his two brothers. Indeed I do wonder if the Three Kings and Oudenarde were intent on serving two masters?'

'Who?'

'Well, if they had revealed what they had found and written up in the "Titulus Regius" to someone like Richard of Gloucester, they could expect even greater reward. I just wonder why they kept two copies, one in the Secret Chancery chamber, the other at St Vedast?' Urswicke shrugged. 'Of course two copies meant they had a guarantee that their work would never be lost. The Three Kings certainly brewed a pot of mischief. Anyway, I came across a final proposal hidden deep in the text. As you know, Richard Neville, Earl of Warwick – the self-styled King-maker – was killed at Barnet. He left no male heir, only two daughters, Isobel and Anne. Clarence, like a hog at its trough, married Isobel so as to seize the Neville inheritance. Richard of Gloucester, or so rumour has it, intends to marry Anne and, of course, demand that half the Neville patrimony be given to him . . .'

'Clarence would fight.'

'Of course, Reginald. So the Three Kings recommended that Anne Neville should disappear.'

'Disappear?'

'Yes, my Lady. Be abducted by Clarence's retainers, hidden away in some nunnery or even a tavern here in London. It might take months, even years to find out where she was, and who would really search for her? Richard of Gloucester? Clarence would hamper that. It would be like searching for a needle in a haystack. People would whisper that Anne Neville had been abducted, murdered or, out of sheer grief, killed herself. If she cannot present herself in court to claim her rights, then those rights must go to the last surviving member of her family, namely Isobel, Clarence's wife.'

'A witch's brew indeed,' Margaret declared. 'The stuff of civil war, the long, encroaching shadow of Cain against Abel, brother fighting brother.' She glanced at Urswicke. 'And so hangs your tale.'

'And so hangs my tale, Mistress.'

'You did well.' She leaned over and stroked Urswicke's face. 'You did so well against truly deadly adversaries.'

'And the "Titulus Regius"?' Bray demanded, pointing at the richly embroidered calfskin tomes.

'Oh very clever.' Urswicke took one of the book of hours, placed it on the table before him and opened it. He pointed to the inside of the front cover and the 'Teste Me' of Stillington. 'You know the reason for that; I will not share such knowledge with anyone else. Anyway, look at this tome. See how it is made up of different chapters or sections, all self-contained. The spine of the book is tough, hard leather, the best you can buy, reinforced with strips which will keep it firm. Observe.' He turned the book so they could clearly see the spine and he tapped it. 'This contains the chapters which are expertly sewn together with twine; these are placed within the spine which is broad enough to accept them. We are all skilled in matters of the chancery: this is the work of experienced craftsmen, the Three Kings and their fellow countryman, Oudenarde the parchment-seller. He fashioned this tome, its pages and the spine. He would then seal them using suitable twine and carefully binding. I suspect each of the Three Kings took responsibility for one of the secret scandals involving the House of York which I have already described to you. Now I have done so in brief, summarising what is written here, but the Three Kings carefully copied out their hidden narrative. Ostensibly they were transcribing the contents of an ordinary book of hours, yet they used this to hide their secret chronicle. Every so often they would change the colour of ink from black to red or from green to blue and so on. By themselves these verses mean nothing, but start running them together according to colour and they tell a tale to catch the heart and startle the mind. For example, all they had to do regarding the incident involving Stillington and Brother Joachim was to find the words 'priests', 'marriage oath', 'betrothal', 'witness', and so on. These, along with other phrases, when put together describe, in detail, the stories of Eleanor Butler and Elizabeth Woodville.'

'But they are not named?' Margaret asked.

'Of course not. Like Stillington's, their identity is hidden beneath the phrases "first betrothed" and "second betrothed". Edward of York is simply described as a "Prince of the White Rose". Again, such a phrase is broken up and scattered throughout the manuscript.' Urswicke paused and leafed through the book of hours. 'A most significant example is the story about David lusting after Bathsheba and arranging for that woman's husband to be killed in battle. The verse I found, when it's assembled together according to colour, reads as follows: "And the captain of archers lay with the duke's wife and she conceived a son, their eldest." This verse is made up of phrases all written in black on a page where the rest of the writing is in blue, and so it goes on: a secret chronicle describing the scandals of the House of York lies hidden away in this book of hours. Now,' Urswicke shrugged, 'I concede many of the witnesses to such an account are dead, but the four most powerful are not.'

'Four?' Bray queried.

'Stillington, the two Barnabites, especially Brother Joachim.'

'And the fourth is Edward of York,' Margaret declared.

'In truth he is,' Urswicke agreed. 'And that is something we should concentrate on. Edward of York knows exactly what happened. He must be fearful for himself, his wife and any possible heir. If Clarence seizes this information and uses it, I doubt if his royal brother will show any mercy. Anyway, Brother Joachim is now wandering the countryside; indeed, he may probably be abroad. Stories about scandals in the House of York will begin to seep through, the usual whispers and chatter, but the seed has been sown. God knows what harvest it will bring.' Urswicke paused and sat staring at the countess, who was lost in her own deep thoughts.

'Mistress?' Bray demanded.

'Time passes on,' she replied in a half-whisper. 'Margaret of Anjou and her son had to go into the dark.' She glanced sharply at Urswicke. 'Your intervention at Tewkesbury was crucial. Somerset's suspicions about Wenlock and his execution of that lord may have turned the tide against the Angevin. Poor woman!

Jasper Tudor, I know, would not have been waiting for her across the Severn; she could expect little help from him. At my request, he had dismissed his levies and been given one task and one task only, to spirit his nephew out of this kingdom. The Angevin and her son could have fled abroad but that would have meant more war, more agitation and yet, I know here,' Margaret struck her breast, 'how the Angevin and her son would never have been accepted in this kingdom. Our saintly King Henry, as expected, did not survive a month after Tewkesbury. Poor man, he has gone to his rightful place amongst the saints.' Margaret paused. 'Only my son,' she added fiercely, 'now sheltering under the protection of Duke Francis, will become the standard around which the rest will rally. Nobles such as De Vere of Oxford.' She smiled thinly, 'I have also been busy elsewhere. John Morton, a leading figure at Westminster, is one of us, and he will draw others in. We must not fritter away our time or wealth on feckless uprisings or surprise landings along some neglected stretch of coastline. Time will pass. Henry will grow older: come the moment, come the prince, and we must prepare for that. Now Christopher,' she leaned across and grasped his hand, 'what are your sharp wits plotting? Moving like the swiftest greyhound to keep its quarry under eye? In a word, how will you present all of this to that demon-incarnate Clarence?'

'Mistress, I hear what you say.' Urswicke gripped the countess's hands and kissed her fingertips.

'And yet what, Christopher?'

'The game is stacked strongly against us. Edward of York is triumphant. He has a fertile wife who will provide a brood of children and present him with an heir. Edward also has two brothers who would fight to the death for their inheritance. What real chance do we have?' He let go of the countess's hand. 'Please don't doubt my fealty or my passion, but what chance do we really have?'

'We have Christ's own words, Christopher, and I believe them. A house divided against itself cannot stand. A house built on sand will not survive the coming storms and tempests. Such prophecies accurately describe the House of York, and I intend to prove such predictions are correct in all their details. Now, as for Clarence . . .?'

PART SIX

'The Duke of Clarence caused the girl Anne to be
concealed so his brother would not know where she was.'
Crowland Chronicle

C hristopher Urswicke gently dug in his heels and his horse,
  snorting at the pungent smell of burning, picked its way
  across the blackened, crumbling remains of the priest's
house at St Vedast, on that stretch of desolate moorlands north
of the city wall. Urswicke stared around. From the information
he had learnt in his father's chancery at the Guildhall, the fire
which started here had been devastating. Wafted by a stiff breeze,
the flames had moved to catch and consume the church, reducing
it to a tangle of scorched stone and timber. Urswicke peered
through the dark. Somewhere nearby lay the blackened remains
of the Barnabites he had killed. Urswicke crossed himself, even
as he promised the spirits, who must be crowding around him,
that he would have a chantry priest sing three requiems for the
repose of their souls – wherever they might be.

He gently urged his horse out of the ruined house and across
through a huge rent in the crumbling walls of the ancient church
of St Vedast. He guided his mount up along the remains of the
gloomy, ghostly nave. Wisps of smoke still swirled. Tendrils of
river mist gathered and mingled before drifting apart. Urswicke's
horse made its way up into the fire-blighted sanctuary where the
clerk dismounted and stood listening. Outside the sun was setting,
a burst of dying light still strong against the gathering night.
Urswicke hobbled his horse and went into the apse behind the
ruined high altar. He sat in the alcove reserved for servers and
listened keenly. He heard a sound, the clip of high-heeled boots
and the jingle of spurs. A figure emerged out of the murk and
Urswicke rose to clasp hands with George of Clarence before

leading him into the enclave, gesturing that he sit on the ledge opposite. Clarence, ever watchful, sat down.

Urswicke opened the saddlebag he had brought across, took out four squat candles and, using his tinder, lit them, watching their flame leap fiercely. He then drew out the book of hours he had brought and laid this on the floor beside the candles. Clarence watched carefully before he rose, unstrapping his warbelt, placing it on the ledge beside him as he retook his seat.

'You are well, my Lord?'

'I am.'

'You came alone?'

'As you asked and as I promised.'

Urswicke nodded understandingly. It had been a week since his conversation with the countess, when they had discussed the secrets contained in the 'Titulus Regius'. Since then, he and Bray had been busy plotting, doing what they could to agitate the city fathers by demonstrating that the Lancastrian cause was not dead. Notices proclaiming this as a truth had been pinned to the cross in St Paul's churchyard and the Standard at Cheapside. All such declarations had warned about a coming time of deep distress and agitation. How fresh storms were brewing and how the House of York would not survive them. In the main, this had been Bray's work on behalf of Countess Margaret, who had urged them to stir the pot even if it was just for the sake of the stink.

'Well, Master Urswicke,' Clarence made himself more comfortable, flicking at the ash on his cloak, 'as you asked, I came alone.'

'Though you have men hidden away who could be with you if you wanted?'

'Of course, but your message was stark and clear. I was to come alone to this devastated church.' Clarence tapped his cloak. 'Of course, beneath this I carry a hunting horn.' He leaned forward, smiling through the gloom, so close Urswicke could smell his wine-drenched breath.

'And you carry that, my Lord, just in case matters do not proceed as smoothly as they should?'

'Master Urswicke, you are an enigma. I wonder, as do the whisperers, whom you really serve? Do you know, Master Christopher, we have a lot in common, don't we? You serve yourself and what do you hope to gain?'

'My Lord, I don't know, but when I find it I shall tell you.'

'And so matters will run smoothly?'

'Oh they will, they will,' Urswicke soothed, picking up the book of hours and handing it to Clarence. 'For you, my Lord, a gift, a pledge of my commitment to the way things should be. Now listen,' Urswicke, tapping the book of hours Clarence now held, repeated what he had told Countess Margaret and Master Bray. How the Three Kings and Oudenarde had written and concealed a chronicle narrating a series of devastating scandals about the House of York. How they had used the Barnabites who had sheltered here, to bring witnesses and other evidence to their chamber at The Sunne in Splendour. Urswicke, however, was careful. He made no reference to either Stillington or Joachim's involvement in the secret betrothal ceremony between Edward of York and Eleanor Butler. He also explained how he had found the identity of this woman. Amongst other things, her first name had been included in a prayer for former queens of England, whilst the surname Butler had also had been mentioned in a prayer for officials of the royal household. As for the Woodville woman, Urswicke explained how that was easy to guess, pointing out the references including a prayer for the royal family and, here again, Elizabeth Woodville's name had been cleverly delineated in a different-coloured ink.

Urswicke secretly congratulated himself for discovering further information over the last week, and he still believed he had not fully unearthed all the evidence that the 'Titulus' contained. Clarence, who had sat with that constant cynical smirk on his face, changed dramatically. He leaned forward, mouth slack, eyes blinking, lips moving soundlessly as he listened to Urswicke's revelations and the precise details he described. Urswicke, who had rehearsed his speech time and again during the preceding day, was almost word perfect, explaining how the Three Kings used their ink and styles of writing both to communicate as well as conceal their secret chronicle. Once he had finished, Clarence sat shaking his head, his face a mask of disbelief.

'By all the saints,' he breathed, 'of course I know some of this rumour, hearsay, tittle-tattle. I asked the Three Kings to investigate and they became as busy as ferrets searching out this person or that. They assured Mauclerc that they were gathering evidence, but nothing like this, the detail, the precision. According to this,' Clarence opened the book of hours Urswicke had handed him, 'my brother Edward has no claim to the throne, whilst his marriage to the Woodville bitch is nothing more than a pretence. The chronicle gives dates and times for this and that.'

'My Lord, I agree. In fact,' Urswicke decided to tell the truth, 'I suspect there is more hidden away here which I haven't found. Perhaps some other secret pattern but, for the moment, you have enough.'

'But why didn't the Three Kings inform me? Surely Mauclerc must have suspected?'

'My Lord, I shall come to that by and by. You do recognise what the "Titulus Regius" contains? It is called that,' Urswicke pressed on, 'because the secret chronicles, as I shall call them, mount a serious challenge about who in the House of York should wear the Confessor's crown.'

'Which is myself,' Clarence snapped.

'Of course, my Lord. Perhaps the Three Kings and Oudenarde were simply waiting for the correct moment to present you with the finished task. I think they were close to that, although,' Urswicke held up a hand, 'for all I know, there may have been fresh revelations about the duchess, your esteemed mother, or the true status of Elizabeth Woodville.' Urswicke pulled a face trying to conceal his elation at leading a man the countess hated along the path to judgement.

'What?' Clarence demanded.

'My Lord, I just wonder . . .' Urswicke, now thoroughly enjoying himself, pointed at the psalter. 'Your brother Edward, if he gave his troth plight to Eleanor Butler, did he do so to another woman? Think, my Lord, how the King has laid siege to many a noble lady who acted like the damsel in the tower, refusing to open their door until certain promises and assurances were made. Think, my Lord, reflect and remember. Refurbish your Secret Chancery. Use your trusted clerks to dig out fresh nuggets of gold, priceless information. My Lord you know the hymn,' Urswicke waved a hand, 'and I am sure you can sing it better than I.' Urswicke let his words trail away.

Clarence sat, licking his lips. He opened the book of hours

and hungrily leafed through its pages. Urswicke watched even as he strained his ears for any strange sound. The evening was drawing on. Urswicke felt satisfied with the way matters were progressing. He had prepared his lure, set his snare and he was confident that this arrogant lord would blunder deeper into the traps awaiting him.

'So.' Clarence put the book of hours down, though he continued to stare at it. 'We have the evidence about what happened in that chancery chamber but not the names of those responsible for killing my faithful retainers.'

'Faithful?'

'What do you mean?'

'As I have said, let's leave that for a while. However, my Lord, you know who is responsible for those deaths? From what I have learnt, it must be the work of your own brother, Richard of Gloucester, assisted by the taverner Tiptree. As for him, I suspect he's either dead or been spirited away to some remote part of this kingdom. Gloucester's name was certainly mentioned during the pretended abduction of Tiptree and his kin. I say "pretended", because Gloucester wanted to save that taverner from falling into your hands.'

Clarence nodded, rocking himself backwards and forwards. 'Little Dickon,' Clarence rasped. 'I shall deal with him soon enough. The Three Kings were correct: Anne Neville must disappear and that can be arranged.' He edged forward on the stone seat of the enclave, jabbing his finger in Urswicke's face. 'But come now. You talked of matters that you'd return to by and by. Well?' Clarence jibed. 'We have reached by and by. What is it? What do you have to tell me?'

'The Three Kings.' Urswicke chose his words carefully. 'They may have seriously considered that the chronicles they had collected could be passed on to others who would pay lavishly to be given such invaluable information.'

'Such as?'

'As I have said, Richard of Gloucester, the King himself, the Woodvilles, foreign powers hostile to this kingdom. After all,' Urswicke shrugged, 'successive kings of England have made great play of how the inheritance to the Crown of France, by due law and process, rightfully belongs to the Plantagenets, kings of this realm and their successors. Can you imagine the damage such opponents could inflict upon your house and its claims with this information? They would argue that the House of York has little or no right to the Confessor's crown, let alone that of France kept in its tabernacle at St Denis.'

'Do you think Gloucester's men seized a copy of the "Titulus Regius" when they murdered the Three Kings?'

'No. They may have hastily searched but they had little time and, as you can now see, the "Titulus Regius" is cleverly concealed.'

'And Mauclerc? You begged me to come alone and not inform him. Why?'

'I am very wary.' Urswicke pulled a face and shook his head to show he was uncertain about what he was about to say.

'Master Urswicke, tell me what you think.'

'Well, shouldn't the Three Kings have been better guarded? After all, Mauclerc – perhaps more than you and me – realised the importance of what the Three Kings were doing and yet, on reflection, your Secret Chancery had very little protection. Shouldn't Mauclerc have been more aware of Tiptree's treacherous nature? Didn't Mauclerc notice anything untoward in the days before those murders at The Sunne in Splendour? Or even afterwards? And the Barnabites who sheltered here or poor Spysin? Couldn't they have all been better guided and guarded? I concede that this is just petty suspicion, yet how many times, my Lord?' Urswicke fought to keep his face solemn, his voice low and sombre like that of any prophet of doom. 'How often do men play the Judas even to a most gracious lord such as yourself?' Clarence, who drank praise as if it was part of his birthright, nodded in agreement, his face so serious and knowing that Urswicke had to curb the laughter bubbling inside him.

'I am not,' Urswicke spoke slowly, 'saying Mauclerc cannot be trusted. However, my Lord, you asked me to investigate these mysteries. I simply put forward possible solutions as well as further questions which must be answered, sooner or later, now or in the future.'

Clarence, however, was lost in his own thoughts. He seized the book of hours and rose, pulling his cloak about him before imperiously extending his ring hand. Urswicke knelt and kissed the sharp diamonds which Clarence pushed against his lips.

'You,' Clarence whispered, 'have done me great service, Master Urswicke. Continue to keep a sharp eye on Mauclerc and, as for that little Beaufort bitch, the one you pretend to serve so faithfully, our enmity is to the death. You agree, Christopher?'

Urswicke clasped the proffered hand. 'My Lord,' he declared loudly, 'you have my solemn word on that.'

'You will be rewarded.' Clarence waggled his fingers. 'Until then.' And, spinning on his heel, Clarence left the sanctuary. Urswicke watched him go, listening intently. Once he was certain Clarence had left, he crossed to his hobbled horse, took the small wineskin and linen food parcel out of his saddlebags and returned to the enclave. Urswicke made himself comfortable and stared at the sack he'd also taken from his panniers containing the second copy of the 'Titulus Regius'. He and Bray had begged Countess Margaret to let them use this as bait, adding that on no account could it be found in their possession as it might prove to be their death warrants. Moreover, Urswicke had insisted, he had copied his own memoranda in a special cipher which summarised the secrets of the 'Titulus Regius'. Urswicke chewed his food, comforting himself that, when this business was done, he would dine on freshly caught salmon, grilled and sweetened with herbs, whilst both he and Bray would drink deep well past the chimes of midnight.

Urswicke reflected on what was happening in London. Bray continued to disseminate stories about the sanctity of the murdered martyr King Henry. Lancastrian sympathisers were still active in the city, spreading stories of unrest, fictitious or otherwise; about risings in Wales, landings on this coast or that, disturbances in the north under this rebel leader or another. Countess Margaret was determined on brewing this mischief. However, she was also determined to leave London to tend to her sick husband, adding that her two henchmen should continue their work before joining her in Woking.

Urswicke took a mouthful of wine, wondering what would happen to Sir Humphrey and whether Margaret would truly accept the hand and protection of Lord Stanley. Urswicke took another gulp of wine, heard a sound and stiffened. He put both food and wineskin away, got to his feet and walked to the edge of the sanctuary. A figure had appeared at the far end of the nave, carrying a shuttered lantern. Urswicke watched the three darts of light, one after the other. He returned, picked up one of the candles and turned, swaying it so the new arrival could clearly see the dancing flame. Again, the shuttered lantern replied with three sharp bursts of light. Satisfied, Urswicke walked back into the sanctuary. He placed the candle down and waited for the dark, shadowy figure to cross the sanctuary and join him.

'Good evening, my Lord.'

'And good evening to you, Master Urswicke.' Richard of Gloucester pulled down his visor and pushed back the hood of his cloak. He and Urswicke clasped hands, Gloucester taking the seat in the enclave, Urswicke sitting opposite, as he had with Clarence. Urswicke picked up the sack, took out the book of hours, cradling it as Gloucester made himself comfortable.

'I saw my brother Clarence leave. He had horsemen close by, hidden in a copse, you do know that?'

'As your men wait?'

Gloucester laughed softly. 'Whom do you really serve, Urswicke?' Gloucester beat his gauntlets against his thigh. 'Whom do you really serve?' He repeated. 'Me? Clarence? The King? Your father? The Beaufort woman?'

'All of them, because I serve myself, as do you.'

Again Gloucester laughed softly.

'You are wary, aren't you?' Urswicke pressed on. 'You are suspicious and rightfully so. Clarence is dangerous, but you fear other demons, don't you? Not your brother the King, but the Woodvilles who shelter behind Elizabeth the Queen, a greedy and ambitious horde of relatives led by the cunning Earl Rivers.'

'True, true,' Gloucester murmured. 'But as long as my brother the King lives and thrives, I am safely protected.' He laughed sharply. 'Which is more than can be said for my brother George. The King, Hastings and others are determined on that. I betray no secret as it must be obvious to everyone except George, that if he returns to his perjuring, his Judas ways, like a dog to its vomit, he will not be spared. So?'

Urswicke stared down at the ground. He was aware of the shadows of those who haunted this derelict place, those dark clouds of souls, gathering to watch. Something about Gloucester's words started an idea, like a hare that abruptly bursts out of a field of long grass. Something he must follow and pursue to its logical conclusion.

'Well, Master Urswicke? You have brought me to the ring, so dance we shall.'

'My Lord, we certainly shall.' Urswicke picked up the second copy of the book of hours and pressed it into Gloucester's hands. The prince glanced sharply at him. 'My Lord, hold that and let me tell you the tale it contains. For this is the "Titulus Regius", as well as evidence of your brother Clarence's malevolent mischief towards you, your brother, indeed his entire family. Now listen and listen well.'

Urswicke then described what he had already told to the countess, though, as with Clarence, he omitted any reference to Bishop Stillington and Brother Joachim. The Barnabites were simply described as couriers and messengers of the Three Kings and their accomplice Oudenarde. More starkly, he described the murders at The Sunne in Splendour as the work of Clarence, who was also responsible for the killing of Spysin. At that Gloucester held up a hand.

'Master Urswicke, I understand why Brother George should use my name to conceal his wickedness. But why would he kill five trusted henchmen?'

'Very easy,' Urswicke retorted. 'Your brother George is like a cock on a weather vane. He turns, he changes, according to whatever favourable wind is blowing. Yes?' Gloucester just nodded. 'I suspect,' Urswicke spread his hands, 'though I have very little evidence for this, that Clarence decided that the creators of this chronicle, the Three Kings and Oudenarde, as well as their courier Spysin, were no longer needed. Your brother George simply decided to remove them.' Gloucester, still holding Urswicke's gaze, nodded; the clerk noticed how the duke's fingers had fallen to the hilt of his dagger. 'No need, no need my Lord,' Urswicke soothed. 'I speak the truth, you know I do. Clarence has acted the Judas before and he will do so again. The "Titulus Regius" is complete, or almost so. Study it yourself. The Three Kings, Oudenarde and, I suspect, Spysin had served both their time and purpose, so Clarence's paid assassins, aided and abetted by his former retainer Tiptree, despatched them into the dark.

For all I know, Tiptree followed them. Who else could be responsible for their deaths? You certainly weren't. And who would use your name to conceal their act? Only Clarence, no one else.'

'This,' Gloucester lifted the book of hours, 'is cleverly and intricately done.' He paused. 'I will not indulge in any outburst but, believe me, Master Urswicke, I seethe at what you have told me. My brother George has impugned my father's blessed memory as well as my brother the King, not to mention my beloved mother. And yet, at the same time, if these revelations are true, then my brother should not be King and any male heir of his has no right to succeed.' He took a deep breath. 'Ah well, I agree. Clarence is as treacherous as a viper.'

'My Lord, if you are shocked, can you imagine what others would think? The Three Kings knew that. They could sell such information to any lord both within this realm and beyond.' Urswicke paused; for a brief flicker of time he noticed a shift in Gloucester's eyes, a tightening of the mouth, as if concealing a smile. 'Tell me, my Lord,' Urswicke decided to gamble, 'did the Three Kings make an approach to you?' Gloucester glanced away. 'My Lord?'

'Recently,' he replied. 'They began to show great friendliness to my henchman Francis Lovel. Chance meetings, or so they appeared to be, before and after Tewkesbury. Of course, I did wonder. Never mind.' Gloucester tapped the book of hours. 'Clarence thinks he has the only copy, yes?'

'Of course.'

'So where did you get this?'

'Hidden away at St Vedast where the Barnabites sheltered.'

'Were you responsible for the destruction of this church and the old priest's house?'

'Yes, along with others of Clarence's household. Mauclerc had decided that they too had outlived their usefulness. They all had to die; that's when I finally concluded that the deaths at The Sunne in Splendour were also their work. That's logical isn't it?'

'Yes, yes,' Gloucester replied testily. 'But I still find it difficult to accept that my brother should silence so many faithful retainers.'

'My Lord,' Urswicke silently prayed that his nimble wits would protect him from stumbling into a mistake, 'think about what has happened. Tewkesbury was a great victory. Your brother is now King triumphant. The Lancastrians are in utter disarray . . .'

'Even though their proclamations appear all over the city, whilst treasonable chatter and gossip are rife throughout London and the shires? Weeds grow faster than the grass.'

'That will pass,' Urswicke retorted. 'George of Clarence couldn't care about such nonsense. He realises Tewkesbury was a decisive victory. He would like to shut the door on the past. Seal off all memories about his days with the House of Lancaster. Above all, he has the "Titulus Regius". You know Clarence, my Lord? Once he has no need of you, then God help you. Think of all those mouths silenced. Think of the Three Kings: they nurtured scandal about your family, did this also include Clarence?'

'I agree,' Gloucester scratched the side of his face, 'the Three Kings, Oudenarde and the Barnabites were all involved in the creation of the "Titulus Regius". But why Spysin?'

'A household courier, my Lord, sent here and there by Clarence with this message or that. Words committed to memory which Spysin would never forget.' Urswicke schooled his features to conceal his enjoyment at this dangerous game of hazard. 'Rumour has it that Spysin was to be despatched abroad. Was he being sent out of the way? Did Clarence change his mind and decide on a more lasting solution? Remember, Spysin was a messenger, he would know a great deal, perhaps too much for comfort. Moreover, we must not only think of Clarence but also his henchman Mauclerc. He too joined his master in deserting the House of York and entering the Lancastrian camp. Mauclerc is a killer. He would not tolerate a clacking tongue or, indeed, anyone who might prove to be a threat.' Gloucester nodded his head in silent agreement. Urswicke decided to change the flow of conversation.

'And the other matter, my Lord? The possible disappearance of Anne Neville. I saw your grimace as I described what the Three Kings recommended. It could prove a great blow to your ambitions.'

'Yes, and I must deal with that, though it's difficult. The Lady Anne lives with her sister Isobel who, of course, is Clarence's wife. Since the death of her father, Anne clings very close to Isobel. Consequently it would be easy for Clarence to arrange matters against her and very difficult for me to offer protection.'

'True, that is a matter for you, my Lord. I have told you what I have learnt. You know how to unlock the cipher within the book of hours and read its contents.' Gloucester weighed the book in his hands, staring quizzically at Urswicke.

'What you say is logical,' he declared, 'and yet . . .?'

'Yet what, my Lord?'

Gloucester, head back, peered under half-closed eyes at Urswicke. 'Something is not right,' he whispered. 'Something is very wrong. Never mind. Not for now.' Gloucester chewed the corner of his lip. 'I shall ask my most trusted clerk to translate and transcribe,' he touched the book of hours, 'what is hidden here. Once that is completed, I shall reflect.' He turned and spat into the darkness. 'I shall certainly teach George a lesson. How dare he dishonour my parents!'

'And what about my mistress, the countess? I have loyalties to her and she must see me working on her behalf?'

'I will protect her interests from both within and without,' Gloucester replied. 'I shall use my influence to advance her affairs with my brother the King. You have my word on that, Urswicke.' Gloucester, gripping the book of hours, rose and walked out of the sanctuary, through the ruined church wall to where his horse stood hobbled in the cemetery.

Urswicke listened until he was sure his visitor had truly left. He then returned to his place, picked up the lighted candle, and went to stand in the gap in the church wall. He stood holding the candle, its flame fluttering vigorously in the night breeze. He waited until he heard the three harsh calls of a night bird echoing across the desolate cemetery. He smiled in satisfaction and strode back to the apse, where he waited for Bray, all cloaked and hooded, to join him.

'So the fish rose to the bait?'

'Faster than I thought,' Urswicke replied. 'I personally took messages to Clarence and Gloucester inviting them here. Clarence now thinks he has the only copy of the "Titulus Regius" but, of course, Gloucester and ourselves know different. All we can do is wait and see what happens. Both brothers are fired with bounding ambition. Gloucester at least has honour and talent but Clarence truly is a midnight soul absorbed with himself. But listen, my friend,' Urswicke gripped Bray's shoulder, 'to a possible future.' Urswicke sat down in the enclave, Bray opposite.

'Your story, Master Christopher?' Bray demanded, pushing back his hood and loosening the chain on his cloak.

'Oh, so many threads to pull. What if we abduct the Lady Anne Neville, hide her away but make it known that Clarence is responsible? We'd send Gloucester on a wild hunt through the taverns and nunneries of both this city and the kingdom. He would be furious. The rift between him and Clarence would deepen and, of course,' Urswicke paused to laugh softly, 'we could also be the ones who secretly find her and so enhance our relationship with my Lord of Gloucester.'

Bray rubbed his face and grinned at Urswicke. 'The countess is correct about you, Christopher. Your mind constantly teems with mischief, most of it on her behalf – why?'

'You know why. The debt I owe her cannot be measured. I shall never forget her kindness to my darling mother or to me. Such a memory burns like a flame within me.'

'And where does that flame lead you now?'

'Why, Master Reginald, to Edward of York, our warrior King. He is the vital piece in this never-ending game of chess. Clarence is dangerous but he is also a fool. He'll make his move and he will fail. This time Edward of York will not prevaricate. Brother or not, Clarence's head will roll, and so the stage will be cleared.' Urswicke turned and stared into the dark. 'Only Edward and his younger brother Gloucester will remain.'

'They are very close. Richard adores his elder brother.'

'Aye and so he does, but he hates the Woodvilles and they respond in kind. Now Master Reginald,' Urswicke plucked at Bray's sleeve, 'imagine you are Gloucester: as long as your crowned brother lives, you are safe from the deadly malice of the Woodvilles. But what if Edward suddenly dies, what would happen then?'

'Edward's heirs?'

'If he has a male issue which survives and, even if the boy does, at this moment in time, it would be a further fifteen or sixteen years before he becomes an heir in his own right.'

'A regency?'

'Of course, but who? As I suggested, if you were Richard of Gloucester, would you tolerate a Woodville regency, men like Earl Rivers and his host of greedy kinsmen? If cornered, if he was threatened and isolated, would Duke Richard reflect on what

I have handed him today? Why should he wait for the Woodvilles to strike? Why should he accept his brother's heirs, who, according to the "Titulus Regius", are the offspring of an invalid marriage in the eyes of Holy Mother Church? Such children would be illegitimate bastards, as perhaps his elder brother may have been, not the offspring of Richard of York but the by-blow of some lowborn captain of archers. If that is the case, and Clarence is gone, Richard is the legitimate heir. Master Reginald, it's just a theory like those you propose in the schools of Oxford. What if this happens . . .? What if that happens . . .?'

'Our mistress is correct,' Bray whispered, 'a pot of mischief is being brewed, thickened and boiled in the heat of deadly rivalries; that pot will bubble over and all this will end in blood.'

'Aye,' Urswicke agreed. He rose, tightening his warbelt, 'this will end in another Tewkesbury, the horrid clash of battle.' He stood up. 'Pray God we have victory that day because this truly is *à l'Outrance* – to the death.'

AUTHOR'S NOTE

Dark Queen Rising is of course a work of fiction, but it is based on historical evidence.

- The Battle of Tewkesbury is as described in the narrative. Somerset did kill Wenlock for refusing to commit his forces. The fighting in the abbey and the summary trials and bloody executions which followed did take place, Edward of England watching the proceedings from an upstairs window of the house he was sheltering in. If you visit Tewkesbury today you can still see marks of violence in the abbey and, according to local tradition, even the faded bloodstains where the Lancastrian Prince Edward was stabbed to death.

- Margaret of Anjou and her son were captured. Edward, of course, was immediately killed. Margaret was imprisoned in the Tower and eventually released, returning home due to the good offices of the French King.

- I believe the personalities of King Edward and his two brothers Clarence and Richard have been accurately conveyed. Richard was completely loyal to both his brother and House but Clarence seemed to be constantly attracted to treachery and betrayal.

- My description of the flight of Jasper Tudor and Henry to Brittany is a work of fiction but I have never really understood the published version, that somehow or other, young Henry was allowed to slip out of Pembroke and safely journey across the Narrow Seas.

- The 'Titulus Regius' is not a work of fiction. The scandalous stories mentioned in the narrative did eventually emerge into the public forum due to Clarence's treacherous meddling as well as Richard of Gloucester's attempts to protect himself in the hurling days following the sudden death of his brother, King Edward IV. Eleanor Butler, Bishop Stillington, the stories about Duchess Cecily and the disappearance of Warwick's daughter, Anne, are mentioned by the chronicles of the time.

- I have tried to faithfully convey the personality and attitude of Margaret Countess of Richmond: her three marriages, her love of her manor at Woking and her constant patronage of the arts. Cambridge University, in particular, owes a great debt to Countess Margaret. Reginald Bray and Christopher Urswicke were principal members of her household. Some people even regard Urswicke as the founder of the British Secret Service.

- Finally, the murder of Henry VI, is I believe based on the evidence available. As regards the possible desecration of his corpse, I refer you to 'The Discovery of the Remains of King Henry VI in St George's Chapel at Windsor Castle', a report drawn up by W. H. St John Hope and published in Volume 62 of the learned journal, *Archaeologia* (London, 1911). A most interesting passage from a report by a leading physician at the time reads as follows:

5 November 1910.
The following report contains all the information gathered from the skeleton which I examined yesterday.

The bones are those of a fairly strong man, aged between forty-five and fifty-five, who was at least 5ft. 9in. in height (he may have been an inch taller, but I give the minor limit).

The bones of the Head were unfortunately much broken, but as far as they could be pieced together they were thin and light, and belonged to a skull well-formed but small in proportion to the stature. Some of the roof bones (occipital and temporal, frontal and parietal) had become ossified together at the sutures. The few teeth found (second molar upper right, and first molar upper left, second bicuspid lower right) had their crowns very much worn down. The portion of the one side of the lower jaw found had lost its teeth some time before death.

There were nearly all the bones of the trunk, of both legs, and of the left arm; but I found no part of the right arm.

From the relative positions occupied by the bones, as they lay in the leaden casket when opened, it was certain that the body had been dismembered when it was put in. If the body had been buried in the earth for some time and then exhumed, it would account for their being in the condition in which we found them. It might also account for the absence of the bones of the right arm, as well as for the accidental enclosure of the left humerus of a small pig within the casket.

I am sorry that I can add nothing more. The state of the bones was so unsatisfactory that I could not make any trustworthy measurements.

© Paul Doherty OBE November 2017